A PERFECT DAY FOR A DRIVE

"Now, place your hands behind mine and take hold of the reins."

Charlotte did as directed, but in truth, her attention was more taken up with her guardian than with the team she was driving. She underwent the oddest sensation as he put his hands over hers. Their warmth, even through his gloves and hers, was comforting, and there was the strangest fluttering in her stomach as she felt the strength of his arms pressing on either side of her waist. The hardness of his chest behind her shoulders was so solid and reassuring. Charlotte had never been so close, so intimate with a man before. . . .

It was all she could do not to lean back and relax in his arms and revel in the sensation of being taken care of, enjoying the knowledge that for once someone else was there for her, to hold her and protect her should anything happen. She wanted to give herself up to the feeling of closeness and security, if only for the mom

The
Gallant
Guardian

Evelyn
Richardson

A SIGNET BOOK

SIGNET
Published by the Penguin Group
Penguin Putnam Inc., 375 Hudson Street,
New York, New York 10014, U.S.A.
Penguin Books Ltd, 27 Wrights Lane,
London W8 5TZ, England
Penguin Books Australia Ltd, Ringwood,
Victoria, Australia
Penguin Books Canada Ltd, 10 Alcorn Avenue,
Toronto, Ontario, Canada M4V 3B2
Penguin Books (N.Z.) Ltd, 182–190 Wairau Road,
Auckland 10, New Zealand

Penguin Books Ltd, Registered Offices:
Harmondsworth, Middlesex, England

First published by Signet, an imprint of Dutton NAL,
a member of Penguin Putnam Inc.

First Printing, November, 1998
10 9 8 7 6 5 4 3 2 1

To
Edoardo and Eleonora

Chapter 1

"Letter for you, my lord. It was delivered here by a solicitor's clerk." Felbridge, trusted servant to Maximilian Stanforth, Fifth Marquess of Lydon, tapped gently on the library door before offering the heavy cream-colored missive to the man seated at the desk behind a mound of papers.

"Thank you, Felbridge." The marquess raised one quizzical dark brow as he took the letter and opened it. Felbridge, his grizzled face impassive under his lordship's penetrating gaze, stood woodenly while his master hastily scanned the contents.

Long accustomed to his master's work habits, Felbridge would ordinarily never have intruded upon his lordship. Whenever the marquess retreated to the library, he worked with the same intensity that he played, and he did not take kindly to interruptions once he was immersed in the morning's affairs.

There were some aspects about this particular letter, however, that were unusual enough to warrant special consideration. First and foremost, the handwriting was obviously that of a woman. That in itself was not surprising, for his lordship, rich, handsome, and dashing, with a past murky enough to intrigue even the most romantic of ladies, was frequently the recipient of missives from the fair sex—some discreet, some not so discreet. These other missives were usually heavily scented and the handwriting full of ornate whirls and flourishes calculated to entice the reader. This script, on the other hand, was purposeful rather than graceful, and the paper, though of the finest quality, was plain and businesslike, as though the writer were doing her best to disguise rather than emphasize her femininity. There was, however, no mistaking the sex of the correspondent.

Not possessing any sisters, cousins, aunts, or female relatives of any sort, Lord Lydon never received anything but letters of assignation or admiration from the fair sex and certainly nothing of a serious nature. When the letter arrived, Felbridge had been intrigued in spite of himself and, like his master, was extremely curious as to the nature of this communiqué.

"My lord," the letter began, "Having been informed by my late father's solicitor that you have been appointed to act as guardian to me and to my brother William, I naturally anticipated your immediate arrival at Harcourt. As we have had no word from you, I assume that you are at present out of town or seriously indisposed. This letter is merely to inform you that we shall remain at Harcourt until such time as you have returned from the country or recovered from your indisposition. We look forward to your calling upon us in the near future upon the assumption of your duties. Sincerely, Charlotte Winterbourne.

"Of all the . . ." Lord Lydon hurled the letter to the floor. Rising, he pushed his chair back from the desk, strode over to the fireplace, where he grabbed the poker and jabbed vigorously at the logs smoldering in the grate. After a few seconds of prodding they burst into flame. He returned the poker to its place with a clang and began to pace the carpet. "Damned impertinent . . ." Then, catching sight of his hovering servant, he halted his pacing. "Just listen to this, Felbridge. Have you ever heard such impudence?" He read the letter aloud, mimicking the shrill and haughty tones of his mother, the now deceased Marchioness of Lydon, with such accuracy that Felbridge was unable to suppress an appreciative grin. In truth, the tone of the letter sounded very much like that of his lordship's demanding mother, and there was nothing so likely to set his lordship's teeth on edge as a reminder of either one of his parents, not that Felbridge blamed him. Neither one of Lord Lydon's parents had ever wasted a moment's thought or concern on their only son, consigning him from birth to the supervision of nurses and tutors, most of whom could have cared less about their unfortunate charge.

Only Felbridge, undergroom at the time, had sensed that beneath the lad's pranks and temper tantrums was a lonely little boy desperate for attention from someone, anyone. Admiring the lad's pluck, he had taken it upon himself to befriend his young master. It had not been easy, for Maximilian, unaccustomed to genuine interest, had naturally been suspicious of the groom's interest in him and had tried Felbridge's temper mightily in an effort to discover his motive. But the groom had withstood these tests with a patience and firmness that had eventually won the boy's trust.

Soon the staff at Lydon Court learned that if *that hellion*, as he was most frequently referred to, was missing, he could be found helping Felbridge in the stables. No matter what anyone said, Maximilian insisted on helping his newfound ally with his duties. "But I like to help you with your work," he would protest when Felbridge, embarrassed by this state of affairs, would remonstrate with him and attempt to explain the master/servant relationship. "You're my friend."

And so they had remained friends, though as the years went by, Maximilian learned that it was more comfortable for Felbridge if they observed the master/servant role when others were present. It was a friendship that had been tested time and time again. Under the groom's tutelage, Max had gained some degree of maturity as he grew from a rebellious boy into an adventurous young man, but he retained a wild streak that drove him to challenge every figure of authority that crossed his path, from his coldly correct father to the masters of Eton and Oxford, until finally the marquess, thoroughly fed up with trying to instill the proper behavior in his son, had thrown him out and cut him off without a penny.

Undaunted, Max had sold his string of hunters as well as his superbly matched bays and booked a passage for himself on a ship bound for Calcutta. Taking his sudden change in fortune in stride, he suffered no real regrets except the prospect of bidding farewell to the only true friend he had, but Felbridge, equally unable to part with his master, had refused to be left behind. The two of them had gone off to conquer the Indian subcontinent together.

And conquer it they had. In the slightly freer society of England's most profitable colony, where many of its members had suffered a fate similar to Maximilian's, his adventurous spirit was appreciated, even encouraged. He flourished in a way that would never have been possible in the rigid confines of the drawing rooms and ballrooms of the Upper Ten Thousand.

The clever mind that had once been derided by schoolmates bent on mindless amusement and jealous of his seemingly effortless academic brilliance, was put to good use. Max quickly made a name for himself among the merchants and bankers, who came to rely on his astuteness. In a very short while he had amassed a considerable fortune and, had he wished to, could have lived in far greater opulence and splendor than he had had back in England. However, he preferred to remain in the simply furnished bungalow that had been home since his arrival in Calcutta.

The allure of learning foreign customs, coupled with the challenge of life in an exotic country, was exactly suited to Maximilian's adventurous nature. He flourished in the atmosphere of intrigue among the local rajahs and the undercurrent of tension between the British and the local inhabitants, the military and the East India Company. Unlike many of his fellow countrymen, he had no particular desire to return to England to settle down and enjoy the fruits of his labors. To him, the enormous wealth he had acquired as a result of his dealings with the local princes, who trusted him more than they did most other Englishmen, was mostly irrelevant—a mere by-product of an existence that was more stimulating and therefore much more enjoyable than the one he had left behind in England.

He had little contact with, and no regrets for, those he had left behind. When five years after he had left England a letter arrived to inform him that his mother had succumbed to a putrid fever, it had as little effect on him as the news that the Prince of Wales had been declared Regent. In fact, to Maximilian, the Marchioness of Lydon was, in many ways, a more remote personage than the Prince whose rebellious stance toward his family was so much like his own.

It was only when his father died, having suffered a disastrous fall on the hunting field, a year after his wife that Max returned home. Forced by his new responsibilities as Marquess of Lydon he took up residence at Lydon Court and visited his other considerable properties, where he spent the minimum amount of time necessary. He had drawn the line, however, at immuring himself in the family mansion in Grosvenor Square, preferring to live in simpler bachelor quarters in Curzon Street while renting the imposing town house to wealthy tenants who wished to cut a dash during the Season.

If the new Marquess of Lydon had been less than enthusiastic about returning to the rigid and insular world of the *ton,* it had not suffered the same reservations about him. Handsome, athletic, and wealthy beyond belief, Lord Lydon had been mobbed from the moment of his reappearance. However, he had been entirely unmoved by the sensation he was causing and, if anything, his popularity only increased his cynicism toward the fashionable world. The only people who did not welcome him with open arms were the mamas of eligible young ladies. They were quick to recognize a dedicated bachelor when they saw one and were well aware of the dangers threatening their susceptible daughters in the form of a charming man with a romantic past whose heart had apparently never been touched by a female.

The marquess was delightfully attentive to all attractive women, spreading his favors and admiration equally among all the beauties of the *ton,* but it was abundantly clear that he had not the slightest intention of settling down now, or ever. Therefore, mothers bent on marrying off their daughters did their best to keep them out of his dangerously disturbing presence in order to concentrate on more likely prospects.

The same could not be said for a group of dashing young matrons to whose lives Lord Lydon added a good deal of spice. With a past spent in exotic places and possessing a daringly unconventional nature, he offered a delightful contrast to their husbands, whose daily routines of clubs and ballrooms, and dubious accomplishments—an exquisitely tied cravat or a well-chosen waistcoat—could not compete with all that the intriguing Lord Lydon had to offer.

The marquess's pursuit of these beauties was bold to the point of impudence. His reckless disregard for the sensibilities of the fashionable world was a welcome antidote to their rule-bound existences. Whispering to each other about his dangerous reputation, they vied for his attentions which, short-lived though they might be, were intoxicating enough to be well worth the risk. In no time, the Marquess of Lydon was as well known in London as he had been in India. His exploits, both athletic and amatory, were the talk of clubs and drawing rooms from St. James's to Berkeley Square.

Through it all, the one remaining constant in Max's life had been the loyal Felbridge, who had followed him uncomplainingly from Calcutta to Bombay, Benares to Madras, negotiating with warring rajahs or wealthy merchants, and at last back to England with its painful memories of a lonely boyhood and a restless, unhappy youth.

"She is not making the usual complaint that females do against you, my lord." Felbridge's weather-beaten features remained impassive, but there was a twinkle in the bright blue eyes alert and intelligent under the shaggy brows.

Max grinned. "No, but she certainly seems to be in a pet about something. Winterbourne . . . Winterbourne . . ." He frowned, trying to recall precisely why the name was so familiar to him. "Of course!" He shook his head at his own stupidity. "She must be

Hugo's daughter. But why on earth . . ." Again the puzzled frown descended as he racked his brains for some explanation of the outraged epistle he had just received.

Then, suddenly, enlightenment dawned. "What a nodcock I am! Hugo must have stuck his spoon in the wall. I thought I had not seen him at Brooks's of late and I naturally assumed that he was rusticating, but apparently not." Now that he gave the matter some thought, however, the marquess realized that during their entire acquaintance he had never known his customary whist partner to leave the metropolis.

Hugo, Earl of Harcourt, was a plainspoken though retiring man whose regular round of existence was confined to his lodgings in Mount Street, his clubs, and Parliament, where he devoted his time and energies to the political issues of the day. Rarely seen at the theater, the opera, or other popular haunts of the *ton,* he was an anomaly among his peers, a hard-working man who took his responsibilities seriously and who put his considerable intellect to work for the good of his country. His single indulgence was the lengthy and triumphant bouts of cards that had made him a legend at Brooks's. It was there that he had begun his unlikely friendship with Lord Lydon.

Vastly different in character, the two men had developed a high regard for one another's card-playing abilities. This had slowly blossomed into a recognition of the lively intelligence that distinguished each of them from his fellows. They made a formidable team at the gaming table and equally formidable opponents in any sort of discussion that might arise, be it economic, political, or philosophical. As time passed, they spent less and less time playing cards and more and more in debating the poor laws, taxation, and the vexing question of a standing army. From topics of general interest and concern, they had gradually proceeded to those of a more personal nature. It was during one of these conversations that the earl alluded to his children and his anxiety over their welfare.

"Charlotte is a bright, capable little thing, but she has her hands full with William. Cecil, pompous fool that he is, would not be of the slightest use to either of them should something happen to me," he mused aloud as he and Maximilian were taking each other on in a game of piquet one afternoon.

"Mmmm," Lord Lydon murmured vaguely as he studied his hand.

This was all the encouragement Harcourt had needed, his cus-

tomary reticence momentarily overcome by his very real worries
and the opportunity to lay them before someone whose advice he
could rely on. "There is no one else in the family, you see, and
after William, Cecil is the heir. A more self-righteous prig you
could never hope to see, and yet . . ." The earl paused to scrutinize
the card Max had just laid down on the baize-covered table. "And
yet, there is something I do not quite like about the man. He is a
havey-cavey sort of fellow for all his mealy-mouthed ways."

"Ah."

"Then you see what I mean. It would never do to leave the children in his care should I meet an untimely end. I can do nothing
about the entail, but I do have some control over their guardianship
and naturally I shall designate someone whose integrity I can rely
upon, someone who can stand up to Cecil."

"Naturally," Lydon echoed as he laid another card on the table.

Max's noncommittal reply was not entirely discouraging and
Hugo, who possessed little or no faith in the intelligence of most
of his fellows and had already mentally cataloged and rejected
everyone else he could think of, was becoming so desperate that
even this lukewarm response was enough to encourage him.
"Would you be so kind? I'm sure there will not be the least need
because I am strong as a cart horse, but of course one never likes
to tempt fate."

"Of course." And that had been the extent of the conversation
that had landed Maximilian in this muddle. Obviously the earl had
not been as strong as a cart horse and now here he was, saddled
with—how many children was it? The marquess glanced uneasily
at a heap of unanswered correspondence piled high on a corner of
his desk. Undoubtedly the full particulars of the case lay buried
somewhere in there, thoroughly explained in an official document
from Harcourt's solicitor. For the past several weeks Lydon had
been too involved in raising capital for his newest venture to pay
much attention to anything else and now he was being suitably
punished for this lapse.

The marquess sighed as he pulled the pile of letters toward him
and began to sort through it. "Thank you, Felbridge. You were
quite right to bring this letter to my attention, though I wish you
had not, for now there is nothing to do but attend to it." Max pulled
out a heavy sheet of crested stationery, scrawled a few lines, and
handed it to the waiting Felbridge. "Here, take this to Mr.

Sedgewick in his chambers at Gray's Inn, if you would, please. He will take care of it."

Having consigned the welfare of Lady Charlotte Winterbourne and her brother to the care of his solicitor, Lord Lydon returned to his own more pressing business concerns without a second thought for the wards he had inadvertently gained.

Chapter 2

The wards, or at least one of the wards, was not about to be so easily dismissed. Hastily perusing the content of a letter from the estimable Mr. Sedgewick some days later, Charlotte Winterbourne frowned mightily and dashed it to the floor with a most unladylike expression of annoyance. The extremely civil tone of this particular letter did not deceive her for a moment. Once again she and her brother were being fobbed off, their care entrusted to the minion of a man too busy to concern himself with their welfare. She should not have been surprised at such a state of affairs, she told herself angrily. After all, her father had been ignoring his children for years, turning them over to an army of well-paid nurses and tutors so that he could forget their very existence while he immersed himself in his own affairs. Why should things be any different when he was dead?

Undoubtedly this Lord Lydon, someone close enough to the Earl of Harcourt to be chosen as guardian of his children, shared the earl's distaste for familial obligations. Oh, she and William had been well enough looked after while her father lived in town. They had lacked for nothing in the way of creature comforts; any wish they had expressed had been granted and they had been given more than ample allowances. In fact, she and her brother William had lacked for nothing, but love. During his exceedingly infrequent visits to the home of his ancestors the earl had made it abundantly clear that his children held no more meaning for him than his vast estates. They were his duty and nothing more, part of the ancient heritage of the Earls of Harcourt that was to be administered and passed on to succeeding generations as his father had done before him. He lavished no more attention on them than he did on pointing the bricks of the chimneys or repairing the fences around the pastures. They were all exquisitely maintained, by her

father's servants, but that was the extent of the earl's concern for
them.

Well she, Charlotte, was not going to suffer such cavalier treat-
ment. She might be passed off and ignored, but she was not about
to allow such a thing to happen to William. As a young man of fifteen and the new Earl of Harcourt, he needed more guidance than
an occasional letter from some solicitor in London.

Charlotte tucked her legs up under her, rested her chin on her
hand, and stared out through the French doors that opened from the
library onto the terrace. The park beyond stretched as far as the eye
could see. Frowning, she tugged abstractedly at one stray dark curl
as she concentrated on her next move. Obviously, mere correspondence was not going to accomplish what she had hoped it
might. Now there was nothing for it but to journey to London herself and set this Lord Lydon straight. Let him try to fob her off on
his solicitor when she appeared on his doorstep. Ignoring her while
she was buried in the country was one thing, but face-to-face was
quite another matter altogether.

Charlotte sighed and the frown deepened. She had not the
slightest wish to visit the metropolis, with its crowds and dusty
traffic-filled streets, but there was nothing for it; her duty lay clear
before her and she had never been one to shirk her responsibilities.
Ever since her mother had died, she had looked after the household
and her younger brother, taking on tasks that were far too difficult
for a child. To be sure, a five-year-old could not do much, but there
had been a housekeeper, nursemaids, governesses, and an army of
servants to carry out the actual work. Then, two years after
William had been born, it became apparent that the protracted and
difficult birth that had killed his mother had also retarded his development and Charlotte's father had deserted them for good, abdicating to all intents and purposes his role as head of the
household in favor of his slip of a daughter.

The Earl of Harcourt had never been around a great deal after
his wife's death, but following the discovery of his son's diminished capacities he no longer bothered to return at all, preferring to
reduce his contact with the family to the written word.

Feeling lost and deserted by a parent whose visits had been infrequent at best, Charlotte had lavished all her attention on her
younger brother, resolving that he should never lack the love and
affection that she had craved so desperately after her mother had
died. She had been amply repaid for her troubles. Slow though he

might be intellectually, William was a handsome, affectionate lad who adored his older sister. He followed her everywhere and hung on her every word. Charlotte had become both mother and teacher to him, devoting hours to coaxing his mind through its painstakingly slow development and fiercely rejecting the opinions offered by her own governess and a score of tutors that he would never be able to read or write.

At last, when she had mastered all that her own governess could teach her, Charlotte had turned in desperation to the local vicar. The Reverend Doctor Joseph Moreland was a gentle, learned man, devoted to his little flock of parishioners, and quite content to eschew the high positions to which his education and abilities entitled him in favor of active involvement in his community. He had welcomed the opportunity to share his scholarship with a pupil as quick and eager as Charlotte and had taken on the challenge of teaching her brother with such enthusiasm that William, at the age of fifteen, was able to say his letters, do his sums, and read and write as well as any eight-year-old.

In fact, thanks to the Herculean efforts of Charlotte and the vicar, William appeared to the casual observer to be a healthy, good-natured easygoing lad with all the energy and interest of a normal sporting-mad fifteen-year-old. It was not until one engaged him in any sort of a discussion that one noticed that his words were simple and often slow to come to him and that his conversation was confined to such basic topics as horses, dogs, and anything else that might engage the attention of an eight-year-old.

The local villagers accepted him and loved him as much for his own sake as for his sister's and he was a familiar sight as he haunted the blacksmith's and the stable at the inn, plying the men with questions about horses, which were his passion.

A common sight in the village, the tall blond boy and his diminutive dark-haired sister offered quite a contrast with one another. He was big-framed and loose-limbed like his father, with bright blue eyes and a smiling, open countenance, while she was small and slim. Her wide green eyes, set under delicately arched brows, were thoughtful and observant, her expression serious. The full lips of a mouth too generous for perfect beauty rarely smiled, but when they did, her face was transformed, allowing the rare observer to see that under the reserved exterior lived a more whimsical, fun-loving creature that had been stifled by responsibilities assumed too early in life. It was a lively face, withal, and her entire being radiated energy and purpose.

It was this energy that prompted her to shake herself, much to the dismay of the spaniel sleeping peacefully in front of her chair. "If I must, I must," Charlotte muttered. Uncoiling her legs from underneath her, she rose and went in search of her brother.

As usual, William was to be found in the stables currying Duke, his own horse, seeing to the care of Charlotte's Brutus and the carriage horses, and exchanging a few words with the lads who were cleaning out the stalls and filling the feed troughs. Ever since babyhood William had been fascinated with the animals, always wanting to pat them whenever he saw them and never showing the least sign of unease with even the largest or most spirited mount. In turn, the horses seemed to sense his fascination and curbed their restiveness or ill temper whenever he was around.

Almost as soon as he could walk, William had escaped to the stables where he seemed to be equally at home with the powerful carriage horses and huge plow horses as he was with his own pony. The grooms and stableboys soon recognized his strange affinity with these animals and left the lad to his own devices when they saw he knew what he was about. They even allowed him to brush out the manes and forelocks of the more docile creatures and feed them bits of apple or lumps of sugar that he had cajoled Cook into giving him.

"Hello, Charlie." William turned to welcome his sister with a wide, endearing smile as he let go of the hoof he had been examining with some concern.

"Hello." Charlotte could not help smiling in return. No matter how lonely and abandoned she might feel, she never failed to be restored by the light in her brother's eyes which told her that one person, at least, not only needed her, but loved her very much.

"I thought Duke had a stone in his shoe, but I cannot find one." He patted the horse, who butted him lovingly and sniffed his pocket in search of any stray delicacy that his master might have overlooked.

"I am glad he does not. William, dear, I am afraid that I have to go to London. I hope to be gone only for the day. Mrs. Hodges will see to it that you are looked after, and of course you will continue your lessons with Dr. Moreland," Charlotte hastened to reassure him.

"But Charlie, may I not come with you?" The big blue eyes regarded her anxiously and there was just the slightest tremor discernible in her brother's lower lip.

"Not this time, dear, for I am very much afraid I shall have to spend the entire day doing boring old business." Then, unable to bear his look of disappointment, she added brightly, "But perhaps some time we may go together and see the Tower and Mr. Astley's performing horses."

"Oh I should like that." Excited by the prospect of such adventure, William immediately forgot any doubts he might have had and turned his attention back to Duke.

Charlotte shook her head, smiling ruefully. She was glad he was so easily reassured. Certainly she had intended for it to be that way, but the instant transition from fear of her leaving to forgetting all about it was disconcerting, nevertheless. Her brother's simplicity could be exasperating at times as it allowed him to forget or ignore problems that kept her awake at night—problems such as her cousin Cecil's impending arrival. Charlotte had been introduced to Sir Cecil Wadleigh and his family briefly many years ago at her mother's funeral, and she had not particularly cared for him or for his interfering wife, who had overwhelmed her with false sympathy and even falser protestations of affection. Nor had she liked Cecil's son, Basil, a slimy young man who kept pulling her curls and poking her when no one was looking. No, Charlotte had not the slightest use for any one of them, not then when young as she was she had mistrusted their air of sanctimonious officiousness, and not now when they were threatening to descend again like a thick fog: dense, cloying, and suffocating.

During her father's funeral and afterward, Charlotte had done her best to act politely toward them, but when Cecil's wife, Almeria, insisted on overriding the instructions Charlotte had already given to the housekeeper for taking care of the funeral guests she had held her tongue with difficulty. Cecil and his family were now back in Somerset at Wadleigh Manor, but not for long. Her cousin had reassured her of that as he had climbed into his carriage. "Once I give the proper instructions to my agent, I shall, of course, return, my dear Charlotte, for it is unthinkable that the estate be left without a man to run it."

Charlotte had refrained from pointing out the obvious, which was that the estate had been left virtually without a man to look after it for the past decade, certainly for the past five years, and had done rather well in spite of this unfortunate circumstance.

Charlotte had not been fooled in the least. She had watched Cecil surveying the vast green fields of Harcourt, the scores of sheep, the neat tenants' cottages, and had seen the unmistakably acquisitive gleam in his eye. She had observed Almeria run her hand possessively over the fine Chippendale sideboard and had overheard her quizzing the butler, Mr. Tidworth, about the family plate, and caught a glimpse of her examining the furnishings in her mother's bedchamber with a calculating expression.

She had also been miserably aware of the disparaging looks cast in William's direction. It took no great feat of imagination on Charlotte's part to interpret those glances. To the Wadleighs, William was less than human; he was something more on the order of a well-behaved pet, but a pet that bore an embarrassing resemblance to themselves. She knew that, in the opinion of people such as the Wadleighs, houses, especially magnificent houses such as Harcourt, were no place for pets. It would only be a matter of time before Cecil would be suggesting, in the most helpful and concerned sort of way, that William would be happier somewhere else, a simple sort of place, like a cottage by the sea, where someone could be hired to look after his particular needs and wants and where his connection to an illustrious family could be kept quiet.

"No! Never!" Charlotte muttered fiercely under her breath as she made her way back to the house where she soon located Mr. Tidworth in his pantry lecturing John the footman on the proper cleaning of the silver.

Having informed him of her decision to journey to London, she went next to see Cook and order a hamper for the trip. Charlotte did not intend to spend the night, and if she did not have to stop for a meal at an inn along the way, she would travel all that much more speedily.

Knowing full well that her reputation was already a topic for discussion in some of the drawing rooms around Harcourt among those who felt it was improper for a young woman to ride about the country on her own without a groom, Charlotte wished to avoid the comment that would arise if she were to put up for the night at a hotel in London. An early departure with no stops along the way would allow her to travel to London and back in one day. It was already bad enough that she was traveling to London on business with only a maid and a stout footman to accompany her. No need to risk further censure by putting up at a hotel.

Chapter 3

The journey to London passed pleasantly enough. After a life spent within the confines of Harcourt and its environs, Charlotte was thrilled at the chance to see another part of the countryside. To be sure, the fields and cottages they passed very much resembled those she knew so well, but they were ones she had never seen before and therein lay their charm.

As they approached the metropolis the traffic increased as did the number of establishments lining the road, a phenomenon that filled her maid, Lucy, with astonishment. "Lawks, my lady, did you ever see so many people! Why they all want to crowd together in such a way is certainly beyond me. It isn't normal." The farmer's daughter could see no allure in a place where one was confined to houses with no gardens and streets jammed with carts, carriages, peddlers selling their wares, and hawkers of every description.

A little better prepared for it all from the prints she had seen by Mr. Hogarth and lesser-known artists as well as the various things she had read, Charlotte was not so overwhelmed as her maid, but she too failed to see what it was that drew people to the place. Now that she had seen it, she was inclined more than ever to think that her father had taken up residence in London to avoid all thought of his family and not because of the charm of the place. Why else, if one had known the peace and quiet, the green spaciousness of Harcourt's particular corner of Sussex, would one voluntarily leave it for the cluttered, noisy, dusty scene that was London unless one wished to escape from those who made Harcourt their home?

At last the carriage clattered up before the somber building containing the chambers of Mr. Sedgewick, and the footman sprang to open the door. Drawing a deep breath, Charlotte emerged, followed closely by Lucy. Until now, all her thoughts and energies had been focused on getting to the metropolis and she admitted to

herself as she scanned the names on the door that she had not truly
given a great deal of thought as to how she was to convince Mr.
Sedgewick to divulge the address of his noble employer. Any solicitor worth his salt would do his utmost to protect the interests of
his client. Certainly she would expect such loyalty from someone
in her employ. There was nothing for it but to try. Desperation
made Charlotte determined. Squaring her shoulders and assuming
an air of cool authority, she opened the door and marched in, head
held high.

"May I help you?"

Charlotte whirled around. In the corner at a high desk sat a
young man who looked to be no older than William.

"I should like to speak with Mr. Sedgewick, please."

The young man untangled lanky legs from the stool he was sitting on and approached her curiously. Generally speaking, Mr.
Sedgewick's clients were of such rank and power that the solicitor
waited upon them at their convenience in their own establishments.

Charlotte endured his scrutiny with barely concealed impatience. The clerk, with his shock of red hair and ears that stuck out
from his head like outspread wings, was not the least impertinent,
far from it, he appeared almost awestruck. She wished he would do
more than just stand there gazing at her. At last, unable to bear it
any longer, she coughed politely.

A vivid red stained the young man's face. "I b-b-beg, your pardon," he stammered. "How may I be of service to you?"

"I wish to see Mr. Sedgewick." Charlotte repeated it politely,
but firmly. Really, she *did* wish he would look more lively, for her
time was quite limited.

"He . . . he's not here."

"Oh." Now what was she to do? In her haste to forestall Cecil
and protect her brother, Charlotte had never stopped to consider
the possibility that Mr. Sedgewick might not be available.

"He has gone to Lord Palgrave's and is not expected back until
tomorrow," the clerk volunteered helpfully.

Charlotte was silent, thinking furiously. Actually, this setback
might be turned to her advantage. In truth, she had been a little nervous about trying to extract her guardian's direction from his solicitor, but this young man was far more approachable than some
respectable gentleman who would surely be bound to protect his

noble employer from inquisitive young women. Yes, the awkward young man might do very well.

Summoning up her friendliest smile, Charlotte moved a step closer to him. "Oh dear. That is most unfortunate, but perhaps you might help me instead," she began in a confiding tone. "You see, he is acting for my guardian and something has occurred that makes it absolutely imperative that I see my guardian today. Ordinarily, of course, he calls upon us, but this is an emergency so I came here. But London is so vast; indeed, it is quite overwhelming, and I have no idea of how to find him, and Mr. Sedgewick has always been so kind to me that . . ." Charlotte allowed her voice to trail off uncertainly.

"Perhaps I can be of some assistance."

"Oh, could you? Otherwise my journey will have been quite in vain and I could not bear for that to be the case."

The clerk was no proof against the pleading expression in the big green eyes fixed so hopefully upon him. He blushed even more brilliantly. "I expect I could give you your guardian's direction," he replied, trying desperately to sound offhand, as though lovely young women threw themselves on his mercy every day of the week.

"Oh, thank you. He is the Marquess of Lydon."

"Ah. Lord Lydon." The clerk nodded sagely. "Then you must be Lady Charlotte Winterbourne."

It was Charlotte's turn to look self-conscious. "Yes. Yes, I am. And who might you be?"

"Jeremy Watton, my lady. At your service. I am clerk to Mr. Sedgewick and, as I have copied some paperwork concerning your guardian, I am familiar with your name. The marquess resides in Curzon Street. I shall furnish your coachman with his direction."

Charlotte was visibly impressed, and the young man could not help thrusting out his chest with pride. It was not often that one was called upon to render assistance to desperate young women and he was glad to think that he had performed creditably. Certainly the young lady appeared to be more than satisfied, smiling gratefully upon him as she allowed him to escort her back out to her carriage.

"Thank you ever so much, Mr. Watton. I am greatly in your debt." Charlotte smiled at him again as he helped her in and then sank back against the cushions as the coachman whipped up the horses. They trotted off toward Curzon Street leaving Mr. Watton gazing after them, a beatific grin plastered across his freckled countenance.

Charlotte could not suppress the smug little smile of satisfaction that rose to her lips and congratulated herself on having successfully overcome the first obstacle that had presented itself. Mr Jeremy Watton was one thing, however; the Marquess of Lydon was quite another. As the carriage slowed and then halted in front of a discreetly elegant building in Curzon Street her newly won confidence evaporated as quickly as it had come. The anger that had fueled her ever since she had received the solicitor's letter receded before the reality of an imposing front door and the imminent possibility of addressing the perfect stranger whose cool dismissal of her and her brother was the source of her ire.

As she emerged from the carriage and slowly climbed the marble steps Charlotte realized just how narrow and sheltered a life she had led, how few real strangers she had ever encountered. It was a lowering thought, but one she was not prepared to let intimidate her after having come all this way.

Mustering her courage she raised her chin proudly as her footman rang the bell. "Lady Charlotte Winterbourne to see the Marquess of Lydon," he announced in stentorian tones to the grizzled servant who answered the door.

Secretly blessing John, whom she had been coaching for several days before their journey, Charlotte sailed proudly through the open door as though she called on single gentlemen every day. She had left Lucy in the carriage, counting on the strapping young footman to lend her respectability. Lucy was a dear, and devoted to her mistress, but Charlotte preferred to deal with the marquess on her own without the softening presence of another female.

Gritting her teeth, she met the shrewd gaze of the servant who had opened the door. His face remained impassive, but the piercing blue eyes that assessed her were bright with curiosity. Apparently she met with favor for Charlotte could just discern a sly twinkle, quickly suppressed with a courteous, "This way, my lady." Well aware of the young lady's identity, Felbridge did not give his master any warning but turned and led her into a library that was well enough stocked even to impress someone accustomed to spending much of her time happily browsing the magnificent collection at Harcourt.

"Lady Charlotte Winterbourne here to see you, my lord," the servant announced with what she thought was the faintest undertone of amusement in his gravelly voice. Before Charlotte had time to puzzle over this, however, the tall figure seated at the enormous mahogany desk rose to greet her.

Well, this man will put Cecil in his place, Charlotte thought gleefully as eyes as cold and gray as the sea in winter scrutinized her. The hawklike face, deeply tanned, with its high-bridge nose and severely sculpted lips, wore the expression of someone accustomed to dominating every situation he might find himself in. The broad shoulders and muscular physique revealed by the beautifully tailored coat and the tight-fitting biscuit-colored pantaloons only added to the power he exuded, and he moved with the grace of a natural athlete.

Everything about the man was likely to intimidate the short, pudgy Cecil, Yes, Charlotte congratulated herself, this man would put paid to any of Cecil's nefarious schemes.

The gentleman's words of greeting, however, quickly dispelled this happy vision. "I had thought, Lady Charlotte, that I had made it abundantly clear to you that any concerns on your part were to be addressed to my solicitor." There was no mistaking the frostiness of his tone or the intense annoyance of his expression. Clearly, the Marquess of Lydon was not about to have any contact with an importunate young female.

Charlotte's heart dropped to the toes of her kid half boots. The man was daunting enough. Not only would he stop Cecil in his tracks, he was very nearly stopping her. She wanted very much to turn and run from the room, away from the scornful look in his eyes and the disdainful curl of his lip, but she concentrated all her thoughts on William and the misery his life would be if Cecil were allowed to interfere.

Strengthened in her resolve, she stood her ground, lifted her chin defiantly, and looked the marquess squarely in the eye. "To be sure you did, my lord," she responded sweetly, but firmly. "But it was such a blatant abdication of your duty as guardian that I felt certain you were unaware of the true situation, so I have come to enlighten you."

Maximilian stared dumbfounded at the young woman in front of him. From Calcutta to Madras he had made men quiver in their boots with the raking gaze he was now directing at Charlotte, but she did not flinch, nor did she drop her eyes in confusion as any normal person would.

Instead, she remained regarding him, matching glare for glare, her green eyes fixed as steadily on him as his were on her. Not only that, but she addressed him in an almost pitying tone as though he were a child lacking in understanding who needed to be set right.

It was indeed an enlightening experience for the marquess. Heretofore the women he had encountered were far more likely to smile coyly at him than glare at him, and there was no doubt that this female was glaring. Nor was this female like the older, more sophisticated females with whom he was accustomed to dealing, for in spite of her determined stance, she looked to be quite young and innocent. There was not a hint of guile in her expression and the delicate flush that betrayed her nervousness drew attention to the smooth skin and softly rounded cheeks that disappeared all too quickly as a girl passed into womanhood.

The marquess was intrigued in spite of himself and he could not help wondering what this unusual female was likely to do next. Telling himself that he was all sorts of a fool for giving in to his rampant curiosity, Maximilian relented. "Then you had better do just that. Pray be seated, Lady Charlotte." He indicated a low wing chair on one side of the fireplace. Then, disposing his lanky frame into the chair opposite hers, he continued, "I await enlightenment."

Chapter 4

Charlotte sank into the designated chair. In her surprise at his sudden capitulation, she could think of nothing to say for a moment. However, speechlessness, which was a rare affliction for one accustomed to stating her mind on any and every issue, did not last long. Recovering quickly, she cleared her throat. "I appreciate that your being named guardian to my brother and me may have been as big a shock to you as it was to me, and no more welcome. Papa tended to do things that way, without consulting anyone. Ordinarily I should protest such a lamentable state of affairs for, as you can plainly see, I have no need of a guardian, but William does, and it is for his sake that I do not dispute this guardianship." Charlotte glanced up at the marquess to check the effect of this little speech, but Lord Lydon remained impassive.

"Go on." Privately, Maximilian thought that any girl mad enough to journey to London on her own and call on a bachelor gentleman in his own quarters did not need a guardian as much as a keeper, but he knew that revealing even the slightest hint of such a thought would prove fatal to this relationship that had been forced upon both of them.

The young lady seated across from him would take instant exception to such an attitude and go flying off in the same precipitate and unexpected manner that she had appeared, embroiling him in an even stickier situation than the one he was in at the moment. Still, he had to admit that it did take courage to travel to the city on her own and take to task a man whom she had never met. For all her youthful appearance, there was nothing youthful in her air of self-possession or the knowing look she directed at him. She had sized up the state of affairs in the blink of an eye and had made him her begrudging ally by acknowledging him as a fellow sufferer of her father's erratic ways.

As directed, Charlotte continued with her story. "Since you have never laid eyes upon us before, and since Papa would never acknowledge it, you could not know that my brother William is simple. Mama died giving birth to him and the difficult birth has somehow affected his brain. To look at him you would think him a normal fifteen-year-old boy, and when one converses with him one does not at first notice anything amiss. It is not until after some time that one suddenly realizes that his vocabulary and speech are that of an eight-year-old. He is the sweetest natured soul and so very obliging, but some people"—here she paused to draw a quick angry breath, her dark brows lowering in a frown so intense it could only be called a scowl. "Some people—my cousin Cecil, for example—think he is not fit for human company and that he should be sent away to live where the world will be able to forget about him."

"And what do you think?" Lord Lydon inquired gently. There was something oddly touching in her fierce devotion to her brother, her willingness to make an uncomfortable journey and confront an unknown gentleman all on his behalf. It had been a long time since the marquess, more accustomed to the frailties of mankind than to its strengths, had encountered such nobility of spirit. He was strangely moved by it. It heartened him to think that somewhere people still possessed the finer feelings and, what was more, acted upon them.

"I think that I prefer William's company to my cousin Cecil's," Charlotte snapped. Then, observing the gleam of amusement in his gray eyes, she blushed guiltily. "Forgive me; I did not mean to bite your head off, but Cecil is . . . is . . ." She groped for words which were rendered quite unnecessary by the look of disgust on her expressive face.

"You have no need to apologize to *me*. Now that you mention him, I begin to recall that the questionable nature of Cecil's character lies at the root of this entire, ah, *situation*."

"It does?" Charlotte asked in some surprise. Apparently her idiosyncratic Papa had possessed more forethought than she had credited him with.

"Yes. I believe that your father thoroughly distrusted the man, though naturally, he did not go on at length painting an unflattering portrait of the person who, after William, is his heir. However, I am convinced that if Cecil were a decent sort of fellow I should never have been burd—er *entrusted* with the guardianship of you and your brother, and we all would be free to continue our lives in much the same fashion as we have been accustomed to."

Lord Lydon's slip of the tongue was not lost on his visitor. Charlotte drew herself up, her eyes flashing. "I assure you, my lord, that I am entirely capable of taking care of William and myself. I apologize for having troubled you." She rose in a dignified manner and, head held high, was prepared to sweep majestically from the room, but the marquess was too quick for her.

Rising and catching hold of her arm before she could take a step, he pushed her firmly but gently back into her chair. "Do not take offense, Lady Charlotte, I meant no reflection on you, but we might as well be honest with one another; the circumstances of your father's will have put us both in an awkward situation."

There was no resisting the teasing quirk of his eyebrow or the rueful smile tugging at the corner of his mouth. When he was not freezing the blood in one's veins with that haughty stare of his, Lord Lydon could be quite attractive, Charlotte admitted to herself. But would he be willing to help her, really help her rout Cecil from their lives for once and for all? She very much doubted it. Charlotte had lived a secluded life, confined as she had been to Harcourt and its environs, her only society being the local gentry and the people in the village, but even her limited experience told her that the Marquess of Lydon was what her brother, copying the parlance of the stableboys, would call an *out-and-outer, top-of-the trees, a real Corinthian.* One had only to look at the superb cut of his coat, the exquisitely tied cravat, and his air of command to know that he was accustomed to a life of far more excitement, adventure, and sophistication than the daily domestic routine at Harcourt and that he certainly would not relish being dragged from his free and easy existence to squelch the Wadleighs' petty pretensions that were upsetting hers.

Maximilian read doubt and hope warring in those big green eyes, observed her gnawing her lip, and found himself subject to the most unusual and annoying twinge of uncertainty. He had spent so much of his life protecting himself from women who were trying to take advantage of his good nature, his wealth, and his position that he had never bothered to wonder whether or not he could live up to anyone's expectations but his own. Now he was not so sure. This chit of a girl had not only arrived unannounced to scold him for abdicating his duties, but now she had the audacity to look skeptical when he was on the verge of offering to take up those responsibilities her father had so blithely condemned him to. It was nothing short of infuriating, but then, she had been infuriating him since the moment she had sent him the imperious summons to Harcourt.

"Very well." His visitor sounded somewhat mollified. "But you must realize that it was never *my* idea to ask for someone to interfere in our lives. However, as someone else is interfering in them already, you might as well make yourself useful and protect us from that person." Her expression was properly demure and she spoke sweetly enough, but there was no concealing the naughty twinkle in her eyes.

She was paying him back, the little vixen, for his previous slip of the tongue. Maximilian grinned appreciatively. It was rare to encounter a woman with a sense of humor. Most of them were far too intent on winning a man's attention and admiration to risk giving offense by teasing him. Obviously, Lady Charlotte Winterbourne suffered no such qualms. He found it rather refreshing and, in a way, far more captivating than the coquettish smiles or alluring glances that were the standard ploys of women bent on enlisting his aid.

"You make yourself abundantly clear, Lady Charlotte, and believe me, if it were not for the complicating issue of William and your cousin Cecil's attitude toward him, I should not dream of offering you my assistance. But obviously Cecil does present a problem, such a problem in fact, that your father asked a relative stranger to look after your welfare. Now how is it that I may do that best?"

Charlotte eyed him suspiciously, but he appeared to be completely serious. "Well . . ." She hesitated. Now that she had succeeded in gaining his attention, she was at a loss as to how to proceed. It did seem rather a lot to ask someone to abandon his own life in order to help someone he had never met before, to protect the rights of a young man who would never be able to fend for himself completely.

Charlotte drew a deep breath. "Well, if you could come visit us at Harcourt you could see that while William is simple, he is not an idiot, and he is able to carry on a normal existence just as long as he has someone to manage his affairs, and"—she

scowled fiercely—"you could keep Cecil from packing him off
to some remote spot. I am quite capable of managing things for
my brother, but I seem to have no effect on Cecil at all. You, on
the other hand, could put an end to any possible schemes he
might have." She beamed approvingly at him.

"I appreciate your confidence in me, but I am not altogether
sure that . . ."

"Oh you will most assuredly set Cecil back on his heels. You
can be quite formidable, you know, and you do have a certain,
ahem, *air* about you that is bound to make him ill at ease. He is
quite short and fancies himself something of a buck. Being confronted with the real thing will naturally put him on the defensive." Charlotte's gleeful tone and her smile of smug
satisfaction gave some clue as to the humiliations she must have
suffered at the hands of her cousin.

"Thank you, I think." The marquess was somewhat nonplussed by her forthright assessment of his qualities and equally
nonplussed by her reaction to them, for it was quite obvious that
while Lady Charlotte considered a formidable appearance and
an air of distinction as valuable assets in intimidating the ob-
noxious Cecil, it was equally obvious from the hint of condescension in her voice that, personally, she had no use for such
things. It was a rather lowering thought and, much to his disgust,
Maximilian found himself wondering exactly what qualities she
did admire in a gentleman.

But he was not to find out, at least not today. Having accomplished what she had set out to do, Charlotte was not inclined to
waste any more time in polite conversation. Drawing on her
gloves, she rose and extended her hand. "Then we shall see you
at Harcourt in the near future?"

Lord Lydon rose as well and took the hand that was offered
him—a slim, delicate hand, but a strong one, with a firm grip,
much like its owner. "I look forward to visiting you and meeting William." Oddly enough, he meant it. It had been a long
time since the marquess had felt that he was crucial to anyone,
but observing the relief in his visitor's eyes, he knew that his
presence at Harcourt was of vital importance to her and her
brother. It was rather gratifying to be needed in such a way. He
had spent a good deal of life avoiding obligations that the world
in general was all too eager to thrust on him, but somehow this
was different. Lady Charlotte was obviously reluctant to depend

on anyone but herself for anything. Circumstances had forced her into this untenable position of dependence, a position she was as eager to escape as he was. Her very disinclination to accept help made Maximilian all the more willing to come to her aid. Besides, she intrigued him, and he could not help wanting to see how it all turned out.

Chapter 5

Charlotte lay back against the squabs of the carriage as it rattled off down Curzon Street toward Piccadilly, and heaved a sigh of relief. It had been a very near thing, but she had managed to carry it off, and now she could face Cecil and Almeria with a fortitude she had not felt before. To be sure, there was still a good deal of work to be done to convince Lord Lydon that, with her help, William was best left to live as he had done for the past fifteen years. After having seen the marquess, she now allowed herself to hope that he would listen to her on that issue. There had been a look in those penetrating gray eyes that told her he was accustomed to observing the world and arriving at his own conclusions unaffected by the prejudices of others. Certainly, he did not appear to be the sort of man to be influenced by Cecil's eternal prosings about propriety and respectability. In fact, from the little he had let slip concerning his knowledge of Cecil, he was far more likely to resent the man who was the root cause of the entire situation than to join forces with him in opposing Charlotte's suggestions for her brother's welfare.

Charlotte wished she knew a little more of Lord Lydon beyond the obvious, which was that his skill at cards seemed somehow to have recommended him to her papa as a likely candidate for guardian to his children. Though the former Earl of Harcourt had often been known to declare that a man's character could pretty well be summed up by the way he conducted himself at a card table, Charlotte was not quite so convinced as her father that a good head for whist or piquet qualified one to look out for the interests of a simple-minded fifteen-year-old boy. However, as she had absolutely no other alternative, she was willing to hope that her father had known what he was about. Certainly, Lord Lydon had not looked her idea of the hardened gamester—far from it. His tanned face, athletic physique, and alert air spoke more of an accomplished sportsman than a bleary-eyed devotee of the Goddess of Fortune.

The only other bit of information concerning her guardian that Charlotte had been able to glean had been the deliciously scandalized gasps of Lady Winslow and her daughters when Charlotte had divulged her guardian's identity to them. Privately, Charlotte thought her nearest neighbors boring in the extreme, but the bluff old baron had given her a great deal of useful agricultural advice, so for his sake she had been her most gracious when his wife and daughters had come to call immediately upon hearing of her father's death. Selina and Emily Winslow had both enjoyed unsuccessful Seasons, but that did not keep them from flaunting their sophistication in front of Charlotte.

"The Marquess of Lydon! How perfectly dreadful!" In fact, the tone of Selina's voice sounded more envious than horrified.

"He is a shocking rake." Emily explained. "Why no self-respecting mama would allow her daughters anywhere near the man."

"But why is that?"

"Lord, Charlotte, you are such a green girl. Because he is only after one thing, and it is not marriage. The reputations he has ruined, why I—"

"That is enough, Emily," her mother, well aware of her younger daughter's propensity for scandalous gossip, forestalled her. "We do not know if anything that is said about him is true and Charlotte is not hoping to make a husband out of him, only a guardian."

Charlotte had been inclined to agree with Lady Winslow that the Marquess of Lydon's amatory adventures had very little bearing on his ability to protect her brother from Cecil, which was the only requirement she had for her guardian.

Now there was nothing to do but bide her time and see. In the meanwhile, there was the threatened return of Cecil and Almeria to steel herself for.

And it was all too soon that Cecil and Almeria reappeared, loaded with so much baggage that there was little need for them to declare their intentions of remaining at Harcourt *until Charlotte and William's futures are settled satisfactorily.*

Knowing that Cecil and Almeria's definition of *satisfactorily* differed widely from hers, Charlotte was forced to exercise heroic self-discipline as she schooled her features into an expression of submissive acceptance and thanked them for their concern. Underneath this meek facade she was fuming as she instructed the housekeeper, Mrs. Hodges, to show them to their chambers, but she knew that at the moment her best recourse was to give way as gracefully as she could in order to muster her strength and resources for the appearance of Lord Lydon. But it was all she could do not to slap the self-satisfied smile off Cecil's face as, rubbing his hands together, he surveyed the magnificent marble entry hall with a proprietary air, exclaiming, "You must not worry your head about such things any more, Charlotte. Almeria can deal with Mrs. Hodges from now on and we shall soon have things in good order."

As it had never occurred to Charlotte that things were in such a poor state of affairs in the first place, she bit her lip and, with admirable self-restraint, resolutely avoided meeting the eyes of Mrs. Hodges, who, rigid with outrage, led them up the sweeping staircase and to their respective chambers.

Sir Cecil Wadleigh was an unprepossessing little man of inferior height, narrow shoulders, unfortunate waistline, thin sandy hair, weak blue eyes set too close together, and a receding chin. However, he made up for all the authority he lacked in his person by adopting an air of pompous superiority. His mother, the former Earl of Harcourt's elder sister and only sibling, had married Cecil's father much against the wishes of her family, for the Wadleighs, though from a most ancient lineage, were far inferior in rank and fortune. However, Lady Anne, who had grown up virtually as an only child and had enjoyed her parents' undivided attention except for the few years between the earl's birth and his enrollment at Eton, had been thoroughly spoiled and therefore was not to be denied once her mind was made up.

Her husband had combined a thoroughly biddable nature with an almost unnatural reverence for his domineering wife, making him a perfect partner for the Earl of Harcourt's imperious sister. Cecil, their only child, had inherited all the defects of his mother's personality with none of her superior understanding or strength of character. He had grown from a self-important and opinionated lad into an equally self-important and opinionated young man who bitterly resented his mother for having married beneath her and for not making a push to secure him a place in the bosom of the family at Harcourt where he could show to his best advantage. But Lady Anne, happy in her complete dominance over her own household, was not about to jeopardize this position by returning to her ancestral home where the earl's word was law and his every whim was catered to. Having no natural affection for a brother who had been raised entirely separate from her, she was content to remain at Wadleigh Manor ruling the lives of her family and her servants with an iron hand.

The eventual birth of an heir to the earldom, after the countess's many miscarriages, had been a severe disappointment to Cecil, who had begun to entertain hopes of succeeding at last to a position worthy of him. His subsequent discovery of that heir's diminished mental capacities had only served to convince him further that a title he had begun to think of as rightfully his did, in fact, belong to him.

So secure was Cecil in these convictions that he had actually begun to picture himself as heir some time before the Earl of Harcourt's demise, and it had come as something of a shock when the will maintaining the deceased earl's son as heir had been read by the solicitor after the funeral. And this was not the worst of it; more appalling still was the fact that Cecil had not even been named guardian of the inheritance for which he was next in line. He had barely been able to contain his outrage at such a sorry state of affairs and it was only by exerting enormous self-control that he was able to maintain his composure under the coolly observant eye of the new earl's sister. The only consolation during the entire thing was that the legal guardian demonstrated such a notable lack of interest in the entire state of affairs that he had not even bothered to appear for the funeral or for the reading of the will, and Cecil had begun to hope that the management of Harcourt might yet fall to him.

His wife, Almeria, had done nothing to dissuade him from this line of reasoning. "For you know what Lord Harcourt was, a loose screw if I ever saw one. Ten to one he appointed some card-playing crony of his who will not make the slightest push to do what is right. As head of the family, Cecil, you have a duty to return to Harcourt and see to it that the place does not come to rack and ruin." At Almeria's urging they had remained back at home at Wadleigh Manor just long enough to pack and to make arrangements for an extended absence before heading back to Harcourt to take up the running of an estate worthy of their abilities.

Ensconced back at Harcourt, they wasted no time. The very next morning Almeria was to be found in the housekeeper's room instructing Mrs. Hodges in the new regime. There were to be no more fires in the servants' bedchambers, nor wax candles in their quarters, and the keys to the storerooms were to be turned over to Lady Wadleigh immediately.

Forewarned by her mistress, Mrs. Hodges listened to these demands with dignified equanimity before refusing quietly to do any such thing.

"Why you impudent creature!" Almeria gasped, once she had recovered enough from the shock of such blatant insubordination as to be able to speak.

"Begging your pardon, my lady, but Lady Charlotte has given instructions that things are to remain as usual until such time as the Marquess of Lydon arrives, and then I am to consult his lordship's pleasure on the running of the household." Mrs. Hodges's expression remained one of respectful servility, but the note of triumph in her voice was not lost on Lady Wadleigh, who immediately turned and swept from the room, her long thin nose in the air, her tiny mouth pursed tighter than ever, and two bright angry red spots burning on her sallow cheeks.

Her husband met with the same lack of success in his conversation with Harcourt's agent. Mr. Sotherton was all deference to Sir Cecil, but not the least inclined to follow his wishes, having already received clear instructions from his mistress to wait until such time as they could benefit from the advice of Lord Lydon.

Frustrated at every turn, the Wadleighs could only fume and possess themselves of the little grace that they could muster to wait until Charlotte and William's guardian saw fit to make an appearance.

Some days after the Wadleighs' installation, as she sat down to yet another interminable dinner punctuated only by stony silence and Almeria's disgusted sniffs, Charlotte thought that her guardian's arrival could not occur too soon for any of them.

In fact, the only person reasonably content with this uneasy state of affairs was William. But even his sunny and confiding nature was considerably dampened by the disapproving stares of his cousins when they sat down to meals. At all other times he was so happily employed exploring the fields and streams around Harcourt or doing his lessons with Dr. Moreland that he had no thoughts to spare for the Wadleighs. At the table, however, contact with them was unavoidable and even William, blithely ignorant as he was, could not help asking his sister, "Charlie, why do not our cousins like me?"

Trying her best to hide her anger, Charlotte thought quickly. "It is just that they are unused to boys your age, dear. I am sure that in time they will become more accustomed to being with a young man your age." She was grateful that her brother's slowness with figures and his general unconsciousness kept him from realizing that it was barely six years ago that their son, Basil, had been just William's age and that the Wadleighs had not had the slightest difficulty in lavishing their disgusting offspring with their fawning attentions.

"Are you sure, Charlie?" William was doubtful. "They both have mean eyes when they look at me."

"What else could it be, dear? You are a most amiable, well-looking, and proper young man; I do not see what there could be to find fault with." *Except that you are the heir to all that greedy Cecil wants for himself,* Charlotte could not help thinking as she smiled encouragingly at her brother. "Just give them time and continue to behave as sweetly as you always do; I am sure they will come around." She was not at all sure of such a thing—in fact, quite the opposite—but Charlotte knew that her brother looked to her for explanations of things.

Despite his mental limitations, William was a sensitive lad and as quick as the next person to sense the feelings of those around him, but he needed his sister's clever mind to interpret and account for the reasons behind his perceptions.

"Do you think Cousin Cecil would like me better if I let him ride Duke?"

"That is very kind of you, William, but perhaps the best thing would be to let Cousin Cecil get to know us and feel comfortable with us first." A lump rose in Charlotte's throat and she blinked to keep back the tears. It was so unfair. Here was William offering his most precious possession in the hopes of befriending the man who wished to deprive him of his birthright, a man who considered him to be something less than human. It made her long even more for the arrival of Lord Lydon and hope even more fervently that he would join her in defending her brother against the grasping schemes of the Wadleighs.

Chapter 6

It was only the space of another day before Charlotte's prayers were answered. Cursing himself for being all sorts of a fool, the Marquess of Lydon bowled down the long gravel drive to Harcourt in his magnificent yellow curricle late in the afternoon of the day after William had voiced his doubts to his sister.

In fact, it was William who brought the news of his lordship's arrival. "Charlie, Charlie, the most bang-up rig you have ever seen," he panted, having run at breakneck speed to find his sister, who was poring over accounts in the library. "And it is come here, Charlie, to see us! I never saw such a pair as there is harnessed to the carriage—they are gray, and such sweet goers. Who can it be? Who can it be?"

Charlie smiled at her brother's enthusiasm. The Marquess of Lydon could have chosen no surer way into her brother's esteem than to be the owner of a well-turned-out equipage and high-blooded horses. It was bound to aggravate Cecil, however, who, though he would agree that a man should own a carriage fine enough to proclaim his consequence to one and all, was such a nervous equestrian that he avoided horses as much as possible and was therefore inclined to be defensive with those who possessed a heart stout enough and hands skillful enough to drive a sporting vehicle. He could often be heard criticizing renowned horsemen as sporting-mad good-for-nothings. Well, there was no use worrying about Cecil's reaction to Lord Lydon. Whatever happened, it was likely to be most interesting. Closing the account book, Charlotte followed her brother to the front portico where the marquess, handing the reins to his tiger, descended to meet the admiring William.

"That is a prime pair, sir. They must be the sweetest goers. How fast can they go when you spring 'em?" William burst forth with a volley of questions before Lord Lydon's booted foot even touched the gravel.

"Why thank you. I am rather pleased with them myself, but please, take a closer look if you wish. By the way," the marquess held out his hand, "I am Lydon."

Already making his way to the horses' heads, William paused, turned back, and, smiling sheepishly, took the proffered hand. "I am William. Have you come to visit us, sir?" He asked incredulously.

"I have." Max grinned at the boy's patent astonishment. "And here, if I am not mistaken, comes my hostess, your sister." The marquess turned toward Charlotte, who was hurrying down the steps to greet her visitor.

But William was ahead of him. "Charlie, Charlie, this is Lydon. He says he has come to visit us."

"And so he has, dear. I invited him."

"You know him?" William was clearly impressed. "But how?"

"Lord Lydon is our guardian. Before Papa died he chose Lord Lydon to look after us."

"Oh." William digested this for a moment. "Then is he our new father?"

Charlotte smiled fondly at her brother. "Not precisely, but I hope he will be our good friend."

The marquess, bemused by this conversation, was brought quickly to his senses by the speaking look in the green eyes now fixed so intently upon him. "I certainly hope to be. But you were on your way to speak to my horses, I believe. Do not let me keep you from that."

"Thank you, sir." And without a backward glance, William hurried back to the horses' heads, where he soon became completely absorbed in petting them and talking to them.

Lydon watched him curiously for a moment before turning back to speak to Charlotte. "He is a nice lad and quite obviously has a way with horses. My team does not stand so quietly for anyone but Griggs, here." He nodded toward his tiger, who was observing William's easy communication with the high-spirited team with considerable astonishment.

Tears of relief and gratitude stung Charlotte's eyes. She blinked them quickly away. "Yes he is a dear, and horses, animals of all kind, are his passion. He spends as much of his time as he can at

the stables hobnobbing with the grooms; and I venture to guess
that he will soon add Griggs to his list of favored companions."

Maximilian, who had spent the better part of his childhood in
much the same way, smiled. "If the grooms and Griggs take a liking to him, then he is a rare person indeed. It is my experience that
those most critical of the human race in general, and one's own
faults in particular, are those who spend most of their time with
horses."

Charlotte chuckled as she could not help thinking of how nervous Cecil made any horse that happened to be near him and of the
barely concealed disdain with which he was treated by his own
coachman and by those who worked in the Harcourt stables. She
heard the crunch of gravel behind her and Cecil, seemingly con-
jured up by these thoughts, appeared with Almeria.

Beaming expansively, Cecil held out his hand. "Welcome to
Harcourt, my lord. We are delighted to have you as our guest; and
may I have the pleasure of introducing you to my esteemed spouse,
Lady Wadleigh."

Seething with indignation, Charlotte gritted her teeth and held
her tongue while her cousin contrived to welcome the marquess at
length to all the glories of Harcourt and enumerated all the ameni-
ties that were at his disposal.

Her fury was not lost on Lord Lydon. One glance at the
Wadleighs was quite enough to assure him that his card-playing
companion had known what he was about when he appointed him
guardian to his children. There was no doubt that Sir Cecil
Wadleigh was a grasping, obsequious little toad with a wife to
match, and that Charlotte, despite her obvious spirit and intelligence, was no match for them. She was one person against two
supremely selfish, ambitious individuals.

Barely acknowledging the Wadleighs, he replied, "Yes, Harcourt appears to be a charming place and Lady Charlotte tells me
that you have been availing yourselves of all the delights that it has
to offer."

The tone of his voice was enough to freeze the blood in anyone's veins, and the air of languid hauteur was calculated to de-
press the pretensions of the hardiest of toadies. Cecil flushed with
anger and Almeria shut her mouth with a snap.

Charlotte could barely refrain from hugging herself with glee as
her guest turned back toward her. Gesturing toward Harcourt's impressive facade, the marquess continued, "But pray, proceed, Lady

Charlotte. I believe you were about to show me around." Bestowing a dazzling smile on Lord Lydon, Charlotte took his proffered arm and led him up the front steps.

When they were safely out of earshot, she chuckled. "Thank you, my lord. That was exceedingly well done of you. I do not know when I have seen Cecil and Almeria so thoroughly put down, and I must say that I found it quite delightful to see them so utterly confounded."

Max smiled down at her. "Come now, Lady Charlotte, I cannot think that you are one to sit tamely by, supporting your cousin's sense of self-importance."

"No . . ." she admitted thoughtfully. "However, I should never dare to give him the cut direct as you did. I dare say that is what comes of being a man. A man is not so subject to the will of others and is therefore more likely to say and do precisely as he wishes without fear of giving offense."

The marquess was silent for a moment, struck by the truth of her statement. From the moment his father had cut him off and he had been forced to earn his own livelihood he had felt free to speak his mind whenever and wherever he pleased—not that he had given much thought to the opinions of others even before parental support had been entirely withdrawn. Before that, however, there had been some constraint there, some consciousness of owing something to his father when he had been more dependent upon him. That sense had vanished completely upon his dismissal from the family. He heartily sympathized with the frustration Charlotte must feel at the necessity of being civil to her poisonous cousin. Of course she was not beholden to Sir Cecil for financial support, but setting herself up in defiance of the Wadleighs would only make her situation more difficult and could ruin her reputation. A young woman on the verge of her come-out could not risk the slightest blemish in that regard if she had any hopes of contracting an eligible alliance and establishing herself in a home of her own.

"I am glad I was able to afford you some satisfaction. From now on I shall consider it my duty as guardian to administer at least one set-down a day while I am here. How is that?"

"Excellent. But I fear that my cousin is so thick-skinned and so determined to manage our lives that it will take a good deal more than a few insults to dislodge him."

Lord Lydon's glance swept the magnificent rose marble entrance hall with its imposing staircase and exquisitely painted ceiling. "I believe you are in the right of it. Harcourt is too rich a prize to pass up so easily. The park and surrounding lands are most impressive. With an estate such as this to enjoy I am astonished that your father did not spend more time at Harcourt."

"We were here."

The terse reply took Max by surprise and he stole a quick look at his companion. Her lips were pressed into a thin white line, her face rigid with some barely contained emotion that he could not quite fathom. "Surely you are mistaken."

Green eyes, dark with pain, glanced briefly up at him and then were hastily lowered as though their owner were afraid of revealing too much. "No, I am not. When it was discovered that Wil— that my brother would not grow into an heir worthy of following in my father's footsteps, he stopped coming to visit us altogether. We had always been something of a burden to him, involved as he was in politics, and he had already found it difficult to get away from town to come see us, but when he learned about William he could not bear to face the situation, so he simply avoided it."

"Leaving you in the care of . . ."

"My governess and William's nursemaid and the other servants. I was almost nine at the time and I was so accustomed to being on my own that at first I was not aware of any difference in his interest in us. Then not much longer after that, when it became clear that his tutor was no help, I began looking after William myself and trying to teach him to talk and, much later, his letters and numbers. I was so busy with William that I no longer noticed my father's absence."

The tale was told simply enough, but a great deal had been left unsaid of the loneliness of a child left without any parental attention. Even the infrequent and always critical attention that Max had received had been more than she had had. The hall they were standing in seemed vast and magnificent to him now, how much more vast and empty it must have seemed to a child of nine, how empty her life must have been if the devotion of her childish existence to a simple brother had formed the sole basis of it. Max looked down at her. What a tiny thing she was, and still so young—too young to have assumed all that responsibility.

His reverie was interrupted by the swish of skirts and the jingle of keys. Mrs. Hodges, notified of the guest's arrival, came bustling up to show the marquess to his chambers and Charlotte, after cautioning him that her brother was likely to be lying in wait to question him further about his horses the minute he reappeared, left him in the housekeeper's capable hands and went off to speak to Cook about preparing something special in honor of his lordship's arrival.

In fact, Charlotte need not have bothered to descend to the kitchen at all, for word of the marquess's arrival had already spread. "He is an out-and-outer, to be sure," panted the stableboy who, fortified with such momentous news, had had the temerity to burst into Cook's sacred domain without bothering to scrub himself thoroughly from head to toe.

"And he is ever so handsome," the youngest scullery maid piped up from her place at the sink.

"And how would you know that, Polly? That sink, which is where you are supposed to be with those potatoes, is nowhere near a window." The kitchen maid reproached her in a lofty tone, safe in her superior position opposite Cook at the kitchen table.

"That must be his lordship, the Marquess of Lydon, guardian to the young earl. Lady Charlotte told me that he was expected." Cook's grand pronouncement effectively silenced all of them. "We must see to it that his lordship is provided a meal worthy of Harcourt. Polly, run fetch me a breast of veal from the larder and two of the pheasants as well. And you"—she turned to the kitchen maid—"had better go and ask Mr. Tidworth for some sherry to put in a syllabub. By now he will have heard of his lordship's arrival and will be ready to bring out the best port." Cook trusted that the butler had managed to maintain the quality of Harcourt's cellars, even though the former earl had not availed himself of its treasures for more than a decade. Still, Mr. Tidworth, ever hopeful of a visit from the master, would have done his best to have something presentable on hand should he happen to appear.

Word of the marquess's arrival had spread like wildfire, from the gardeners trimming the bushes along the drive to the stableboys. Throughout the servants' quarters it had been passed along that he was top-of-the-trees, a true Corinthian, and furthermore, it was widely known that he had given the odious Sir Cecil and his shrewish wife a stunning set-down. Everyone, from the butler to the scullery maid, rejoiced that at last someone had come to put the Wadleighs in their place and restore smiles to the faces of Lady Charlotte and Master William.

Chapter 7

In fact, the guardian himself was thinking along much the same lines as Harcourt's devoted retainers. As he washed off the dust of his journey, Lydon marveled at the change in Charlotte's appearance when she smiled. In an instant she was transformed from an intense, almost dowdy little creature into an intriguing and attractive young woman. The change had taken him quite by surprise. It had been so brief, so transitory, that he was not even sure he had seen a woman underneath. However, the marquess was nothing if not the man for a challenge, and he resolved to try to bring that brilliant smile back to her face as often as he could.

Obviously, the best way to accomplish this was through William. It took no great powers of observation to see that Charlotte doted on the lad, lived for his happiness, and trembled lest he be made to suffer the unkindness of an unsympathetic world. The marquess had seen the way her eyes lighted up when he had called him *a nice lad*. He had felt her eagerness for him to understand and accept her brother when she had spoken of William's affinity for animals. The boy was everything to her, and no wonder, neglected as she had been by her father, left alone with no family to offer her support or sympathy of any kind. Her love for William and his for her must have been the only love that Lady Charlotte Winterbourne had ever known. How well he understood what that was like.

Being ignored by the two selfish, unapproachable people who had been his parents, Lord Lydon had suffered a childhood not so different from Charlotte's. Maximilian only hoped that she had been fortunate enough to have some adult—a nurse or a governess, perhaps—who had given to her all that Felbridge had given to him. Her fierce devotion to her brother was certainly a natural outcome of such an upbringing, and it was through this devotion that Max planned to win her trust and friendship.

The marquess paused in the middle of drying his face. Win her trust? What had come over him? He had left London that morning resenting the unexpected responsibilities that had been thrust upon him, intent on completing a burdensome task as quickly as possible and with as little cost to himself as he could manage. Now, in the space of little over an hour he was thinking about making Charlotte happy. How had this come about?

In part, this transformation was owing to William. There was something in the boy's open countenance and confiding expression that appealed to the marquess in a way that he had never before experienced. And this was further enhanced by his own reaction to Sir Cecil Wadleigh, a creature whose type Lord Lydon had encountered far too many times in his life: self-important, self-serving, and certainly not to be trusted. Seeing the two together, Charlotte and Cecil, innocence, and deviousness, the marquess had experienced a flicker of anger that made him sympathize heartily with Charlotte's passionate indignation at their situation and made him wish to remedy it as quickly and as effectively as possible.

The marquess finished his ablutions and, refreshed and ready to tackle both the Wadleighs, strolled to the door of his bedchamber. He paused to glance in the looking glass and give a final twitch to his cravat before stepping into the hallway. As he opened the door he caught sight of the shaft of sunlight pouring through one of the tall windows, illuminating the bright blond hair of the boy who jumped up eagerly from an enormous Jacobean chair the moment the marquess appeared.

Charlotte had surmised correctly. Her brother had been lying in wait for Lord Lydon. Unable to contain himself, William burst out, "Oh sir, that is the most bang-up pair I have ever seen. Such beautiful action, such deep chests. They must do sixteen miles an hour when you spring 'em. Did you get them at Tatt's?"

Flattered by the genuine admiration glowing in the boy's eyes, the marquess laughed and laid a kindly hand on his shoulder. "Whoa there, lad, one question at a time. Yes they are good for at least sixteen—seventeen if the road is good and they have not been given a good run for a while. And yes, I did get them at Tattersall's. I had been looking for a team for some time and then this one showed up. They belonged to the Earl of Dalton, who lost disastrously at Newmarket and was forced to sell off his cattle or mortgage his estate. He was accounted a fair judge of horseflesh, so I bought them and have been most pleased with them. But perhaps you would like to join me tomorrow and see for yourself what sweet goers they are."

"Would I?" William could barely speak for excitement. Then his face fell. "No, tomorrow is my long day for lessons with Dr. Moreland. That is my day for sums and I am dreadfully slow at them so it takes most of the day." He brightened as a sudden thought occurred to him. "But I could ask Charlie if I might have my lessons the next day instead."

"No, there is no need to apply to your sister to change your schedule. You have your lessons as usual and we can go driving the next day."

"Will you be staying with us the next day as well?" Such a happy thought had not occurred to William and he looked to be much cheered by it.

"I hope so, but it all rather depends on your sister."

"I shall talk to Charlie," William responded confidently. "We never have anyone visit except Cousin Cecil. Charlie frowns a great deal when he is around, but I expect that she would like to have someone as top-of-the-trees as you are as a visitor."

The marquess laughed. "I am not sure that those things that make me an interesting guest for you would make me an interesting guest for your sister, but we shall have to hope I can offer something that she enjoys."

William was silent for a moment, his forehead wrinkled in deep concentration. "You must talk to her of books. Charlie loves books and she never has anyone to talk to about them." He paused for a moment, fixing the marquess with an anxious look. "You do like books, do you not, sir?"

"Yes, I do like books, perhaps not the same sorts of books your sister likes, but I do like books."

"Then it is settled." William beamed, relieved to learn that his new friend was still the paragon he had at first taken him to be. "For Charlie likes all sorts of books—big ones, small ones, with pictures, or without pictures—and she is always reading. Yesterday my cousin Almeria was scolding her for reading poetry by some man who is very naughty, and the day before she told Cousin Cecil that he must not really have read Mr. Roo . . . Mr. Ruu . . . well, anyway, she said that he must not really have read him if those were the ideas Cousin Cecil thought he had."

"I *see*" Maximilian grinned. He could just imagine how happy the Wadleighs would be with an intelligent young woman who read Byron and Rousseau. Truly, his visit was promising to be more enlivening than he had hoped. Armed with the information William had just supplied him, he looked forward to a most interesting conversation at the table that evening. Undoubtedly the freethinking Lady Charlotte was a supporter of Mary Wollstonecraft and William Godwin, and he felt quite certain that the very mention of either or both of these names was likely to make the Wadleighs exceedingly uncomfortable.

With this in mind, Lord Lydon complimented his hostess at dinner that evening on the fineness of Harcourt's library. But before Charlotte could draw breath to reply, Almeria broke in. "Why yes, we have a superb library here at Harcourt. The carving is by Grinling Gibbons himself and there is none finer to be found anywhere in the country."

"Most fascinating indeed, but I confess that I find the books themselves more worthy of interest than the room, as, I have no doubt, does Lady Charlotte. I took the liberty of examining it this afternoon and I can see that it has been the work of generations of collectors going back in time a good deal farther than Mr. Gibbons and continuing to the present day. Is that not so, Lady Charlotte? The collection of contemporary volumes must be the result of your tastes, as I know that your father spent little time at Harcourt."

Effectively silenced, Lady Wadleigh subsided with an audible sniff while Charlotte, directing a grateful look at Lord Lydon, could barely repress a smile at the wicked twinkle dancing in his eyes. It was all too clear that he was baiting Cecil and Almeria— successfully too, if Almeria's heightened color and angry expression were any indication.

"Why yes, I have continued the work of previous Winterbournes, though I have also added the volumes from Papa's library in London. Reading is one of my chief pleasures." Here she darted a defiant glance at her cousin that the marquess was hard put to interpret. In all probability Cecil and Almeria might have criticized her for cultivating tastes that were far too intellectual and too liberal to be attractive in a female, but the expression in Charlotte's eyes hinted at something deeper than that. Maximilian wondered what it was and resolved to delve deeper.

"Surely that is a most admirable pursuit." He probed delicately.

"Admirable indeed, if not carried to excessive lengths, as our dear Charlotte is inclined to do. She is too studious by far, which cannot be good for her health." The heartiness and concern in

Cecil's voice was belied by the coldness in his eyes. Obviously there was an issue of some importance here, so critical that his wife could not refrain from adding her opinion.

"I have warned our dear Charlotte that she is in danger of becoming a bluestocking, which would never do. Men of the world, as you well know, my dear Lord Lydon," she simpered grotesquely at Max, "do not like a young lady to be forceful in her opinions, and they certainly would never marry such a one. We must see to it that Charlotte goes about in society soon, before she becomes too eccentric."

"Which is of little account in this case, as I have no desire or need to marry, though naturally, I thank my cousins for their concern." Charlotte smiled sweetly enough, but her eyes were flashing, and the iciness in her voice gave fair warning that this was dangerous ground indeed.

Max's eyes gleamed. So that was their game! They wished to marry off Charlotte and take the care and supervision of William into their own hands while they enjoyed all the luxuries of Harcourt just as much as if Cecil had actually inherited it. It was a clever enough scheme and might very well have worked if Charlotte had had the tastes of an ordinary young woman. But Lady Charlotte Winterbourne was no ordinary young woman, nor was she likely to be talked out of any course of action on which she had set herself. The marquess had seen enough of his ward to be sure of that.

"Then it sounds to me as though there is an end to your worries. If Lady Charlotte is fully alive to the terror that a learned lady strikes in the hearts of prospective suitors and stands ready to accept the consequences of pursuing her unfashionable interests, then I see no difficulty here. But"—the marquess turned to Charlotte and intoned in mock seriousness—"be aware, young lady, that an intelligent young woman is a most forbidding person indeed and is very likely to wind up completely independent and on her own."

Charlotte sighed inwardly with relief. Knowing the marquess's distaste for his newly acquired responsibilities, she had become rather nervous the moment the question of marriage had been introduced, for marrying her off would certainly be one way to insure her future and take her mind off William. To be sure, the general consensus among Harcourt's neighbors was that she should find a husband and relinquish the care of her brother to someone more suitable, but Charlotte would have none of that.

First and foremost, she could think of no one who understood William's needs better or had his interests more at heart than she did, and, secondly, she had not the least inclination for handing her life over to the whims and dictates of someone else. Having to answer to a guardian was bad enough—a husband would be ten times worse. But for now, she smiled gratefully at Lord Lydon, thankful that at the moment it appeared she had a guardian who appreciated her and understood her.

Chapter 8

Charlotte was not entirely correct in this. Though Lord Lydon heartily sympathized with her lack of enthusiasm for the married state, he did not fully understand this reluctance, so unusual in a young woman. His experience had taught him that single females, young or old, were all eager to rush into matrimony. In fact, most females seemed to make it the goal of their existences. He pondered this anomaly as he prepared himself for bed that night, but his curiosity was piqued. The next morning the marquess sought further enlightenment on what was a highly unusual outlook by approaching his ward as she was pruning roses in the garden.

"I have no need to be married," Charlotte replied matter-of-factly as she snipped a heavy pink blossom and laid it in her basket.

Max had never quite thought of it in these terms before. Every unmarried female he had encountered thus far had been so intent on remedying the situation that he had naturally assumed that women became wives out of inclination rather than necessity. Still, there was something in the bald finality of her statement that made him suspect that there was more to it than that. He pondered a moment. "I feel certain that any man worthy of your regard would welcome your brother into his house."

At last she looked up at him. Her face, shadowed by the broad brim of her chip bonnet, was grave. "I suppose so. However, it is not only William that I am concerned about. At the moment I am content as I am and since I do not need a husband to support me or care for me, I do not see why I should have to have one."

The logic was unanswerable, but still the marquess sensed that there was more to it than that. "There *are* other reasons to marry, you know. Even those most desperate to gain a fortune or raise their rank in the world give at least some credit to the power of love. And these days, most modern young ladies will insist on having love, or at least the romantic appearance of it, and will have none of a match without it."

"Oh *love*." Charlotte swiped at another fragrant bloom and added it to the pile in the basket.

"Do you not need love in your life?" The marquess was incredulous.

"No. I *have* love. I have William and he has me. He needs me and is happiest when I am with him, and I love him dearly." A tender smile flitted across her face at the thought of her brother. She turned to her interlocutor. "Do *you* need love, my lord?"

Maximilian was nonplussed. "Why, of course . . ." He faltered under the steady, questioning gaze. Did he need love? Until this moment, love was what he assumed he had been seeking in his numerous liaisons with the fair sex, but now that he considered it, he realized that it was not love at all, but something else, something even he, worldly and sophisticated as he was, was not prepared to discuss with this clear-eyed young lady.

Though Lord Lydon had begun the entire discussion, he now admitted to himself, for the sole purpose of shaking that cool self-possessed air of hers, to make her blush and lose countenance, the result was that he was losing his own. Such a thing had never happened to him before, at least not within recent memory. The conversation was not going at all as he had planned. "Ah, but we were not talking about me. I asked you. And I was not speaking of the love between a brother and a sister." There! Now he had her.

Charlotte smiled faintly. Though he had neatly side-stepped the issue, her guardian looked distinctly uneasy, and she had the satisfaction of knowing she had at least disconcerted him. "The love and affection William and I feel for each other is more than enough for me, and far more than one finds in most marriages, I dare say."

But there was a strangely shuttered look in her eyes as she responded to his question that made Max think it was more complex than that. There was something she was avoiding, something she would not or could not discuss, and he resolved to get to the bottom of it, though he could not have said why it mattered to him whether or not she wished to share her life with a man other than William. But for some strange reason, it did matter to him. Perhaps it was because he had witnessed that very affection between brother and sister that she had spoken of. Having observed her warm and loving nature, he found it difficult to believe that sisterly affection was enough for her. Even odder still, he did not want it to be enough for her. He had seen firsthand her passionate protectiveness of her brother, her intense devotion to his welfare, and he did not like to think that such passion would never have any other outlet than a simpleminded brother, that such a vibrant young woman would live out her days as a spinster buried in the countryside without ever having experienced all the richness—both emotional and physical—that life had to offer. It seemed such a waste somehow.

A slight cough startled the marquess out of his reverie and he glanced down to see Charlotte regarding him curiously.

"I had not thought my observation was such an unusual one, but it seems to have given you pause for reflection," she remarked.

"What? Oh, the fondness one finds in most marriages, or the lack thereof."

"How many of the unions you know were founded on love, or give any indication that love exists between those involved?" She demanded.

Max mentally reviewed the couples with whom he was most familiar, beginning with his parents. Certainly his mother and father had appeared to live in different worlds entirely as did most of his acquaintances in London. The men escaped to White's or Brook's in order to find true companionship and the women gossiped together over innumerable cups of tea.

"You see? People are forever urging marriage on single men and women, touting it as a blessed state, but if one stops to consider how things truly are, one comes up with a different perspective on it altogether. Surely as an eligible bachelor you must constantly have people telling you to *find a proper young lady and settle down.*" Charlotte shot a triumphant glance at him.

The marquess chuckled. For a young woman who had spent her days quietly at Harcourt, she had a keen grasp of society at large, but he still could not rid himself of the sense that she was avoiding something.

But all speculation was put to an end as William burst around the corner of the stone wall protecting the rose garden. "Charlie, Charlie, Mr. Griggs let me give an apple to . . ." He came to a full stop upon seeing his sister's companion. "Oh, excuse me, sir, I did not know you were here." He subsided into respectful silence for a moment, but then, unable to contain his enthusiasm, he continued, "Mr. Griggs is ever so nice, isn't he, sir? He allowed me to feed your team and showed me all their finest points."

"Yes. Griggs is as knowledgeable a man as you could hope to find where horses are concerned. If he takes a liking to you, as he seems to have, he can teach you more than anyone I have ever known about blood stocks and breeding, the ins and outs of knee action, how to raise horses that don't shy. You cannot go wrong with Griggs as your teacher. He was an orphan and grew up on a stud farm in Yorkshire. I was lucky to persuade him to come to me when his master was forced to sell out. I offered to pay him handsomely, but truth to tell, he finds life a good deal more dull with me. Training horses is his true interest and he only bears with the tame life I give him because I pay him so well and I have promised to set up a stud farm of my own some day."

"A farm of your own? For race horses?" William was quite pale with excitement.

"Yes. I have one or two particular ideas of my own about breeding and training that I should like to try, though at the moment I am too involved in other things to give the project my full attention."

If Lord Lydon had been a hero in William's eyes before, he had now reached the status of a demigod. "Do you go to Newmarket? Jem and Tim have told me that that is the place to see the fastest horses. How I should love to see it. I have asked Charlie if we may go some time, but she says that it is not the sort of place for young ladies to be seen."

"And she is entirely correct in that." The marquess directed a rueful smile in Charlotte's direction. "But we shall have to see what we can do about that. In the meantime, remember you *did* agree to go out driving with me," again he directed a meaningful glance at William's sister, "after you have finished your lessons."

Charlotte smiled fondly at her brother. "It was very good of you to remember your lessons when Lord Lydon offered you such a splendid invitation."

"I was good, wasn't I, Charlie?" He responded proudly. "But Lord Lydon said I could go with him another day."

"And so you shall, but now you had better run along. You do not want to keep Dr. Moreland waiting."

William looked as though he would not mind in the least making the vicar wait when such stimulating company was to be had, but he gave in with good grace and, bestowing a quick hug on his sister, went off toward the schoolroom.

"You are very good to take him driving, my lord, but you must not let him tease you. In general William is very well behaved, but horses are his passion and he tends to forget his manners in his excitement over them."

"I do not mind in the least," the marquess hastened to assure her. "I enjoy driving, and from the little I have seen, I can tell that William seems to understand highbred cattle thoroughly enough that he is likely to be a good passenger." Maximilian was gratified to see the anxious look fade from her eyes.

Charlotte's devotion to her brother was unlike anything he had encountered before. He was touched and humbled by her selfless dedication to the welfare of someone whom most ordinary people would simply ignore. For a moment the marquess wondered, almost wistfully, what it would be like to be loved so completely and disinterestedly.

Chapter 9

Maximilian had not been wrong in his assessment of William's capacities as a passenger. The boy's face was alight with happiness as they bowled down Harcourt's tree-lined drive the next day. He sat quietly, his eyes fixed for the most part on the marquess's hands. "You must have to be very strong to keep them in check when you spring them," he observed.

"Yes it does take a good deal of strength, but they have very sensitive mouths and respond very quickly. The thing is to plan ahead so that you pace them correctly and do not have to make any sudden moves. One should never have to haul on the reins so much as to lean back or to stand up. A good deal of that can also be prevented by being sure you have chosen the height of the seat correctly so that it gives full support to the back and legs should you have to rein in your horses. A driver should always remain straight in his seat."

"I *thought* that was the way it was supposed to be." William nodded with a good deal of satisfaction. "Cousin Cecil always leans way forward. He told me that is the way an alert person handles his horses, but I think he does not like to drive. He usually has his coachman drive; he says that being driven commands the proper respect from tenants, but *I* think he is afraid of horses." William lapsed into silence as they emerged from the drive onto the road and picked up speed, but after some minutes of what appeared to be deep thought he turned to the marquess. "Do you like Cousin Cecil, sir?"

Here was a question indeed, and Lord Lydon, for all his usual address, found himself at a standstill. The blue eyes fixed so trustingly on him begged him for some sort of an answer, but he knew not what. "I only just met him so I hardly know the man well enough to form an opinion." He hedged. For one who constantly scoffed at the polite lies that members of the *ton* traded with one another, Maximilian was finding it remarkably difficult to admit the truth, which was that he found Sir Cecil Wadleigh to be a rather nasty piece of work, and he chided himself for his lack of courage.

"I think he does not like me. I try to be nice to him and I told Charlotte that he could ride Duke if he likes, but she says that perhaps he is not used to boys my age and I should let him get to know me better. What do you think?"

Privately, Maximilian thought that he was in thorough agreement with the sentiment once expressed to him by Charlotte; he infinitely preferred William's company to Cecil's. At this particular moment he wanted to do nothing so much as tear William's slimy cousin from limb to limb for causing the look of hurt bewilderment in the boy's eyes. "I expect that your sister is in the right of it. Your cousin Cecil seems to be a bit starched up. He must have had some unfortunate experience with rag-mannered young people and therefore expects you to act the same way."

"Oh." William did not look convinced. "But he looks at me with mean eyes. I wish he were more like you, sir. You are a great gun, aren't you?"

Maximilian chuckled as he neatly feathered a corner. "There are not many who would agree with you. In general, I am looked upon as a shocking loose screw."

"You, sir? But you are top-of-the-trees. Anyone can see that."

"Why thank you, William. But in most company, it takes more than an eye for well-bred horseflesh and light hands to be accepted."

"But you would not want to be liked by people who did not admire those things, would you, sir?"

The marquess's lean, tanned face twisted into a sardonic smile as he recalled the disapproving stares of the town tabbies, marriage-mad young misses, and mothers of eligible daughters. "No, William," he replied slowly, "I would not. You are quite in the right of it."

Max gave the horses their heads as he mulled the entire conversation over in his mind. There was something strangely gratifying about the boy's unhesitating and unquestioning admiration. It had been a long time since someone had simply appreciated Maximilian for the person he was. Too often he was subjected to the disdainful looks of people who, without bothering to know him, accepted the general hearsay that he was a sad rake. Or he had endured the calculating smiles of women who cared nothing for the man, but only for the envy they would inspire in the breasts of others by attaching someone who was known to be unattachable.

With William the marquess felt the way he did with Felbridge and Griggs and with the horses and dogs he had loved over the years; that he could just be himself, Max, and that that was sufficient for them to enjoy his company. Responding to this comfortable feeling, he surprised himself by turning to the boy. "Would you like to hold the ribbons for a while?"

William was breathless with the honor of it all. "Could I?" he eventually managed to gasp.

Telling himself that he must be thoroughly and completely mad, the marquess nodded. "Here, sit closer to me and put your hands on the reins behind my hands, holding them just as I do."

William edged carefully over on the seat, doing just as he was told, his brow furrowed in concentration as he gently took the reins.

Slowly, carefully, Lord Lydon loosened his grip and withdrew his hands, watching closely and tensing himself to grab them back should the lad upset the horses with any unexpected movement.

He need not have worried. William, who always found quicker acceptance among animals than humans, was well aware that any sudden movement or change in the pull on the mouths of the horses could have disastrous effects. He remained as calm and steady as the marquess could have wished, hardly daring to let himself breathe. In fact, the team seemed to be entirely unaware that any change had occurred. They continued on as before without even so much as the flick of an ear to betray their sense of a new pair of hands on the reins.

They drove several miles this way, William sitting ramrod straight, his hands and arms maintaining the precise angle that the marquess's had, his eyes fixed steadily on the road ahead of him. Lord Lydon heaved a sigh of relief that the kindly impulse he had yielded to had not brought them to any calamity.

They approached a more winding, hilly stretch of road and William, never taking his eyes off the team, broke his silence of concentration. "I think you had better take over now, sir." He maintained his position steadily until the pressure on the reins in front of his hands slackened as the marquess took them back into his capable grasp. Then he slid smoothly back to his place on the seat. "Thank you ever so much, sir."

The blue eyes shone with gratitude and his entire being glowed with happiness. "You are so kind. I cannot wait to tell Charlie that I took the ribbons. She will be so surprised. They are very strong, are they not, sir? It must be most tiring to drive a very long way as you do." Then, overwhelmed and not a little worn out by his experience, he fell into silence for the rest of the drive, content to observe the countryside and enjoy the thrill of riding in a magnificent sporting vehicle behind a superbly matched team of horses.

His excitement burst forth, however, the moment they halted on the gravel under Harcourt's portico. Carefully climbing down he once again thanked his guardian and then raced up the steps shouting, "Charlie, Charlie, I drove, I drove! Charlie, Lord Lydon let me drive his curricle!" His voice echoed through the entrance hall as he raced off to the library in search of his sister.

The marquess climbed down more slowly and handed the reins to Griggs, who had materialized the minute the brilliant yellow of the carriage had flashed through the stately line of ancient elms along the drive.

"How did it go, sir?"

"Very well. I was even rash enough to let him take the ribbons."

The tiger's weather-beaten features puckered into a rare grin. "I imagined you might, sir. He is horse-mad, that boy, but he is a good lad and I'll wager he handled himself fine."

"Yes he did. He seems to have an instinctive feel for the animals."

"That he does, sir. It is a rare gift that I have not seen above a few times in my life. The horses seem to sense that he understands them and they trust him. Your Ajax was meek as a lamb yesterday when I let Master William brush out his tail."

"Ajax? Why even I take care to see that he is in a mellow mood when I approach him. The high spirits that distinguish him on the hunting field can also make him rather difficult to deal with."

"I know, sir, but he and the lad just took to each other, you might say."

"And you, too, Griggs. It is a rare person who wins your favor. You can be as touchy as your horses."

Griggs bobbed his head and chuckled as he began to lead the team back to the stables. "That is a fact sir, but I like the lad. Which I can't say the same for *some*," he muttered as he caught sight of Cecil emerging from the hall.

"Good day, Lydon. I see that you have been touring the coun-

try. We have some rather pleasant drives around here, and though
nothing in the surrounding countryside can compare with Harcourt, there are some rather fine houses which I should be delighted to show you."

Cecil's ingratiating smile was wasted on the marquess, who
thanked him briefly and turned to follow Griggs to the stables and
continue their discussion of William, but Cecil, having captured
the marquess's attention, was not about to be brushed off so easily.

"Tidworth tells me that you took young William driving with
you this morning. That was most kind of you, but there is no need
for you to devote your precious time to the boy. Almeria, who is
very good at these things, has come up with a proper companion
for him. Our housekeeper at Wadleigh, a very good sort of woman,
has recommended her cousin as being a person precisely suited to
acting as companion for a young man of William's ah, er, *condition,* and Almeria has written to her."

Companion? Keeper, more like, Maximilian muttered savagely
under his breath. "That is very thoughtful of Lady Wadleigh, but
entirely unnecessary. William's sister and I have discussed the
matter thoroughly and I see no reason not to leave things precisely
as they are."

"Leave them as they are?" Cecil was aghast. "But the boy is an
idiot!" Lord Lydon's raised eyebrows and incredulous stare silenced him, but only briefly. Smiling nervously, he continued,
"Come now, my lord, we are both men of the world and we can
admit to ourselves that the boy is not right in the head, nor will he
ever be. He is not fit for polite society and will be far more comfortable off somewhere else where he will not be exposed to the
agitating influences of the outside world. The housekeeper's
cousin is a capable girl with a good deal of sense about her. With
her and perhaps a maid to help out, William should do quite nicely.
I am sure we could find a nice little cottage in the country, say
Devon or Cornwall, where the air is healthy and the lad could be
quite happy away from the prying eyes and gossips he is subject to
here."

"You are *too* considerate." Maximilian did not bother to soften
the biting ironic edge to his voice. "But believe me, there is not the
least need to go to such trouble on his behalf. Lady Charlotte assures me that he is quite content here and, as to the good people of
Harcourt, why they accept him for what he is and like him for his

good nature. It is quite unnecessary for you to bother yourself on his behalf."

The sarcastic tone was not lost on Cecil. He flushed uncomfortably, but he refused to be daunted and tackled the problem from another angle. "You know as well as I do, my lord, that Charlotte cannot spend her life wasting away in the countryside looking after a simpleton. It is high time she is properly settled down in an establishment of her own, but she cannot hope to do that without a proper Season and that is out of the question if she is hampered by that . . . that boy. If his existence is kept quiet, she should take quite well. While it is true that blondes are all the rage at the moment, she is not ill-favored and she comes with a considerable enough portion that someone is bound to take·her."

Having been warned by Charlotte, and having already formed his own unfavorable opinion of Cecil, Lord Lydon was not so surprised or disgusted at this callous disposal of Charlotte's future as he might have been, however, he was surprised at the exception he himself took to Wadleigh's description of Charlotte. *Not ill-favored.* Why, when she was not on her high horse she was a taking little thing and when she smiled that conspiratorial smile at him as she occasionally did, she was truly enchanting. *Not ill-favored.* Maximilian found himself longing to wipe that condescending smile off Cecil's face in a most ungentlemanlike manner, however he restrained himself. "There is no need to put yourself out to such a degree, Wadleigh. As their guardian, I shall insure that the futures of both my wards are amply taken care of."

"Ah yes. This, er, guardian agreement. It is an agreement of some long standing, I collect?"

With difficulty, Max controlled his rising annoyance. The man's impudence knew no bounds, but then, Harcourt was a rich enough prize that it gave courage to even such a miserable coward as Cecil Wadleigh. "Since it had never occurred to me that a *gentleman* might question another gentleman's word, naturally I did not bring proof of my guardianship with me. However, you may consult with Harcourt's solicitor and my solicitor to allay any misgivings you might feel on this score." And without deigning to do so much as glance in Cecil's direction, the marquess turned on his heel and strode up the wide marble steps.

Cecil was neither particularly quick-witted, nor thin-skinned, but he did sense the implications of this stinging retort and, realizing that he had gone too far, hastened after Lord Lydon. "No offense meant, my lord. It was but a natural concern for the well-being of my young relatives that inspired me to voice my misgivings. But I am sure your lordship . . ."

The marquess did not bother to acknowledge his apologies with so much as the shrug of a shoulder and, nodding at the footman holding the door, he disappeared inside.

Chapter 10

Having seen more than he cared to of the Wadleighs, and with his sympathies now lying totally with Charlotte and William, the marquess began to devote his energies to ridding his wards of their cousins' presence—not such an easy task where such determined self-interest was involved and the stakes were so high.

Almeria felt compelled to point out these stakes to her husband when he later confessed to having questioned the validity of Lydon's claims of guardianship. "Really, Cecil, that was most ill-judged of you. Just because *you* were not aware of a guardian's existence until after your cousin's death does not necessarily cast doubt on his lordship's position. And whether or not it is all that is proper is immaterial. The Marquess of Lydon is a leader of fashion and a most powerful man; it would behoove you not only to accept his claims without a murmur, but to cultivate his good will. As usual, you have mishandled the situation completely. I must see what I can do to remedy it."

Consequently, Lady Wadleigh was more cordial than ever to the marquess at luncheon. Positively oozing conspiratorial friendliness, she attempted to compare notes with him on the fashionable world, referring to Lady Jersey and Mrs. Drummond-Burrell as though they were her closest friends, calling Lord Lydon a *sad rake* and smiling coyly at him as though they had shared innumerable intimate conversations at countless *ton* functions. She went on to the point that Max was hard put to decide who annoyed him most—the impertinent Cecil, or the fawning Almeria.

It did not help matters in the least that when at last he was able to look away from Lady Wadleigh, he encountered a pair of green eyes, brimming with amusement, fixed on him and his loquacious partner. The amusement was transformed into surprised gratitude when Maximilian, prompted as much by an urge to discompose the Wadleighs as to encourage William, turned to the boy, remarking, "William and I had a most enjoyable drive this morning. He was kind enough to show me the countryside." He nodded encouragingly at William.

"Yes and Lord Lydon let me take the ribbons and I drove for a way without making any mistakes, didn't I? His team is bang-up. The action is smooth and the—"

"Thank you, William. I am sure it was most kind of Lord Lydon to allow you such a privilege, but you need not describe it to the very last detail." Cecil hastened to stem the tide of William's enthusiasm, but his efforts were wasted as Maximilian, refusing to allow this bald-faced exclusion of the boy, chose to continue the conversation.

"William is quite a good judge of horseflesh and he is entirely correct in praising my pair. They are certainly unique and I spent a good deal of time and effort tracking down horses that were so perfectly matched, not only in size and color, but in pace and stride."

"Lord Lydon says it is almost impossible to acquire grays and that one must pay an extra price to get them," William could not help adding.

Charlotte, thoroughly enjoying her cousin's discomfiture at being preempted in the conversation, threw in her own comment for good measure. "So that is why it is said that grays are unfashionable; it is not that they are so much out of favor with the *ton* as they are beyond the reach of most people."

Max grinned. "One might say that, if one cared what the fashionable world thought. Color was the least of my considerations when purchasing them, however."

"I wager it did them no harm in your eyes that they were beyond fashionable." The teasing glint in Charlotte's eyes became even more pronounced while the saucy smile hovering at the corners of her mouth lent a piquancy to her usually serious expression.

"*Touché!* I am discovered at last. But as you also insist on avoiding that world altogether, I stand in no fear of having my secrets spread throughout the *ton.*"

It was Charlotte's turn to chuckle. Really, the marquess, when he was not ignoring one completely or acting odiously overbearing, could be quite amusing.

However, Almeria and Cecil, completely excluded from the conversation in general and the repartee in particular, did not share her appreciation of Lord Lydon's charm. In truth, they were not a little put out by his ready acceptance of William and his easy camaraderie with William's sister; however, there was very little they could do except smile and bear it with as good grace as they could muster.

"And how long can we hope that you will be with us, my lord?" Almeria inquired sweetly, gritting her teeth at the conspiratorial glance exchanged between the marquess and his ward. Really, he was allowing the girl to act far too familiar with him. If he were not careful, she would lose all respect for him and he would have no authority over her whatsoever. Charlotte was already inclined to be pert enough as it was toward her elders and held far too little appreciation for their superior wisdom; the last thing she needed was encouragement.

"Why I expect that I shall stay long enough so that you and your husband feel satisfied that you are leaving your cousins in good hands and are comfortable enough to return to Wadleigh Manor without any qualms on their behalf," he responded just as sweetly; however, there was a firmness in his voice and a steadiness in his eyes that left no uncertainty in anyone's mind that he expected this to occur in the very near future.

"Oh, but we would not dream of leaving poor, dear Charlotte all alone in this vast place until, until . . ." Almeria faltered under the marquess's ironic gaze. ". . . until suitable arrangements have been made," she finished lamely.

Charlotte opened her mouth to point out that having spent her entire life *all alone in this vast place* she stood in no need of *suitable arrangements* just because the father who had never visited them had passed away, but she was quelled by the look from her guardian.

"Naturally you are concerned for your relatives' welfare, but there is absolutely no need, and they must not grow to depend on two people whose responsibilities lie elsewhere."

Even Almeria did not have the temerity to respond to this clear dismissal. "Well, it is indeed true that Cecil has a great deal to attend to in Somerset. There is always some quarrel among the tenants, and our bailiff, Winklemere, though an honest person as far as that goes, is not so forceful with them nor so clear-sighted as Cecil."

Charlotte was hard put not to giggle, for the dumbfounded expression on Cecil's face revealed more clearly than any words how little accustomed he was to being given any credit at all by his imperious spouse.

"Then I think you may be able to assure Mr. Winklemere that you will be relieving him of his more onerous duties within a week."

Charlotte could have cheered, but as it was, she was afraid even to glance in the marquess's direction for fear that her jubilation at such a prospect would show. Much as she despised Cecil and Almeria, she truly did wish to avoid alienating them. Who would have thought that a guardian could turn out to be such a useful sort of person after all?

She said as much later to the marquess when they followed William down to the lake to feed the ducks. "I must thank you, my lord, for routing the Wadleighs. It seems that guardians are not such a bad thing to have."

Max gave a shout of laughter as he lofted a piece of bread over the heads of the crowd of ducks pecking at each other furiously to one lone duck too timid to join in the fray. "Aha, so I am not such a burden, then. Perhaps your esteemed Papa knew what he was about. However, they have not left yet."

"No, but I feel certain that they will for Almeria would never have admitted they were needed in Somerset if you had not routed her completely. It is only in the most dire of circumstances that she will allow that Cousin Cecil is good for anything, so you know that if she feels his presence to be needed at Wadleigh Manor you have won your point completely."

"Am I to gather then, that Cousin Cecil lives under the cat's paw?"

"If I were a cat, I should consider that an insult, but in general, yes, it is Almeria who disposes of things according to her view of the world, which leaves Cousin Cecil nothing to do but come the great man over William and the servants."

The marquess cocked a quizzical eyebrow. "You are far too acute for a young woman who has not been about in the world. It is no wonder that they are concerned about attracting an eligible suitor for you. Any young miss as outspoken as you will put all the self-important young bucks in a perfect quake. Though I have not bothered to look over your finances, I trust that your fortune is large enough to overcome this shocking defect?"

Charlotte could not help but laugh. "How lucky it is, rather, that I have fortune enough so that I do not need a husband, if that is indeed the way of the world. However, I cannot believe that an honest man would ever be frightened off by plain speaking."

"I count myself as honest a man as any, but even I entertain some favorite illusions about myself that I would prefer not to have dispelled by some overly perspicacious young lady."

"You, my lord? Surely not. I thought you were a *sad rake,* one of those men who cherishes no such illusions." Charlotte tilted her head to smile impishly at him.

"And where did you get . . . ? Ah, yes, Almeria. Now I know that you do not believe a particle of the good advice she lavishes on you, so why would you suddenly take everything she says about me as the absolute truth? You are not such a ninnyhammer, Lady Charlotte, and if you think you can tease me into sharing any of my particular illusions I might have about myself with you, you are fair and far out."

"Oh." Charlotte sounded disappointed, but only for a moment. "It is not only Almeria, but Emily and Selina Winslow also say that you have a reputation as a shocking libertine."

"My thanks to Emily and Selina, whoever they may be."

"Oh they are Lady Winslow's daughters, and very carefully brought up young ladies, both of them. They had a Season last year, you know, and are forever pointing out what a dreadful rustic I am. I must say that it set them back a bit when word got around that it was you who was to be our guardian." Charlotte's reminiscent smile suggested that this revelation had settled several old scores with the Winslow girls. "If one *must* have a guardian, I suppose you are not a bad one, and at least you are not a prosy old bore like Cecil."

"Thank you. If ever I feel that my character is in need of repair, I shall be sure to call on you to attest to it."

At this point, their conversation was interrupted by William who, having thrown in all his bread, came over to identify the different types of ducks to Lord Lydon. "Charlotte says that in St. James's park in London they have ever so many different kinds. We are trying to do that here, but we do not have too many as yet. She also says they have tame deer that will let you feed them and pet them just as if they were dogs. I should like that. Have you ever seen that, sir?"

Lord Lydon acknowledged that he had seen the deer, but much to William's disappointment he had not actually fed them.

"Do you know how they do it, sir, make them tame, I mean?"

"No, I am sorry to say that I do not, but I expect that they do it much the same way as they do with horses, slowly and carefully, gaining the animals' trust over time. But you know how to do that, William. Griggs tells me you have become great friends with Ajax, and he is an animal who does not take kindly to most people."

"He even eats carrots from my hand now, Charlie," William informed his sister proudly. "Do you think we could have deer here, Charlie?"

"I do not know, dear. I do not think that any live close enough to us for us to tame them."

"But you would know where we could get some, wouldn't you, sir?" He turned to his guardian, confident that the man's obvious authority where horses, tailors, and carriages were concerned, extended to everything else.

Maximilian was touched. Ordinarily, the more people expected of him, the more he resisted their expectations; however, William was different. His expectations arose not so much from a wish to exert control over the marquess as from an absolute faith in his omnipotence, a faith that was as irresistible as it was flattering. He smiled. "I expect I might. I shall have to make inquiries, though."

"Oh would you, sir? That would be famous!"

It was Charlotte's turn to smile, as she shook her head, murmuring, "Now you *are* in the basket, my lord, for he will not forget, nor will he let you rest until you discover something."

"I do not mind. I would like to do something for him. He is a nice lad." And strangely enough, Max meant every word.

Chapter 11

But it was not only William's wishes that the marquess wished to gratify. The more he saw of William's sister, the more he found himself wanting to do something that would enrich and enliven her life. Though Charlotte seemed perfectly satisfied looking after her brother and running both the household and the estate, to Maximilian, it seemed a lonely and cheerless existence. He began to observe her more closely. But the more he observed her, the more he realized that Charlotte enjoyed what she did and that he had done her a disservice in thinking her life hard because it seemed so in comparison to the frivolous, fashionable rounds pursued by the rest of his female acquaintances.

In fact, her life was not so very different from his own. She arose early each morning and, usually accompanied by William, rode for an hour or more after breakfast. Then she retired to the library to read and look over accounts. The afternoon was spent dealing with the housekeeper, the butler, the bailiff, and various tenants. In fact, it was a productive and energetic existence, so why did he feel the urge to add some gaiety and more companionship to it or to give her things that would make her life more like those of other women?

Charlotte was already more than grateful to her guardian for having removed what she considered to be the only flaw in her existence. Not very many days after the discussion at luncheon, the Wadleighs had departed, protesting loudly at the irregularity of a situation in which a bachelor of questionable reputation was left to look after a young woman not ten years his junior while blood relatives of the highest respectability were cast off without so much as a by-your-leave.

"For that is what we have been, Cecil, utterly cast off and ignored." Almeria climbed into their traveling carriage and settled herself huffily against the squabs. "It is a most improper situation for which I hold your mother completely accountable. If she had shown the proper sisterly regard for her brother, he would never have behaved in such a unnatural fashion, leaving his children to the care of . . . of . . . well, it does not bear thinking of."

Cecil, who mourned the loss of Harcourt's luxuries more than he did the possible slur on the family name, was left with nothing to say. He was not a strong man, and being pushed around by the combined forces of Lord Lydon and his wife had left him feeling most unfortunate and ill-used. It was bad enough that the idiot boy should succeed to all that rightfully should have been Cecil's, but to be virtually ordered off by the idiot's guardian, and then to be blamed for the entire thing by his wife was more than he could bear.

Cecil slumped dispiritedly in the corner of the coach thinking gloomily that life was most unfair. The farther that Harcourt and its magnificent park receded into the distance, the more injured and resentful he grew until at last he could endure it no longer. Crossing his arms in front of him he straightened up and began to think. He would not suffer silently such an unlucky situation, but would stand up for himself, take charge, and take back what he deserved. At the moment he was not precisely sure how all this was to come about, but he was determined that it would, and soon.

Cecil was not the only one whose plans had been severely disrupted by Lord Lydon's unexpected role as guardian to the Winterbournes. In the silken boudoir of a slim, elegant house in Brook Street, Isabella, Lady Hillyard, was listening intently to the most interesting report brought to her by her maid, Marie. A pert young French woman whose air of *à la modality* was second only to her mistress's, Marie was far too august a personage to have involved herself in anything so vulgar as espionage, but she had bribed an admiring housemaid who aspired to be a lady's maid with offers to teach her the art of coiffure if she would become friendly with the grooms who looked after the Marquess of Lydon's horses.

"Nancy informs me that Lord Lydon has gone into Sussex to a place called Harcourt." Marie was rhythmically brushing her mistress's blond tresses.

"Harcourt?" Lady Hillyard's blue eyes widened in surprise. The very little she had heard of the Earl of Harcourt did not offer any reasonable explanation for Lord Lydon's sudden departure. In fact, he was so rarely seen at fashionable gatherings that Isabella, who knew the ancient and illustrious title well enough, was hard put to recall the man. Yes, now she had it, a tall man with a serious expression whose only companions were men of politics, hardly the sort of person to offer diversion enough to lure the pleasure-seeking Marquess of Lydon into the country, especially when she, Isabella, remained in town.

The beauty's delicately arched brows snapped together in an irritated frown. Lord Lydon, skilled as he was in the art of love-making itself, often proved to be a frustratingly elusive lover, frequently failing to show the amount of devotion that Lady Hillyard required. In fact, it was very like him to disappear without so much as a line to her; he was so exasperatingly independent that Isabella sometimes wondered why she put up with him. However, he was so very rich that someone whose widow's jointure was disappointingly small could not afford to overlook him. Besides, there was no denying that he was devastatingly attractive. Just one sardonic smile or a lazily appreciative glance from those penetrating gray eyes could make her quite breathless with desire.

To be sure, the marquess, both by reputation and by his own admission, was a dedicated bachelor, but Isabella was certain that given ample time and opportunity, she could change all that. After all, it had not been so very long ago that she had taken the *ton* by storm during her first Season. With her golden curls, deep blue eyes, retroussé nose, exquisite complexion, and elegant figure, she had been lucky enough to appear on the scene just as dark beauties were falling out of favor in the fashionable world. Hailed as an incomparable from the moment of her introduction to society, she had had her choice of suitors. Governed by prudence and her parents' worldly experience, she had selected Sir Walter Hillyard.

Physically, Sir Walter was not nearly so prepossessing as his stunning bride, being an average-looking man of medium stature with an amiable, though undistinguished countenance. However, what he lacked in rank and physical appearance, he more than made up for in fortune. As he owned several prosperous coal mines and held a major interest in several canals, he was reckoned to be one of the warmest men in England. He had fulfilled his young wife's expectations, catering to her expensive tastes and furnishing her with ample pin money while turning a blind eye to her ever-increasing circle of admirers. Unfortunately, he had been killed suddenly in a carriage accident and thus Isabella, who had failed to provide an heir for her benefactor, was forced to live on her widow's portion while a distant married cousin enjoyed the full benefits of the inheritance.

Obviously, the thing to do for a woman who found herself in such an unfortunate situation was to remarry, but this had proven to be rather more difficult the second time than the first. It was not that Isabella had lost her looks; if anything she was even more stunning than when she had taken the *ton* by storm her first Season. Her figure had matured into voluptuous curves and her flirtatious smile had grown into a seductive invitation. In truth, more men crowded around her now than had ever before, but none of them was offering marriage. The dashing young widow soon discovered that while men thoroughly enjoyed a delicious dalliance with a sophisticated widow, they preferred to take younger, more innocent, and more biddable women as their wives.

Even Isabella, ordinarily so certain of her charms, had almost begun to feel discouraged when the Marquess of Lydon had appeared upon the scene. Possessed of a rather racy reputation himself, he appeared to pay not the slightest heed to the gossip whispered about Isabella among the town tabbies. Neither was he the least bit disconcerted by the throng of admirers that constantly surrounded her, never even bothering to acknowledge them whenever he sought her out. He always strode up to her boldly in a masterful way that brooked no denial. In any other man, such a calm assumption of his power to charm her would have infuriated Isabella, but where the devastatingly attractive Lord Lydon was concerned, this touch of arrogance only added to his charms and she found herself intrigued rather than annoyed.

His dedication to the bachelor state, however, was not so attractive, but Isabella, fully confident of her own captivating beauty, felt sure that it would only be a matter of time before she became the Marchioness of Lydon. This latest disappearance was something of a blow, but Lady Hillyard was a woman of infinite resource and in a situation where the stakes were high, she stood ready to spare no effort or expense in keeping herself informed. To this end, she had already liberally bribed the servants, both his and hers, but now it looked as though further outlays were called for. Nancy was summoned and questioned thoroughly and it was established that she had a younger brother who, for a handsome fee, would be willing to journey to Harcourt in order to learn more. While it was not unusual for Lord Lydon to disappear without notice, it was not like him to stay away for any length of time, and

Isabella was determined to get to the bottom of this mysterious behavior.

It was several days before Ned reported back to Brook Street, and the interval during his absence was most uncomfortable for all members of the household. At best, Lady Hillyard could only be called impatient and, under the strain of her lover's desertion, her temper deteriorated rapidly until Marie was the only one with enough temerity to face her; even she had had a Sèvres figurine hurled at her for venturing to suggest that Madame should perhaps concentrate her efforts on a more susceptible admirer, such as Lord Atwater.

"Lord Atwater!" her mistress had screamed. "What is a mere baron to a marquess?"

"Available." It was this reply that had brought the Sèvres figurine crashing to the wall behind her, and the maid, who ordinarily held herself aloof from the rest of the household, was inspired to remark to the rest of the servants at dinner one evening that Madame was far gone this time. "It is the marquess she wants and the marquess she will have and no one else."

"Well she won't get him," Nancy responded gloomily. "Everyone knows he has never kept a mistress for more than six months and has vowed never to get caught in the parson's mousetrap. The mistress will not be worth living with if she sets her sights on him." She sighed heavily, and the rest of them at the table nodded in silent agreement.

Everyone in Lady Hillyard's household had completely underestimated their lady's determination. The longer the marquess remained out of town, the more her determination increased until one day she astounded Marie by ordering her to see that things were made ready for a prolonged visit into Sussex.

"Sussex?" The maid echoed blankly. "But what about Madame's engagements—the Countess of Northcote's ball, Lady Featherstonaugh's rout, the Venetian breakfast . . ."

"I shall have to cancel them. My relative, Lady Marling, writes me that she is rather low and in desperate need of company, so I have decided to pay her a visit."

Marie, who had never known Lady Hillyard to yield to a humanitarian impulse in her life, gazed at her mistress in astonishment. "Lady Marling?"

Isabella looked just the slightest bit self-conscious. "She is my mother's second cousin, but we were close . . . almost as though we were aunt and niece."

Unable to hide her skeptical expression, the maid bent low over a flounce she was mending. Madame barely had any contact with her older brother, a highly respectable gentleman who refused to leave his estates in the country. That she could suddenly develop a fondness for a distant relation who happened to live in Sussex was as ludicrous as it was transparent.

Though she abhorred the country with the passion of a native Parisian, Marie was forced to admit that the pursuit of the Marquess of Lydon was bound to prove instructive, if not highly entertaining. "Very good, Madame, I shall begin the packing. Shall I alert the rest of the staff?"

Isabella colored ever so slightly under her maid's ironic gaze. "I suppose so. Though except for the coachman, it hardly seems necessary. We shall be gone for such a short time."

Chapter 12

Totally oblivious of his impending doom, Lord Lydon was discovering for the first time what a delightful companion a woman of sense could be. In fact, he often stopped to marvel in the middle of a morning ride, or as he was doing now, mulling over a move in their nightly game of chess, how comfortable he felt with Charlotte, more comfortable than he had felt with anyone ever before except perhaps Felbridge.

"It is your move, my lord," Charlotte said, breaking into his reverie.

"Hmmm." Seeming to ponder his strategy, Max tried to cover up his fit of abstraction, but it was no use, as the next move was an obvious one.

Charlotte glanced over at him, a twinkle in her eye. "That won't fadge, my lord. Come, admit it, you were woolgathering."

He grinned self-consciously. "Is it so obvious, then? Yes, I was. I was thinking how much I enjoy your company."

"My company!" It was Charlotte's turn to look slightly self-conscious.

"Yes, your company. I have never met a woman like you. You are comfortable to be with. Most women expect a constant stream of flattering speeches and admiring remarks about their persons and their attire."

"Oh." Charlotte digested this slowly. She had never aspired to be the sort of woman he was referring to; on the other hand, *comfortable* seemed hopelessly dull. "I suppose that when I have someone else to talk to I would rather discuss something other than myself, something interesting."

"A rare female indeed, unique, in fact."

"But surely your mother, or aunts, or cousins, did not expect constant flattery from you."

"On the contrary, my mother, when she noticed me at all, demanded nothing but that."

There was no hiding the bitterness in his voice. Charlotte's eyes softened. Poor little boy, she thought. Even now she could hear the loneliness in his voice. It was strange to think of the dashing Marquess of Lydon as a neglected little boy, but the bleak look in his eyes and the dispirited hunch of his shoulders gave him away. Oddly enough, Charlotte found herself wanting to make it all up to him, to give him the care and attention he had apparently never had from his mother and the warmth of feminine nurturing. She had been only five when her mother had died, but even she, despite all the intervening years, could remember the love and comfort that had been her mother. How very sad never to have known that.

"And checkmate." Charlotte's train of thought was rudely interrupted as Lord Lydon took her king.

"Blast! I should never have allowed you to distract me so. That is what comes of allowing one's head to be turned by flattery. I should have been warned by your ruinous reputation, but I ignored it, and to my peril. I *never* lose at chess."

Maximilian could not help chuckling at her discomfiture. It was such a refreshing change to find a woman who made no excuse for employing her intellect, but was proud of it instead. "Now where had you any news of my reputation?"

"Oh, it is common enough knowledge, my lord," Charlotte responded airily as she slowly picked up the ivory and ebony chessmen.

"As though you ever listened to common gossip, or were even in any of the ballrooms and drawing rooms where such rumors have their beginnings."

"Very well," she admitted, "In addition to the Winslows, Cousin Almeria said that you were accounted a shameless flirt and that no lady of any character would have anything to do with you."

"Ah, the oracle."

"Well, Almeria *is* concerned for my welfare." Charlotte shot a teasing glance at him. "And naturally, I am too."

"What a plumper! And you are nothing of the sort. It is my belief that you, clever witch, are trying to discover just what it is that I have done to earn that reputation."

The man was entirely too acute, Charlotte acknowledged as she schooled her features into an expression of prim astonishment. "Why I would *never* . . ."

"I warn you, Lady Charlotte, I *am* more than seven, you know."

"Very well, then, what *have* you done to deserve your reputation?"

Her about-face caught him completely off guard. "Well, I . . . well . . ." he began helplessly. "Dash it, Lady Charlotte, no man talks to a woman about such things, especially a guardian to his ward."

"Oh pooh. You just finished telling me that I was not like other women."

He was no proof against the teasing light in the big green eyes. In fact, as she sat there, elbows on the table, chin resting in her hands, she looked more like a mischievous sprite than a young woman who had been shouldering the cares of a large estate and a simple-minded brother for the last ten odd years. She looked . . . adorable, and at the moment, he wanted nothing so much as to plant a kiss on the tip of her pert little nose.

What was wrong with him? Ruthlessly he squelched the thought. He was her guardian and she, for all her intelligence and capabilities, was little more than a girl in so many ways. Perhaps it was only an avuncular kiss that he wanted to give her, he comforted himself. An elusive dimple hovered at the corner of her mouth as her lips parted in a tiny smile, and he knew that the kiss he wanted to give her had nothing to do with avuncular feelings.

"I expect you are considered dangerous because you are not married, and as far as most women are concerned, men exist only to marry them. You are unnatural, my lord."

"No, merely interested in things other than flirtation. I have better things to do with my time than dance attendance on some demanding beauty."

"What things?"

Maximilian shot a suspicious glance at her, but she was no longer teasing; she was genuinely interested and, much to his surprise, Lord Lydon found himself telling her all about his life in India and even about his business affairs in London. Threatened by the enervating boredom of life in the *ton,* the marquess had maintained his interest in commerce and affairs that had been sparked in India. It was perhaps fair to say that he was just as well recognized and sought after in the City as he was in the ballrooms of society's most fashionable hostesses.

Charlotte listened with a good deal of amazement and dawning respect. Her incredulous expression showed Max more clearly than anything she could have said that heretofore she had considered her guardian to be nothing more than a frivolous man of the world—intelligent perhaps, but a useless fribble, nonetheless.

"Then you, my lord, are the perfect person to ask about the article I just read in *The Edinburgh Review* entitled "An Inquiry into the practical Merits of the System for the Government of India under the Superintendance of the Board of Controul.""

It was the marquess's turn to look surprised. That his ward was very clever he had no doubt, but he did not expect her to be quite so well informed or curious about the more complex affairs of the day. "And what is it that you wished to know?"

"It appears from the article that there are two differing philosophies in regard to the English presence in India: one, espoused by Lord Wellesley and the Board of Controul that, in the hopes of eventually increasing profits, the English should increase the territory in India that is under their influence despite the increased cost, and the other, held by the Court of Directors and the Marquess of Cornwallis, that the English should limit acquisition and then devote attention to the establishment of good government, the development of a sound system of justice, and the creation of a thorough understanding of the situation. Which philosophy do you prefer?"

For a moment Max was more intrigued by the tiny wrinkle that appeared between her eyebrows and the way her right eyebrow rose higher than the left when she considered a serious problem. He had flirted with countless women, had been beguiled by coquettish smiles and lascivious glances, he had observed them in court dress and abandoned déshabillé, but he had never actually watched one think before, and he found it oddly attractive and somehow more intimate than many of the more physically familiar scenes in which he had actively participated.

The questioning look deepened, and Charlotte's right eyebrow rose a fraction of a degree higher. He realized that she was waiting for a reply. "Oh, er, Cornwallis or Wellesley . . . well, the author of the article makes it appear a simple choice between the two when in reality it is not. What works in Bengal does not necessarily work in Madras, and it depends so much on who is doing the deciding that it is difficult to say which is correct." Lord Lydon could see the disappointment in her face and was acutely aware that his ward was relegating him to the ranks of adults who, when they could not be bothered to explain a thing, blamed it on the questioner's lack of intelligence or experience. As a bright, inquisitive child, he had suffered from that far too often to do it to someone else.

"Forgive me, I do not mean to sound condescending or to avoid the question, but the thing of it is, if there were a simple answer, it would have been done long ago and no article would have been written."

"And I expect it also depends on answering the question of why the English are in India at all. If they are there to make a profit, then one answer is correct; if they are there to bring peace and order, then the other is."

"Precisely." The marquess leaned forward as he thought for a moment, gazing into the fire, a faraway look in his eyes. "But it is also a question of immediate profit or later profit. At the moment, what England really needs is a market for manufactured goods. Napoleon has closed the continent to us and unfortunately, India is not yet advanced enough to use our manufactured goods. It only provides us with raw materials, but in time, with good administration and development, it could grow to need the manufactured ones."

There was an excitement in his voice that Charlotte had never heard before, and the intensity of his pose, the thrust of his head and shoulders as he stared into the flames, revealed a pent-up energy that was carefully held in check, hidden skillfully under his mocking pose of cynical boredom. This was the real Lord Lydon. This was the man her father had chosen as their guardian. No wonder Cecil had decamped so quickly and with so little protest, for the marquess was a force to be reckoned with. Charlotte wondered briefly, if irrelevantly, what Cecil would do when the marquess returned to London, but she pushed that thought quickly out of her mind as something too unpleasant to be considered at the moment.

"Then you must agree with the philosophy that says the English should concentrate on settling and administering the territories already within their sphere of influence rather than expanding further."

"And why do you think that?" The gray eyes, dark as slate, seemed to bore into her.

"Well . . . well . . ." Suddenly unsure of herself under his scrutiny, Charlotte faltered. After all, who was she, a country-bred young woman who had barely traveled beyond Harcourt, to speak of foreign trade to someone as worldly as Lord Lydon. But it was only the hesitation of a moment, as she told herself that there was nothing lacking in her intelligence—only in her experience. "Well, if it is as you say that we need more market for manufactured goods, then the more the English settle in India and export their way of life there, the more India will want the manufactured goods the English have to sell. And besides, war in general, and armies in particular, are so very expensive, even if new territory is gained."

The marquess's eyes gleamed and he chuckled. "Precisely so, and that is why I say it is all a matter of time as to whether or not it is profitable to concentrate on administration. But the politicians who are concerned with the renewal of the East India Company's charter only ask if it is profitable at the present moment; they do not have the foresight to consider how profitable it might be in the future."

"Perhaps that is because they are politicians, and politicians are, in the main, concerned with the present, whereas those involved in commerce and investment look more toward the future. It appears to me that only the truly great politicians try to see what the future holds and then shape their politics accordingly."

"Hmmmm. That is a truly provocative thought. The politicians, however, would not thank you for such a disparaging view of their calling, but I do think there is merit to what you say." Not only was there a great deal of sense in what Charlotte had said, it was the most stimulating conversation Lord Lydon had shared in some time with anyone—man or woman. In fact, the last conversation that he had enjoyed this much had been with Charlotte's father. It was easy to see how she had come by her native intelligence, but what had inspired her to keep herself so well informed? "How does it happen that someone who lives so far removed from all these questions follows them so closely and with such thoughtfulness?"

"You mean, how is it that a mere woman interests herself in things that are the proper concerns of men?" Charlotte fairly bristled with defensiveness.

"No, not at . . . well, yes." Max's apologetic smile was completely disarming. "You must admit that, for whatever reason, most women concentrate exclusively on their clothes, their households, or their gardens, and that makes you a singular woman. How did you come to be that way?"

There was no resisting the flattery of genuine interest, especially when no one had ever before evinced the least curiosity about

Lady Charlotte Winterbourne, her likes and dislikes, her passions and pursuits. "Papa was always devoted to politics, even when Mama was alive. After she died, he dedicated his life to them. When I could read well enough, I discovered that his activities and speeches in Parliament were often mentioned in *The Times,* so I read it every day to follow what he was doing. Then I was able to write him letters that would be of interest to him."

It was explained simply enough, but there was no hiding the longing in her voice or the loneliness in her eyes, at least not from someone who had also longed for attention from distant and disengaged parents in much the same way she had. Maximilian suddenly had a vision of Charlotte as a young girl poring over the papers and scratching out long letters to her father in a desperate effort to reach a man who barely, if ever, acknowledged her existence. His mind flashed back to the former Earl of Harcourt's chambers awash in books and papers and he pictured the stacks of letters that covered the earl's desk. How many of them had been from Charlotte?

The marquess had not yet dealt with the former earl's personal effects. He had felt somehow uncomfortable going through the belongings of someone who was not a relative, but now he was eager to collect them and restore them to the daughter who had been so desperate to know him. For the moment, however, Maximilian resolved that however much the earl might have ignored his daughter, her guardian was going to pay attention to her, to appreciate and encourage the mind that had devoted itself to those worldly affairs that had been her father's obsession. Fortunately, these affairs were equally as engrossing to him, and Lydon looked forward to further discussions.

Now, however, it was time for bed. A glance at his ward in the dwindling firelight showed that her eyelids were growing heavy, and Max chided himself for keeping her up so late when she had had a long day in the fresh air looking over fences with her agent, Mr. Sotherton. "I beg your pardon," the marquess apologized as Charlotte tried, not very successfully, to stifle a yawn. "I have selfishly kept you up amusing me. It is high time you were off to bed, my girl."

Charlotte blinked ruefully. "And I should beg yours, my lord, for being so obvious. I am not accustomed to dissembling, you see, and I fear that I make a poor hostess."

"On the contrary, you are the best of all possible hostesses, for you are genuine enough that I feel completely comfortable and at ease with you." It was, Max thought, a far cry from the way he usually felt with his latest mistress. Isabella was nothing if not exciting, but there was such a thing as too much stimulation. He thoroughly enjoyed her seductive ways and her skilled dalliance, but there were times that he wondered if he was ever allowed to see the real Isabella.

"Good night then." Charlotte rose gratefully and headed toward the door. She was loathe to put an end to such an enjoyable evening, but in truth, she was very tired. Having a stranger in the house, pleasant though it was, did take extra effort on her part, and though her days were more interesting by far, they were also more tiring.

Chapter 13

Maximilian, on the other hand, felt more rested than he had been in some time, accustomed as he was to keeping much later hours than he was keeping here. At this time most evenings he was usually making his way from one hostess's ball to another's rout or to Isabella's perfumed boudoir. In truth, he was finding it rather relaxing to be free from these social obligations and from Isabella's expectations. Lady Hillyard was as beautiful and as skilled a mistress as he had enjoyed in quite some time, but she was becoming rather too possessive.

What had begun as a purely physical liaison was starting to feel as constraining as any formally recognized relationship and Max was beginning to be held as accountable as any husband. As the son of an acknowledged beauty, Lord Lydon had had his fill of demanding women at a very tender age. He was not about to threaten the peacefulness of his existence by allowing another one into it.

Settling himself luxuriously in the comfortable chair in front of the fire in his bedchamber with the latest copy of *The Edinburgh Review*, the marquess decided to give Lady Hillyard her congé the moment he returned to town. It would be inconvenient to look for a new mistress, and undoubtedly there would be tears and reproaches, but these would not last long, if he were generous, and that would be infinitely preferable to the trapped feeling he had begun to experience since he had discovered just how many evenings Isabella expected him to devote to her.

Yes, it was definitely time to remove himself from the seductive but ever-tightening clutches of Isabella. The sense of liberation that accompanied this resolution was a fair indication to Maximilian of the danger that he had been in and he was almost grateful to his friend the Earl of Harcourt for having left him in a position that allowed him to escape the widow's company long enough to put things in perspective.

Lord Lydon would have been a great deal less pleased with himself if he had known that not two miles on the other side of the village from Harcourt Lady Hillyard was regarding her image in the looking glass with considerable satisfaction while Marie brushed her hair, and congratulating herself on having accomplished the first part of her plan.

Lady Marling, though somewhat bewildered by the sudden appearance of her long-lost relative, had nevertheless been delighted to welcome her. Knowing Isabella's propensity for gaiety and brilliant company, especially company of the male sex, Lady Marling had expressed some misgivings, but these were quickly dismissed by her guest, who assured her that she longed for nothing so much as the peace and quiet of the Sussex countryside after the exhausting round of the fashionable world.

If Lady Marling thought it exceedingly odd that such a devotée of fashion was escaping the metropolis before the gaieties of the Season were entirely over, she kept such observations entirely to herself and set about making Lady Hillyard as comfortable as possible.

The second half of Isabella's plan required only patience and an inordinate amount of loitering in the village's meager shop, where she was treated with exquisite deference by the shop's proprietor. Mr. Mapplethorne, entirely swept away by the beauty and sophistication of his newest customer, was soon sending to London for luxurious trifles for her, and he was so diligent in his attentions to her that Mrs. Mapplethorne was beginning to be quite cross with the bemused expression he wore most of the time now as well as with his absent-mindedness. "Really, George," she scolded him after one particularly irritating lapse, "you are behaving like a schoolboy. One would think you had never seen a pretty woman before."

"Now Martha, you know that is not true; I see you every day." George tried to retrieve some of his dignity. "She is most gracious, and I am learning a great deal from her about London styles, which can only benefit our business."

"She is up to something, I tell you. Women like her do not frequent country shops if they do not have to."

"Of course they do not, but she is visiting Lady Marling."

"And women like her do not visit ancient ladies in the country by choice."

"But Lady Marling is a relative of her mother's and a very close friend besides."

"Then why have we not seen or heard of her before? No, she is up to something, I tell you."

"But Martha, if it makes us richer, what does it matter what she is up to?"

"Humph." Mrs. Mapplethorne was not to be placated, at least not where a woman of such stunning beauty and captivating ways was concerned.

The shopkeeper was not the only one enjoying Lady Hillyard's presence. Many the farmer working in his fields took pleasure in watching her as she and her hostess drove about the countryside. Lady Marling was rather surprised at her guest's passion for fresh air, but she was delighted to indulge her for the weather was very fine and the scenery, if not particularly noteworthy, was serenely beautiful with its rich green pastures and tidy cottages.

But for all her attempts to engineer a chance encounter with the Marquess of Lydon, Lady Hillyard was forced to endure a week of killing boredom before she spotted her quarry one afternoon strolling down the high street in the village.

The marquess had taken Ajax to the local blacksmith where he had personally overseen the tightening of a shoe on his right foreleg. After assuring himself that Ajax was taken care of to his entire satisfaction, he had dropped in to the Green Dragon to sample some of the landlord's home brew and enjoy a bit of masculine company.

It was not that he had been bored by Charlotte and William, quite the contrary, in fact. Charlotte's mind was as quick and inquisitive as his own, so much so that there was no fobbing her off with vague references or fuzzy thinking. Sometimes, when she had triumphantly pointed out some fallacy, he even found himself thinking wistfully of the *ton*'s marriage-mad young misses who, in their constant efforts to please, agreed with everything he said. And though William did not challenge the marquess intellectually the way his sister did, his inexhaustible enthusiasm and his unbounded admiration for anything that Lord Lydon did were demanding in another way. Maximilian, who had never tried to please anybody in his entire life, found that trying to live up to William's high opinion of him could be quite fatiguing. Thus, the opportunity to share a tankard of ale in the uncritical atmosphere of the Green Dragon's taproom was too alluring to be passed up.

He had emerged feeling oddly rested and much like his former self when the silvery accents of Lady Hillyard's salutation had reminded him of the drawbacks of his former existence. "Why Lord Lydon, how delightful to come across you in this out-of-the-way corner of England."

For a moment, the marquess felt like nothing so much as some fox run to ground—a wily, clever fox, but a hunted animal, nevertheless. His resolution to give the lady her congé grew even stronger than ever. However, the carefully bland expression he adopted as he turned to acknowledge her greeting revealed none of his thoughts.

If Isabella had hoped for a warmer reception than Lord Lydon's expression of polite recognition, she was disappointed. Beyond agreeing to the amazing coincidence of their both appearing in the same small village in Sussex at the same time and allowing himself to be introduced to Lady Marling, the marquess evinced not the slightest interest in Lady Hillyard's presence in the neighborhood; nor did he offer any explanation for his.

Stifling her frustration at this patent lack of curiosity, Isabella smiled sweetly and expounded upon the beauties of the local scenery and the healthfulness of the country air until the incredulity of Lord Lydon's expression forced her to break off in some confusion and invite him to accompany them on their drive.

"Thank you, Lady Hillyard. Another time, perhaps, I should be honored to join you and Lady Marling, but at the moment I have pressing business to attend to back at Harcourt." It was a mistake, and Max knew it the moment he let his local direction slip.

Isabella was nothing if not determined, and when she had a definite goal in mind, she could be extremely clever. "Ah, your wards. I am longing to meet them—charming children, I am sure. My mother used to be dearest friends with the Countess of Harcourt when she was alive, poor thing. I should have called upon them earlier to tell them how fond she was of their mama, but my devoted hostess here has kept me so busy. Why do we not join you and you can make us known to them. Poor things, to have lived without a mother all these years." Isabella sighed sympathetically and would have dabbed at her eyes with a lacy handkerchief had not the sardonic glint in the marquess's own eyes warned her that this was carrying it much too far.

Maximilian knew when he was caught. There was nothing to do but admit to his mistake and cope with it as best he could. "I am sure they will appreciate your, er, *sudden* interest, Lady Hillyard. Now, if you will excuse me, I shall just stop in and fetch my horse."

And thus it was that half an hour later, William, who was preparing for his lessons, and had been looking longingly out of the window instead of at the corrections Dr. Moreland had marked in his grammar that needed further study, was the first to catch sight of the visitors. Without a thought for his tutor, he tore out of the schoolroom, down several flights of stairs, and burst into the library where his sister was perusing tradesmen's bills.

"Charlie, Charlie, it is Lord Lydon and some visitors."

"Visitors?" Charlotte's heart sank. "It is not Cousin Cecil, is it?"

"No. Two ladies in a carriage, but not so nice a carriage as Lord Lydon's, though."

"Hmm. Thank you, William. And William," she laid a restraining hand on her brother's shoulder, "let us wait until Mr. Tidworth announces their arrival so we can welcome them properly instead of rushing out at them."

"Oh." William plopped down obediently on a stool in front of the fire while his sister racked her brains to guess the possible identities of the women. She knew very well that the marquess had no female relatives and though Lady Winslow called on Charlotte, she never did so without both of her daughters. Besides, Charlotte felt reasonably sure that the Winslows were unacquainted with Lord Lydon.

By the time Tidworth came to announce the callers, Charlotte was almost as consumed with curiosity as William. Lady Marling's name was one she knew, though she had never met her, but Lady Hillyard was a mystery. Instructing the butler to make them comfortable in the drawing room, Charlotte stole out into the hall to glance quickly into an ornate rococo looking glass.

Assuring herself that she had no ink smudges on her nose and that her hair was in reasonably good order, she turned to her brother, but William too was presentable, having spent the day quietly in the schoolroom. Then, knowing they looked as best they could, given the unexpected nature of the call, she led the way to the drawing room to welcome the visitors.

Chapter 14

As they entered the drawing room Charlotte's first perception was that the marquess had somehow retreated back into his shell of cool indifference. Though he was physically part of the trio seated by the window overlooking Harcourt's magnificent rose garden, there was an aloofness in his expression and a rigidity in his posture that declared as loudly as if he had been sitting at the opposite side of the room that he in no way wished to participate in the visit. This expression changed, however, the moment he caught sight of Charlotte and William in the doorway. The gray eyes warmed and the corners of his mouth turned down in a faintly ironic smile. "Charlotte, William, this is Lady Marling and Lady Hillyard, an acquaintance from London who is visiting her. I encountered them in the village and when Lady Hillyard discovered that I was staying at Harcourt she expressed a desire to make your acquaintance. Apparently, her mother and yours were dear friends."

"It is most thoughtful of you to call on us, Lady Hillyard." Charlotte welcomed her visitor pleasantly enough, but with such a lack of enthusiasm that it was perfectly clear to Lord Lydon that she was no more convinced of the supposed intimacy between her mother and Lady Hillyard's than he was.

In fact, Charlotte had taken an almost instant dislike to Isabella. It was not that the lady was unattractive—far from it. Her ripe figure, its curves emphasized by the trimming on her lilac pelisse which crossed the bust Grecian style and drew the observer's eye to the voluptuousness of her bosom, was elegant in the extreme. Her exquisite complexion and deep blue eyes, which were accentuated by the bunch of lilac flowers draped around her white satin bonnet, made Charlotte feel quite drab and shapeless in her morning dress of plain white cambric. It was not that the lady was cold or reserved—quite the opposite. Lady Hillyard was simply charmed by the fortuitous circumstances that had made it possible for her to meet the Countess of Harcourt's sweet young daughter and her handsome son.

Lady Hillyard was beautiful and she was delighted to meet them, but still there was something Charlotte could not like about her. She objected to the air of condescension. Lady Hillyard's words were kind enough, but her entire manner betrayed her sense of superiority to Charlotte, to William, to country ways, to outmoded dresses, in short, to everything Charlotte was. Charlotte felt it all in an instant and her dark brows lowered mutinously.

Maximilian chuckled to himself. His ward was no fool. He watched those alert green eyes taking the full measure of Isabella and it was obvious to him from Charlotte's frigidly polite expression that she was unimpressed. It was equally obvious that Isabella was somewhat chagrined by the coolness of her reception at Harcourt. Accustomed to overwhelming one and all, male or female, duke or dowager, peer or peasant, with her style and beauty, Isabella was entirely unprepared for Charlotte's candid appraisal, an appraisal that, for all its innocence, left no one in any doubt as to her opinion of Lady Hillyard.

Refusing to be stymied by her failure to impress the sister, Isabella turned to the brother with renewed interest. After all, there was not a single male that she could ever recall having failed to reduce to abject adoration with the merest hint of a smile. "And you must be William. Do come and sit beside me." Isabella patted the space next to her on the yellow damask settee.

"Thank you." Smiling guilelessly up at the pretty lady, William obligingly took his place beside her and waited expectantly for her to say something.

"You are a fine young man, William. Your mother would be so proud of you, taking charge of the estate when you must long to be with your friends and—"

"Charlotte takes care of everything," William hastened to reassure her. "And I see my friends Jem and Tim every day when I am finished with my lessons. They wait until Dr. Moreland leaves and then they let me help them with the horses."

"Oh, ah, how very nice for you." Isabella glanced sharply at William, who continued to smile broadly at her. Edging imperceptibly away from him, she turned to bestow a coy smile on the marquess. "It is really too bad of you, Lydon, to deprive the *ton* of Lady Charlotte's charming presence. Surely you are not going to be so gothic as to keep her buried here in the countryside? She should be in London where all the young men can give her the admiration she deserves and where she can find a husband worthy of her."

Charlotte's eyes widened in alarm and she fixed them anxiously on her guardian. Almeria was one thing—smug and self-serving, she was easily resisted. This stunning creature was another story. However unenthusiastic Lord Lydon appeared to be, it was quite obvious to Charlotte that he and Lady Hillyard had once been on intimate terms, for no one, not even an Incomparable, would be so bold as to follow a man who was not a relative into the country.

And there was no doubt that she had followed him. Charlotte had never heard of Lady Hillyard's mother nor seen any letters among her own mother's correspondence, which Charlotte had saved and treasured. It appeared that Lady Marling, who sat so silently beside her houseguest, was just as bewildered by Lady Hillyard's sudden interest in Harcourt and its inhabitants as everyone else was. Certainly, if the barely concealed scowl on her guardian's face were any indication, Lord Lydon had not expected this visit either. How much influence did the beautiful Lady Hillyard have over Lord Lydon? From the little she had seen of her guardian, Charlotte doubted that anyone exercised much control over him, but he was rumored to be partial toward beautiful women, even Charlotte knew that. Would he listen when a beautiful woman told him that his ward should be married?

"Your concern for Lady Charlotte does you credit, Lady Hillyard, but I doubt that she considers herself to be buried in the countryside. I rather think that she likes her life as it is, do you not, Lady Charlotte?" There was just a hint of a twinkle in the gray eyes as Maximilian turned to smile reassuringly at her.

Charlotte let out an audible sigh of relief. She should have known she could trust him to respect her wishes, but still, one could never be sure about a man of his reputation who had so recently and so unwillingly become involved with the Winterbournes. Flashing a grateful smile at her guardian, Charlotte thanked Lady Hillyard for her interest and assured her that she was quite happy as she was.

The tiniest of frowns wrinkled Isabella's smooth white forehead. Such an attitude would not do at all. Besides being unbecomingly eccentric, it simply did not align with her plans. "But my dear, you really have so little experience of the world that you cannot know what you are saying," she admonished Charlotte gently.

"Believe me, as a widow I am well aware of the trials of being a woman alone in the world." Isabella paused to blink hastily once or twice, but as her large blue eyes were visibly devoid of tears, the effect was lost. "I wish you would allow yourself to be guided by me in this case, not only as a woman accustomed to the ways of the world, but as someone who cherished your mother."

Charlotte did not see either the truth or logic in this statement, but she held her tongue.

"But how very silly of me." Lady Hillyard pressed a slim hand to her forehead as if struck by sudden inspiration. "Perhaps you do not know any females in London. Why do you not stay with me? In my lonely state I would greatly welcome companionship, and as someone who is on the best of terms with the *ton*'s most brilliant hostesses I could insure that you would be invited everywhere."

This was stretching it a bit, for society's best hostesses, or at least those with susceptible husbands, had been rather leery of the dashing widow once she had put off mourning.

"Yes, that is it." Isabella clapped her hands in delight. "You must come stay with me and let me introduce you to the world. Not only am I a friend of the family, but I am a longtime friend of your guardian. Nothing could be more perfect."

Light dawned. Now Charlotte understood the motive behind both the visit and the invitation to London. It was not she who was Lady Hillyard's quarry, but the marquess. A quick glance at Lord Lydon's rigidly impassive countenance confirmed this. Refusing to acknowledge Lady Hillyard or her plan, he remained silent, his eyes fixed on his ward. Reflecting on the implications of all this, Charlotte was also silent. She had not the least intention of considering the proposal, but she could not help feeling the tiniest bit amused both by Lady Hillyard's breathless attentiveness and Lord Lydon's barely concealed discomposure.

It was William who broke the silence before it became too awkward. "I would like to visit London, Charlie, and you *did* promise to take me the next time you went. Let us go."

If Charlotte had not been so sensitive to her brother's feelings, she would have laughed out loud at the expression of horror, hastily banished, that swept over Lady Hillyard's exquisite countenance. As it was, she turned to William and replied in a offhand manner that she was far from feeling, "I know you would like to visit London, dear, and we shall. I have not forgotten my promise to you, but I believe that Lady Hillyard is returning rather soon and we will need some time to plan all the sights we wish to see and the things we wish to do. It may also be that Lady Hillyard, though she knows all the things a young lady would like to do in town, is not so knowledgeable about the things you would like to do. I think it would make much more sense to consult with Lord Lydon, decide on what we would like to do, and then plan our trip accordingly. What do you say?"

William, though he found it rather difficult to follow his sister's logic, had heard the words that recommended her plan to him—Lord Lydon—and he looked at his guardian hopefully. "Could you sir? Tell us what to see in London, I mean."

"Why I expect I could, William. There is no doubt in my mind as to what *you* would find most interesting in London, and that is Astley's."

"Astley's? What is that?"

"Why indeed, it is the most wonderful exhibition of horses, riders, and equestrian feats that you could ever hope to see."

"Oh, could we sir? Would you take us?"

"I should be delighted to, and to anything else you would care to see—the Tower of London, the beasts at the Royal Exchange, Madame Tussaud's wax statues."

If the marquess's ready reply to William's expression of interest was meant as a reproof to Isabella, it was entirely lost on that lady, but it was not lost on another. Charlotte smiled gratefully at him. "You are a veritable fountain of ideas for our amusement, my lord. Have care or you will be stuck with us for a month."

"I should enjoy it. I have never seen those things myself."

"What? Not even when you were a boy?"

"I was never allowed to visit London until I went to university."

The quiet finality of his tone expressed more than words possibly could have of the loneliness of a neglected childhood spent isolated on his estates safely away from his parents and the possibility that he might interfere with their lives.

"I am sorry." The words were simple enough, but the look of sympathy and understanding in those wonderful eyes told him everything—thanked him for appreciating her brother and treating him so well, thanked him for standing up to Lady Hillyard, and commiserated with the pain he had felt and the joys he had missed as the unloved and extraneous child of fashionable parents.

A smile flickered in his eyes. "Why thank you."

This intimate byplay was too much for Isabella. Accustomed to commanding all the attention in a room, she was not best pleased to discover the depth of communication that seemed to have sprung up between Lord Lydon and his ward. True, if she managed it correctly, he could be made to feel that acquiring a wife was the best thing he could possibly do for a young woman on the verge of taking her place in society, but from what she had discovered today, Isabella realized it was going to be difficult. She rose to go. "It has been delightful making your acquaintance, Lady Charlotte, and seeing Harcourt where your mother was so happy brings back my own dear mama to me. But, as unexpected visitors we have trespassed on your time too long, and indeed, I am afraid I have taken Lady Marling away from her own errands. I do hope I may call on you again so that we can have a chance to talk more about your mother and mine.

"No, do not ring for anyone to show us out; I am sure Lord Lydon can escort us and hear the news I have of our mutual acquaintances in London."

Occupied as she was by gathering her parasol and her skirts and ignoring William, Lady Hillyard missed the marquess's rueful grimace, but Charlotte did not, and she could not help chuckling to herself.

Chapter 15

Lady Hillyard might have given up for the day, but she had in no way relinquished her campaign. The very next day found her back at Harcourt bearing a locket belonging to her mother that she wanted Charlotte to have. She was lucky enough to find Charlotte in the library with her brother and her guardian, so there was an audience to witness this touching piece of generosity.

A night's reflection on Harcourt's latest visitor had done nothing to advance Isabella in Charlotte's eyes, and she was as reluctant to take the trinket as Isabella was eager to bestow it. As the little gold heart on the slender chain looked suspiciously new, Charlotte did not think she would be rejecting the gift of a treasured family heirloom, but Isabella made such a pretty show of delight in giving it to her, begging Charlotte to let her fasten it around her neck and exclaiming how charming she looked, that there was nothing for it, but to endure the entire scene with as good grace as she could muster.

Certain that the entire episode was staged for her guardian's benefit, Charlotte could not help stealing a quick glance at him and was relieved to find him gazing out the library window in a way that left no doubt as to his lack of interest in the entire scene.

"Lydon, it is too bad of you. You are not attending. Does not Charlotte look delightful in her finery? She is such a credit to you." Charlotte was not the only one who had noticed the marquess's patent lack of interest. "There, do you not see what a crime it would be to keep her hidden down here in the country?"

"I see nothing of the sort. If Charlotte wishes to remain here, I have no objection."

"Men!" Isabella flashed a conspiratorial smile at Charlotte. "They see life in such simple terms. They think that it is merely a question of doing what one wants in life, which is quite possible if one is a man, but a woman is not so free. She has her reputation to consider, and it is not so much a question of what she wants, rather it is what people think of her. It is all very well for Lydon to go gallivanting all over the country pursuing his own interests, seeing only the people he wishes to see, snubbing those he does not. People merely look upon him as dashing and independent, but they are no less eager to be seen with him in spite of his independent ways. However, if he were a woman, he would be labeled a raging eccentric and shunned by the best society." She laid a hand on Charlotte's shoulder. "I know that your guardian has your best interests at heart, but he does not know the world as I do. He needs a woman's perspective to show him all the pitfalls a young girl is faced with, do you not, my lord?"

All the time Isabella had been addressing Charlotte in a tone loud enough to be overheard, but to no effect. The marquess had remained rigidly apart from the entire discussion; now, however, there was no ignoring this direct appeal. "What you say may very well be true, but it applies only to the young woman who wishes to move in the fashionable world. For the young woman who does not, it is irrelevant."

This unerring masculine logic was too much for Isabella. She threw up her hands in a pretty show of exasperation. "You see," she appealed to Charlotte, "there is no reasoning with him. You simply *must* come to London and let me show you about. You will soon understand what I mean."

The conversation and the situation itself was at an impasse. Charlotte had not the slightest intention of visiting London in general, and Lady Hillyard in particular. And Lady Hillyard had not the slightest intention of letting the Marquess of Lydon remain out of her sphere of influence. It was time to call Isabella's bluff by luring her back to London, but Maximilian found himself surprisingly loathe to do so. Strangely enough, he had been enjoying himself in the relaxed and congenial atmosphere at Harcourt, and even stranger still, he had enjoyed feeling that his presence really meant something to Charlotte and William.

There was nothing like the warmth in Charlotte's welcoming smile as he strode into the room or the appreciative light in her eyes when he made some particularly telling point in one of their frequent discussions. And there was nothing so rewarding as William's pride and pleasure at being in the company of *a real Trojan,* as he insisted on labeling the marquess.

While Lady Hillyard in the country was unavoidable, Lady

Hillyard in the city was much more easily ignored. Lord Lydon could see from the determined look in those blue eyes that the flirtation was over. The lady's pursuit was in deadly earnest, and if he wanted to escape her clutches, it was, as he had previous decided, high time to give her her congé.

"Lady Charlotte may do as she wishes, but I must return to London soon. I have left my affairs in the hands of others far too long." Max was almost certain that his removal to London would draw Lady Hillyard back to the metropolis while his ward would remain at Harcourt, but he could not help being gratified by the disappointment he saw in Charlotte's eyes. It was not until he actually saw that expression that he realized how much he had hoped that she and her brother would want him to stay with them at Harcourt. Heretofore, he had worked sedulously to avoid any sense of obligation or relationship in which he would think twice about saying good-bye, but now, inexplicable though it was, he rather relished the thought that he would be missed.

"How convenient. I am just about to return to town myself for I have several social engagements that cannot be put off. I should be delighted to have you as an escort, my lord." Isabella smiled triumphantly.

This was a bold move even for Lady Hillyard, and Maximilian, catching the ironic glint in his ward's eye, could not help looking somewhat shamefaced as he gave in to this barefaced manipulation, but he did so with a marked lack of enthusiasm. "Very well, but I warn you that I travel at a shocking pace, and I travel very light."

Lady Hillyard was forced to be satisfied with this concession and, having gained her point, bade good-bye to Charlotte without even nodding in William's direction, and held out her arm for the marquess to lead her to her carriage. Charlotte and her brother were left to their own rather uncomfortable reflections.

William, at least, was very clear in his reaction to the marquess's upcoming departure. "Charlie, I don't want Lord Lydon to leave. Make him stay with us."

"I cannot do that, dear. His lordship is a very important man with many pressing affairs back in London that need his attention."

"But . . . but, *we* need him and we are having such a good time here."

"We *are* having a good time, but he has many people in town who need him too."

"Maybe if I told him how much we wanted him to stay here he would stay."

"That is very sweet of you, dear. I am sure he knows we want him to stay, but he cannot."

"It is that pretty lady who made him go, isn't it, Charlie? She is very pretty, but I don't think she likes us."

"She is just not used to people like us. Now run along to the schoolroom, dear. Dr. Moreland will be along directly and I must finish the accounts I was working on." Charlotte followed her brother from the drawing room, glad for the distraction of the bills.

William might have been entirely sure of his reaction to Lord Lydon's imminent departure, but his sister was not sure of hers. In fact, she was a mass of conflicting emotions, but the primary one she felt was relief—relief that she would not have to observe Lady Hillyard's fawning attentions to the marquess or endure her condescending air toward herself and William; relief that she would not have to wonder about the hungry look that stole into Lady Hillyard's eyes every time they rested on the marquess, relief that she would not have to speculate any longer on whether or not he felt that same hunger.

At first Charlotte had been certain of Lord Lydon's lack of enthusiasm for Lady Hillyard, but the more Charlotte had observed them together, the more she became convinced that the two of them had a history, had shared some intimate connection in the past, and perhaps shared one now. Charlotte felt distinctly uncomfortable with those observations. It was all very subtle—a glance here and there, an air of familiarity as Lady Hillyard took the marquess's arm—but Charlotte felt it, nevertheless, and suffered a host of conflicting emotions that came along with it. First and foremost among those was a dislike for the lady herself. Charlotte had mistrusted Lady Hillyard's motives and she disliked seeing her guardian under the cat's paw, especially the paw of this particular cat.

From disliking the marquess intensely at first, Charlotte had begun to have a certain grudging admiration for him and now she was beginning to realize that she actually wanted to look up to her guardian. At any rate, she did *not* want to think of him as just some town beau who could be led around by a beautiful woman.

But there was more to it than that. There was an undercurrent—

intense and inexplicable—between Lady Hillyard and the marquess that Charlotte could not really identify, inexplicable but no
less powerful or unsettling. Somehow it made her see Lord Lydon
as a man rather than as a guardian, and a very attractive man at
that. It was as though she were seeing him through the hungry eyes
of Lady Hillyard, noticing things she had never noticed before: the
powerful shoulders, slim hips, long legs, square jaw, and well-
shaped hands. Thinking this way made her feel as though the
breath were being squeezed from her body and there was a fluttery
sensation at the pit of her stomach. Charlotte did not like these sen-
sations; it was unnerving in the extreme and made her feel like
quite another person altogether, not the sensible, capable Charlotte
Winterbourne she was accustomed to being.

Now the marquess's visit was coming to a close and she and
William could return to the peaceful, comfortable existence they
had enjoyed before the arrival of Lord Lydon and Lady Hillyard.
Charlotte heaved a sigh of relief as she turned her attention to the
accounts lying on the desk, but the figures in front of her kept blur-
ring and slipping away to be replaced by mental images of her
guardian, his face intent as he proved some point to her in one of
their after-dinner discussions, or his broad shoulders bent over the
chessboard in friendly competition. In fact, the days and evenings
stretched empty before her, and the life which had previously been
busy and full now appeared dull and sadly flat. It was not an enlivening prospect and it was made even less so by the certain
knowledge that Lord Lydon would not have a thought to spare for
them as he immersed himself in all the delights that London had to
offer.

Charlotte shook her head, blinked, and tried again to focus on
the figures before her. At least the marquess's absence would force
the departure of the odious Lady Hillyard. What a piece of work
she was, so determined to attach Lord Lydon. From the gentleman's reaction, it was obvious to Charlotte that she would catch
cold at that. After all, the Marquess of Lydon *did* have the reputation of being a rake and a libertine; and libertines were not the sort
of men to be easily caught in the parson's mousetrap. He had certainly not bothered to deny his reputation. The one time Charlotte
had been close to learning more about this reputation, she had let
him slip on to other topics of conversation before she found out
anything. What had he truly done to deserve the raised eyebrows

and horrified expressions on the faces of Lady Winslow and her daughters or the knowing glint in Almeria's beady black eyes?

There had been nothing in his conduct at Harcourt that was not perfectly gentlemanly, but perhaps that was because Charlotte was not the sort of person men did ungentlemanly things to. She sighed. Perhaps she and William were better off without him. People rarely changed, and undoubtedly his libertine propensities would have asserted themselves sooner or later and she would have felt responsible for any repercussions in the neighborhood. Yes, it was better that he was going, but still she could not help wondering how he acted with a woman to whom he was attracted, for there was no denying that the Marquess of Lydon was a fine looking man—*a real Trojan,* as her brother would say. Charlotte smiled at the thought.

Chapter 16

Much as his ward had predicted, Maximilian reverted to his libertine propensities almost immediately upon returning to the metropolis, but this arose less from an inclination for these rakehell pursuits than from a wish to avoid the presence of a particular female.

The night after his arrival in town he put in an appearance at the theater with the intention of selecting a new mistress from the *corps de ballet*. As luck would have it, there was a performance of *Othello* and Max, a fervent admirer of the bard's skill in portraying the weaknesses of humanity, became so involved in the drama of jealousy and treachery that he almost forgot the purpose of his visit. Fortunately, a glint of candlelight on a blond head in a box opposite him reminded him of Isabella and her determined pursuit and brought his mind back to the issue at hand.

Act Three brought the appearance of Bianca, whose coyly seductive air toward Cassio betrayed an actress who was either very good at her profession or perfect for the role the marquess had in mind for her. His mind now at ease, Lord Lydon had a note conveyed to the lady requesting permission to visit her in her dressing room after the performance and expressing the hope that she might join him for a delicious private supper.

Ordinarily Maximilian preferred to woo his mistresses more slowly and seductively, but circumstances were pressing, and if the lady were to respond favorably to such a bold invitation, he would know he was dealing with someone experienced enough to know what she was doing.

He had chosen well. Madame Dufour was a woman of the world. The former Betty Trimble had left her village in Yorkshire in the wake of a traveling theater company at the tender age of fourteen, attracted as much by the free and adventurous life of traveling performers as by the charms of the French actor and dancing master Monsieur Dufour. It was unclear, even to members of the troupe, as to whether or not the nuptial knot had actually been tied; certainly they had lived together as husband and wife and she had been the picture of wifely outrage whenever his roving eye was attracted to other women. As this had occurred more often than not, their relationship had grown as antagonistic as any real marriage and had served to convince anyone who knew them that they were in fact husband and wife.

The strain in an already dramatic relationship was only increased by the rising popularity of Betty and the declining health of her *husband,* who was as fond of the bottle as he was of pretty women. Eventually, having fallen headfirst into a small brook during a drunken stupor, he departed this world leaving Betty with a suitably exotic name, a smattering of French and charmingly accented English, and a healthy cynicism where men were concerned.

Her success in the provinces had encouraged Betty, now Madame Dufour, to try her luck in the capital. Bidding a fond farewell to the troupe who had, to all intents and purposes, been her family for the last six years, she had signed on as understudy to one of the lesser actresses at the New Theatre Royal. Her cheerful personality and her ability to get along with even the most temperamental members of the company soon won her friends as well as the gratitude of the management, who saw to it that she was rewarded for her diplomacy by giving her bit parts that allowed her to demonstrate a genuine acting ability. This recognition allowed her to put into action the second half of her plan, which was to attract the attention of a wealthy protector, or if possible, several.

It was no time at all before Madame Dufour had captured the eye of a Mr. Bickerstaff, a successful banker with a penchant for aping his betters. Having built himself a mansion in Russell Square and acquired both a barouche and a curricle, he concluded that the next step toward establishing himself as a man of the world was to begin a liaison with a mistress—not a mistress so fashionable and so well known as to be demanding and expensive, but someone recognizable enough to make his friends green with envy. Madame Dufour was the perfect choice. In fact, the only drawback to the entire affair was that the lively thespian refused to let him set her up in a snug little house in Marylebone, but only allowed him to shower her with expensive trinkets. "For though I am extremely grateful for your generosity, sir," Madame had explained graciously, "I should never wish to take you so much for granted as to depend on you for my support. Such arrangements inevitably kill all possible romance." She had fluttered her dark lashes at him in a most affecting manner, one that never failed to make his pulses quicken. "And I, as you well know, am incurably romantic."

If the truth were told, Madame Dufour had resolved never to be entirely beholden to one man again and had deemed it expedient to keep all her options open, should a more lucrative or more attractive situation present itself. Fingering the thick creamy paper and observing the forceful flowing script of the marquess's invitation, she decided that just such a situation had presented itself. Betty, or Lise, as she preferred to call herself, smiled dreamily at her reflection in the looking glass as she removed the last vestiges of paint. Lord Lydon—she had certainly heard of him, but she could not quite remember him. Her delicately arched brows drew together in a charming frown as she tried to place him. No matter—she pinched her cheeks and bit her lips to bring just a little attractive color to them—he was the Marquess of Lydon, and that was enough for her.

Her pensive frown deepened. No matter who he was, she was not going to be so easy as to allow him to take her to dinner upon their first encounter. No, a woman had to have standards, no matter how attractive the proposition.

"My Lord Lydon," her maid announced. And as Betty rose to greet her admirer, she acknowledged to herself that the Marquess of Lydon was an *extremely* attractive proposition.

Surveying the tall, athletic figure, lean, tanned face, and gray eyes set deep under dark brows, Betty at last was able to place him. She had heard his name often connected with the dashing matrons of the fashionable world. "This is a most unexpected pleasure, my lord. Gossip says that customarily you confine your, ah, *interests* to the ladies of the *ton*."

Maximilian grinned. There was no false coyness here. He was going to enjoy dealing openly and honestly with this mistress for a change. "For once, madame, gossip is correct. However, situations change. Ladies of the *ton* are demanding. They expect nothing less than love or marriage for their attentions."

"How very fatiguing for you, my lord."

"Precisely. When I am with a woman, I wish to relax and enjoy myself and,"—his eyes traveled slowly from the dark ringlets tumbling over smooth, white shoulders to her voluptuously rounded bosom, slim waist, and the long line of her thighs—"I trust I do the same for them."

Betty smiled slowly, luxuriating in the delicious tingle that his admiring gaze sent racing through her. "I am sure you do," she murmured, licking her full bottom lip.

"Perhaps I could do the same for you."

"Perhaps." He had not moved an inch closer, but Betty could feel the heat from his body warming hers. Lord, he was handsome! She had not wanted a man so much in years, but she was not going to let a little thing like raging desire cloud her judgment. "We must discuss this further, my lord, but at the moment, I am desolated to say that I am late for an engagement. However, you may call on me tomorrow if you like. I shall be at home in my lodgings in Cadogan Place tomorrow in the afternoon after three o'clock."

"I look forward to it eagerly." Lord Lydon bowed low over the plump white hand that was extended to him before turning toward the door. He had not truly expected to be able to take this charming ladybird to dinner that very evening, but it had been worth the attempt. He had seen the desire in her eyes and sensed it in the parting of her full red lips. Her pride and her experience might have warned her not to accept his first invitation, but she wanted him, he had no doubt of that. Smiling to himself, he turned back just as he reached the door. "Until tomorrow, then."

"Tomorrow," she responded huskily.

Tomorrow proved to be as satisfactory as each of them had anticipated that it might be. By the time the marquess left the slim house in Cadogan Place the sky was tinged pink with the setting sun. Madame Dufour, reclining languidly on her peach damask couch, was reflecting with a good deal of satisfaction on the skills of her latest lover. Not only was he wealthy, he was devastatingly attractive and knew exactly how to please a woman. Betty stretched luxuriously and smiled dreamily.

Not since the earliest days of her brief infatuation with Monsieur Dufour had she actually enjoyed lovemaking. Since then, all her relations had been as much a career as her acting had been and she had viewed them with the coldly professional eye of a business woman. But this, *this* had been different—not that she was in any danger of falling in love with Lord Lydon. In spite of what she might tell her lovers, Betty was not the least romantic, but the hungry gleam in the marquess's eyes as they had rested appreciatively

on her bosom, the insistent pressure of his lips on her skin as he
had kissed her hand and then turned it over to kiss her palm and
plant lingering kisses up the inside of her wrist, had left her shiv-
ering in anticipatory delight. In truth, he had taken not much more
advantage of her than that, but his air of barely suppressed passion
had made her as breathless and excited as if he had done a great
deal more, and she looked forward eagerly to the time when he
would do that great deal more.

Sauntering back toward Curzon Street and his own chambers,
Maximilian was reflecting on his interlude with the charming actress with equal satisfaction. The sensuality she had exuded even
on stage had not been an act. The red lips invited kisses; the seductively lowered lids hinted at the desire sparkling in her eyes;
and the sensuous stretch of that magnificent body as she draped
herself on the couch begged him to run his hands over its ripe
curves. And he would do just that; oh, he would, but not quite yet.
Seduction was an art, and rushing it only ruined the pleasurable anticipation.

He chuckled to himself. Freeing himself from the clutches of Isabella was proving to be more than merely regaining his independence; it was going to be extremely enjoyable. There was no
question that Isabella would find out about his latest inamorata; the
servant who had tracked him down at Harcourt for his mistress
would have no trouble discovering the marquess's liaison with
Madame Dufour. In fact, he might be being followed at this very
moment. Max did not even bother to look around. The only question was whether or not this relationship with the actress would
make Lady Hillyard angry enough to break off with him or if Max
would be forced to make the break.

In the meantime, he had a great deal to do outside of his amatory adventures. There was a stack of correspondence to answer,
various merchants to contact about his next shipload going to
India, and the former Earl of Harcourt's chambers to deal with.
That would not involve much for he would have the furniture and
other belongings sent down to Harcourt and turn over any compli-
cated affairs to his solicitor, but he did wish to go through his late
friend's correspondence to make sure that there were no nasty sur-
prises, no unfinished business that might surface later to cause
Charlotte grief. She had not alluded to anything that might cause
her embarrassment or unhappiness, but the picture she had painted
of the earl as a cold and distant parent left Max with the impres-

sion that she knew very little about her father and was hungry for
any information that might make him more real to her. He felt certain that she would pore over all of her father's letters in a desperate attempt to know him better, and he did not want her
discovering anything that would tarnish her image of her father.
The marquess had seen the loneliness in those deep green eyes,
heard the longing in her voice whenever she spoke of the earl, and
he was determined to leave her with the best memories of her father that he could possibly give her.

Chapter 17

The next morning found Lord Lydon at the former Earl of Harcourt's lodgings in Mount Street. Seating himself at a battered mahogany desk littered with papers, he began to go through the drawers carefully and methodically. All of the earl's current and most pressing correspondence would naturally be on top, but the marquess was more interested in unearthing documents that would reveal something more about the man, letters that would have been important enough to him to save. Even a man so single-mindedly devoted to politics as the earl had been must have had some memento that he treasured, something that kept special memories alive for him.

Max opened the top middle drawer, which contained nothing but old keys, a pistol, and a few broken writing implements. The top drawers on the side revealed only old account books and a pack of cards. Finally, in the bottom right-hand drawer, way at the back, he felt something. Reaching deep inside the drawer, he pulled out two packets of letters, yellow with age and bound with a faded blue ribbon. Carefully he undid the ribbon and opened the first one, gently unfolding it and smoothing out the creases. It was covered in a childish scrawl, the words straggling haphazardly across the page at an oblique angle. *Dearest Papa*, it began, *We are well. I hope you are too. I am doing my lessons just as you told me, but I wish you would come home to us. We miss you. Your loving daughter, Charlotte.*

The script on the next one was smaller and neater and the sentences marched smartly across the page. It thanked the earl for William's pony and spoke glowingly of his progress with riding lessons. It went on in some detail about the writer's own lessons with Dr. Moreland. Again the writer begged the earl to visit Harcourt, but there was no mention of missing him and it was simply signed *Charlotte*.

There were others of increasing length and complexity and demonstrating improvement both in grammar and style. As they progressed, there was less and less mention of Harcourt, William, or any of the affairs at home and greater and greater discussion of the politics of the day. Maximilian could picture Charlotte poring over *The Times* and *The Edinburgh Review* searching for topics of interest to her distant parent. Had he answered her? the marquess wondered. There was never any reference to letters received, and Charlotte's were all dated at six-month intervals. Had she gone on faithfully for years and years writing to a father who never replied, striving to discover a topic of sufficient interest to him to make him answer her?

Lord Lydon finished the last of the letters and stared blankly across the room into the cold dark fireplace, but he was not seeing the sooty bricks; instead, he pictured a pair of wistful, dark-fringed eyes and heard a soft voice saying *and after I could read, I discovered that his activities and speeches were often mentioned in* The Times *so I read it every day to follow what he was doing and to be able to write him letters that would be of interest to him.* His heart ached for the serious young girl who had tried so desperately to please her father.

Why had the earl not responded? Any man would have been proud to have such a daughter: capable, intelligent, demanding none of the gewgaws and pin money or the London Season that most gently bred young women considered their birthright. Had the earl been so cold and selfish, so bent on living his own life, that a daughter's devotion meant nothing at all to him? Maximilian cast his mind back to the evenings spent at the card table with Hugo, trying valiantly to remember conversations, expressions, anything that might give a clue as to his feelings. True, the man had been single-mindedly devoted to his politics, but he had not been inhuman. In fact, the political causes he had given his support to were all humanitarian ones. He had been an outspoken and unremitting adversary to the slave trade and had worked tirelessly at reforming the poor laws. Why had someone so benevolent in spirit toward society at large been so begrudging of his interest and concern toward his own flesh and blood?

And what did he, Maximilian, care, anyway? The marquess shook his head ruefully. He had come a long way from wishing to hand over Lord Harcourt's affairs to his solicitor to poring over his private papers in an effort to bring some happiness to his children.

What magic had Charlotte Winterbourne worked on him to effect such a complete change?

Carefully, Lord Lydon put the letters back in order and gently retied them with the ribbon before turning his attention to the other packet. This one contained more than letters, for on the top of it was an oval-shaped object, wrapped in silk—also yellow with age. Gingerly he pulled away the folds of material to reveal a miniature of . . . Charlotte. No, it was not precisely Charlotte, for on a second glance he could see that the features were more delicate, the mouth not quite so generous, the lips more delicately sculpted, the cheekbones not quite so high, and the forehead not quite so broad. But the eyes were the same—deep green, dark-fringed, eyes that revealed a lively mind and an inquisitive nature, eyes that looked directly into one's soul.

Slowly Maximilian let out his breath, which he had been holding since opening the packet. He turned the picture over. On the back in a flowing hand was written, *My darling Maria 1770–1795*.

Now he was beginning to understand. Hurriedly, he turned to the letters, opening them gently, reverently. They were written in two hands, one delicate and spidery and beginning *My dearest Hugo* and the other bolder, stronger, and addressed to *My darling Maria.* For a moment Maximilian hesitated, overcome with the uncomfortable feeling that he was intruding in a private and very sacred place, but then his glance fell again on the portrait, seeing those eyes, but not those eyes—other eyes, Charlotte's eyes, filled with loneliness and yearning. Max read on, leafing carefully through the yellowed pages of shared dreams and tender outpourings.

In those days the earl's absences had been kept to a minimum and he had obviously chafed at their necessity, looking upon the affairs that required them as a duty rather than a pleasure and something that detracted from his home life rather than replaced it. But as Maximilian read on, he began to notice that though the earl inquired after his infant daughter, all his solicitude, all his anxieties over health and happiness were for her mother, and it almost appeared as though he asked after Charlotte simply to bring pleasure to Charlotte's mother, his beloved Maria.

Max paused over one line in particular. *I am distressed to hear of your being so anxious over the baby. You must take care that you do not wear yourself to a shadow over this. There are others who can help with the nursing, and you must not ruin your own delicate health, my love, in looking after her. Please take the utmost care of yourself and allow Tibbs to bear the burden of her care. You are not strong and I am frantic with worry over your own well-being.*

The marquess gazed off into space, the letter clasped loosely in his fingers. That must have been it. Harcourt, with all its happy memories of Maria, would have been too much to deal with after her death. And the sight of his daughter, such a constant reminder of her adored mother, would have been more than the earl could bear. It had not been a lack of love, as Charlotte seemed to think, that had kept her father from Harcourt and his family, but an excess of it. Unhealthy though it might have been for Hugo to be so wrapped up in his wife at the expense of his children, it at least showed him to be a man capable of love instead of the cold and distant figure of Charlotte's memory. And, following this line of reasoning, it also appeared that it was Charlotte and the memories evoked by her resemblance to her mother, not William and his disability, that the earl had been unable to face, that had kept him safely away in London and buried in his work.

The marquess sat wrapped in deep thought for some time. In a way, he almost envied Hugo's near obsessive love for his wife. Maximilian could not ever remember caring for anyone or anything with even a fraction of the fervor that the earl had felt for his Maria, but on the other hand, he had been able to remain remarkably level-headed and cool during most of his life—quick to act and able to make decisions without being blinded by his feelings—while he had seen many of his friends, some of them highly intelligent, rendered perfect idiots by a beautiful face or a charming manner. Max had never been a fool in his life.

Until this moment, he had been exceedingly grateful that he had never fallen victim to this sort of paralyzing passion, but now, reading these letters, he was not so sure. He felt very much like an outsider looking in, like a poor street urchin peering through a window at a sumptuously laid table and a warm fire on a cold winter's night. And if the coldly cerebral Hugo had once been madly in love, what was wrong with Maximilian, Lord Lydon, that he had never experienced the tender passion? Tender, no; passion, yes, he amended, and grinned as he remembered the way Madame Dufour had licked her lower lip in anticipation, how her magnificent bosom had risen and fallen with her quickened breaths as she had undressed him with her eyes in the silken drawing room of her house in Cadogan Place.

Yes, there had been a great deal of passion in the marquess's life. Women had been casting alluring glances at him since he had been a tall and gangly youth of fourteen, with his bold eyes and smoldering air of pent-up anger and frustration. He had been more than happy to oblige one and all, but none of the women who had thrown themselves at him had ever made his pulses stir with anything more than purely physical desire. Did he envy Hugo his all-consuming love, a love so overwhelming that when the object of it had died, the earl had, to all intents and purposes, died as well?

Max carefully refolded the last letter. No, he did not wish to be so obsessed by anything or anyone that he would cease to exist as a person in his own right; however, it would be nice to look forward to something as much as the earl of Harcourt had looked forward to seeing his wife after a long absence in London, to long for something as much as Hugo had longed to hold Maria in his arms.

How curious it was to look back over his own life in the light of these letters and realize that, despite an existence filled to the brim with travel and adventure, passion and excitement, in a certain sense he had never really lived. With the exception of Felbridge, Max had never really cared a great deal about anyone, never felt great regret at having to say good-bye or great excitement at the prospect of seeing someone. This certainly had kept him free from entangling relationships, but on the other hand, it had made him rather rootless—a man who never truly belonged anywhere. Until this moment, that sort of belonging had never mattered to him—he had actually avoided it—yet now he wondered if he had made a huge mistake in avoiding so assiduously all those ties that might have made him feel part of something.

He watched the motes of dust dancing in the sunlight that filtered through a crack in the drapes. The pain of loss must have been intolerable for Hugo to give up the vast green fields and spacious magnificence of Harcourt for these sparsely furnished and dimly lit chambers. At last Lord Lydon gathered up the packets of letters and the portrait, locked the door, and descended the stairs out into the sunlight.

Strolling along Mount Street he puzzled over how best to share his discovery with Charlotte. Surely the knowledge that her parents had loved each other dearly would wipe out some of the bitterness she seemed to feel toward her father, and surely an understanding of her father's real reasons for avoiding his family would erase some of her mistrust of love and marriage in general, and men in particular.

And what had these discoveries done for him? That they had had an effect on him Max was certain. What that effect was, was more difficult to articulate.

This somber and reflective mood was quickly banished the moment Lord Lydon entered his own chambers in Curzon Street. He had barely settled down at his desk before Felbridge handed him a heavily perfumed letter addressed in Isabella's unmistakably flowery script. *I do hope this finds you at home though it has been such an age since I last saw you, I fear you have left town again. At any rate, I expect to see you at Lady Charlton's rout. Isabella.*

It was as desperate a note as Lady Hillyard had ever written. Accustomed to being able to pick and choose among her admirers, she had never been forced to sit at home and wait for one to call on her, which was precisely what she had been doing since she and the marquess had returned from Sussex. It had been a humiliating and enraging experience. Life in the elegant house in Brook Street had been unbearable for all those forced to endure her ladyship's ill humor.

Isabella had expected the shared experience in the country to bring her and Lord Lydon closer together and in fact, when she had first set out on her journey to Harcourt, she had fully expected to return to London as the future Marchioness of Lydon. Not only had this happy state failed to materialize, but she had not laid eyes on the marquess since their return. Marie's optimistic observation that if she had not seen Lord Lydon at any of the *ton* functions, at least that meant she had not seen him with any other fashionable beauty, had only earned the maid a scolding in language that would have made a sailor blush.

At last Isabella had resorted to this note, a step she had never been forced to take in her life, and one that did her already questionable temperament no good. She labored mightily over it and by the time she handed it to the footman to deliver she was so fatigued by her travails that she was forced to retire to her darkened boudoir where a solicitous Marie made sympathetic noises and bathed her ladyship's aching head with lavender water as she lay in bed, prostrate from having to sink to such desperate measures.

"He cannot help but call now," Isabella muttered as her maid removed one sweetly scented compress to replace it with a fresh one.

"Even he, oblivious as he is to these things, knows that Lady Isabella Hillyard never begs for the attention of any man. I vow I shall make him pay for this."

"Hush, Madame. Lie still now. You are working yourself up." Marie dabbed gently at her mistress's brow and rubbed her temples soothingly.

"But Madam, surely you do not wish to have it thought that you are willing to share his lordship with an actress?" Nancy, bringing in a fresh bowl of lavender water, spoke up despite the murderous looks directed at her by her superior.

"*What!*" Isabella shrieked, sitting bolt upright in the bed upon which she had been reclining so limply.

" 'Tis nothing, Madame. Now lie back." Gently but firmly, Marie tried to force her mistress back against the pillows. "Calm yourself, Madame, it is only an empty rumor."

"I will not be calm." Isabella struggled against the restraining hands on her shoulders and turned to face the hapless Nancy. "Where have you heard this, girl?"

" 'Tis but common knowledge, Madam. Everyone knows that Lord Lydon can be found at the New Theatre Royal every night. Why he has seen *Othello* three times running, all to catch a glimpse of Madame Dufour. And it is also said that he is the only one among her crowd of admirers that she admits to her dressing room after the performance."

"Is this true?" Isabella looked to Marie for confirmation.

The maid nodded.

"I shall go mad! All that time wasted! Those endless boring days with Lady Marling in Sussex! Ooooooh," Isabella moaned, sinking back among the pillows while both maids applied cool compresses to her brow.

"Madame must not waste another thought on such a scoundrel. Madame must appear tonight at Lady Charlton's rout more beautiful than ever and looking as though she had not a care in the world. And Madame must be seen on the arm of my Lord Atwater, who is just as wealthy and of a family far older and far more distinguished than that of Lord Lydon's. While it is true he is only a baron, his—"

"Be quiet, Marie," Isabella snapped. She sat up and pressed her fingers to her temples. "Leave me now, both of you. I must think."

The two maids crept out silently, closing the door behind them so carefully that even the click of the latch could not be heard. But once outside, Marie turned on her underling with a vengeance. *"Quelle Bêtise! Stupide!"* she hissed. "How could you upset Madame so? Now our lives will be a misery, and all because of your tongue. You will never be a true lady's maid, for that requires the utmost of discretion, of which you have none!"

However much she was in awe of Marie, Nancy was not about to suffer such accusations in silence. "Perhaps I have no discretion, as you call it, but at least I am kind. Far better that Madam knows the truth than that she make a fool out of herself going after that one. *He* is not one to get caught in the parson's mousetrap; and since Madam will settle for nothing less, she is better off without him." Nancy smiled slyly. "Not to say that he is not a handsome devil, though. If I were Madam, I should forget about marriage and enjoy him; better to have a lover like the marquess than a dull dog of a husband like Lord Atwater."

Marie snorted disdainfully. "In Madame's world, reputation is everything. A husband of Lord Atwater's standing is not easily found."

"All the more reason to forget the marquess and look for some-one better, if marriage is what she wants."

Though she would never go so far as to admit it to anyone else, Marie acknowledged to herself that Nancy had been right in telling their mistress of Lord Lydon's perfidy—not that they were not all going to suffer from it, but the sooner Lady Hillyard's mind was turned to more productive channels, the better. Long ago Marie had planted the notion of Lord Atwater's availability in her mis-tress's head; it was time to concentrate on that.

Chapter 18

The Marquess of Lydon was also intruding entirely too much in the thoughts of another woman, but unlike Lady Hillyard, she was trying to focus them elsewhere. Back at Harcourt, Charlotte was trying to concentrate on some of the things she had not paid attention to during their guardian's visit, but it was turning out to be a more difficult task than she had imagined. The man had only been part of her life for less than a month, but his impact on it was as profound as if she had known him for years. She constantly caught herself wondering what he would think of this or what he would say to that.

It bothered her intensely that he kept interrupting her thoughts in such a manner. Perhaps Almeria and the Winslows were right after all and a Season would do her good. If she were to go to London she would be exposed to lots of men and then perhaps one man in particular would cease to preoccupy her to the extent that he did now. She would be able to put him in perspective, forget about him, and continue on with her life as before. William needed her and she had no energy or thought to waste on anyone else if she were going to help him take his place in the world.

As it was, she had been remiss in assisting him with his lessons. In order for him to absorb or remember anything, she really needed to go over in the evening what Dr. Moreland had taught him during the day. It was agonizingly slow, and her patience was frequently tried as she grappled with different ways of explaining the same thing to him in a desperate effort to make him understand. Sometimes she was forced to give up, as she had today when her brother had protested. It made her head ache to recall the entire scene. William had been trying so hard, but he could not help feeling discouraged, nor could she. "But Charlie," he had protested, "why shouldn't I spell *through* 'thrue' like *blue,* or even 'throe' like *shoe,* when it sounds the same if you say it?"

"Because it just *is* that way, that is all."

"But why?"

"I do not know, William."

"But that does not make sense, Charlie."

"I know, dear." Charlotte rubbed her aching head as she struggled to come up with some logic that would help him remember such illogical spellings. "To tell you the truth, I cannot explain to you why it is that way; it just *is,* and the only thing you can do is to commit it to memory."

"Oh." William looked doubtful.

"You can do it, dear. I know you can."

"If you think so, but it is very hard." He sighed and ran his hand through hair so rumpled already that he looked as though he had been dragged backward through a hedge.

Yes, it took everything Charlotte had to help William cope with the world. The last thing she needed was to be troubled with thoughts of a man who at this very moment was probably out carousing, a man who had probably ceased to remember their existence the minute his curricle had passed through the gates of Harcourt.

Charlotte sighed and forced her attention back to the copy of *The Times* she was reading. Ordinarily she treasured these hours in front of the library fire after the rest of the household had gone to bed and she was alone at last, free to think her own thoughts and read whatever caught her interest. However, what had formerly been an oasis of peace and quiet from her crowded routine, now gave her some of the most unsettling moments she had yet experienced as she relived the evenings she had spent with the marquess as they had shared her special time of day in the warm and intimate atmosphere of the library—her sanctuary in the vast magnificence that was Harcourt.

These once-treasured hours of tranquility now seemed more like hours of emptiness. For the first time in her life, Charlotte began to question whether the existence she had chosen for herself was enough. At the moment, she was kept busy with the demands of the estate and her efforts to give William as normal a life as she could, but what about the future when her brother had learned all that he could and gained all the confidence she hoped to give him, what then?

Charlotte sighed again, laid down the paper, banked the fire, and headed toward her bedchamber and the welcome oblivion of sleep.

Perhaps she was just tired. A good night's rest was bound to dispel her melancholy state of mind.

The next day, while it did not bring answers to the questions troubling her, certainly brought diversion. Charlotte was in the housekeeper's room discussing the inventory of linens that they had been conducting when William came bounding in. "Charlie, Charlie, there is a man out there with a horse and . . . and . . . he says it is for me, and he says it is a present from Cousin Cecil, and it is all for me! Come see, come see!"

Casting a rueful glance at Mrs. Hodges, Charlotte excused herself and hurried along to keep up with her brother as he raced back down the long echoing corridor to the entrance hall, out through the wide portico, and onto the drive where an enormous bay stallion was tossing its head, rolling its eyes, and shifting uneasily from one foreleg to another. "Look Charlie, isn't he wonderful? And this man says he is mine."

The scrawny, weaselly looking man, who was holding the bay's reins with some difficulty, touched his cap with exaggerated deference. "Tom Piggott at your service, my lady. I am here on the instructions of Sir Cecil to deliver this here horse to the young master." He glanced nervously at his charge as though he expected at any moment to be dragged the length of the driveway or trampled to death.

"You see, Charlie, Cousin Cecil *does* like me after all."

However, Tom Piggott's ingratiating manner was lost on Charlotte, who eyed him skeptically. "And how is it that Sir Cecil has suddenly become a fancier of fine horseflesh, and even more suddenly overcome with generosity?"

The groom began to shift as uneasily as the animal. "As to that, my lady, I could not say. All I was to do was to bring this horse and help the young master ah, er, get to know him."

"I doubt if William needs your assistance in that." Charlotte looked over at her brother who, having extracted one of the ever-present lumps of sugar from his pocket and offered it to the horse, was now chatting earnestly with the enormous stallion as it licked greedily at his hand.

The groom's jaw dropped in amazement, but he recovered quickly enough. "Well," he laughed with forced heartiness, "they seem to be in a fair way to getting to know each other, but this is one spirited animal and he wants looking after by someone as what is wise to all his little tricks, and there is no one who knows them better nor Tom Piggott does, my lady; of that you can be sure."

"Very well, Mr. Tom Piggott. You will find the coachman, Mr. Speen, in the stables and he will direct you as to the proper quarters for the horse and for yourself. In the meantime, why not leave your charge here and William can look after him while you see to your lodgings."

"That is very kind of you, my lady, but I hardly think the lad is up to handling . . ."

"I have every confidence in my brother's ability with horses. You need not concern yourself," Charlotte replied serenely as she turned to join William in welcoming his new acquaintance.

His protests effectively squelched, Tom Piggott swallowed his chagrin at being so quickly and easily dismissed, touched his cap, and led his own horse toward the stables while Charlotte took a closer look at the unexpected present from Cousin Cecil.

"Isn't he magnificent, Charlie? Just look at those shoulders— and those hindquarters. He should be a very sweet goer. Just look, Charlie."

"I *am* looking, dear." But while William exclaimed over the powerful shoulders and hindquarters, his sister was viewing the rolling eyes, tossing head, the nervous twitching of the tail, and the stomping of the wicked-looking hooves with some dismay. "Perhaps we should let Speen take a look at him, dear. He appears rather ill-tempered to me, and you know that if a horse is vicious there is nothing that can be done to change it."

"No, Charlie, please. He is not vicious. I know he is not. *Please* may I keep him? I know he and I can be friends."

Charlotte would have been hard-put to resist the pleading in her brother's eyes, but then he softly stroked the stallion's nose and she could see the animal relax under his reassuring touch. There was no doubt that William had a gift where horses were concerned, and if anyone could calm this nervous, high-strung animal, most certainly he could. Besides, she did not have it in her heart to deny him. He asked for so little and tried so hard to please. Though he was not aware of it, life had deprived him of so much, the least she could do was to give him a chance with his new present. "Very well; you may keep him, but I want you to be guided by Speen in all of this. This horse is more horse than you have ever had to cope with and I want you to be careful."

"I will, Charlie, I will." His face bright with happiness, William turned to whisper into his new friend's ear all the fine things they would do together.

"I expect you had better choose a name for him." Charlotte smiled fondly at her brother's excitement. "Why don't you and he discuss it while I go and tell Speen about the latest addition to our stables."

Charlotte found the coachman overseeing the stabling of Tom Piggott's horse. "I hear the young master has received a surprise," the sinewy leather-skinned old man greeted her. "I have just instructed the lads to show Mr. Tom Piggott to their quarters and make a place for him there."

"Thank you, Speen." Charlotte directed a significant look at the coachman, jerked her head toward the door of the stable, and walked toward the cobbled courtyard.

Speen followed her out into the sunlight and waited until they were well out of earshot before turning to his mistress. "What is it, my lady? Something is troubling you for certain."

"It is this horse, Speen. For one thing, you know as well as I do that my Cousin Cecil is as uncomfortable around a horse, a pony even, as a rabbit is with a fox, and a more thorough-going nip-cheese you could not hope to find. Furthermore, he detests William. Now why would a man like that suddenly give William a very expensive present, especially a present that is as nervous and temperamental as this animal looks to be? I do not like it. No, I do not like it in the least, but William has his heart set on keeping the animal and we shall just have to do what we can to keep him from getting hurt. But what is Cecil up to, I wonder?"

"Nothing good, if you do not mind my saying so, my lady." The coachman scratched his head. "It is a puzzle to be sure. Here is a man who would not give the time of day to someone and now he has sent a horse. It does not make a particle of sense. I'll keep an eye on the lad and the horse, though from what I see, there is not an animal alive as does not take to Master William. As I see it, the boy has some kind of magic in him."

Charlotte's eyes filled with sudden tears. "He does, doesn't he, Speen? And we must see that he gets a chance to do the best he can with that gift."

"We will, my lady. I promise you that." The sudden gruffness in the old man's voice was not so much for the boy, who was too simple ever to suffer anything more than a transitory and easily comforted sorrow that a child suffers, as it was for the sister, who endured the constant sorrow of trying to make a place for him in a cold-hearted world—a place where he would feel accepted, understood, and happy with who and what he was. It was a crying shame that such a lovely young woman as the mistress should have such a heavy burden to bear all alone with no one to confide in. Certainly, her relatives were of no help—a pair of scavenging dogs snapping at her heels, trying to get as much as they could of Harcourt for themselves. Lady Charlotte was right to mistrust the shifty-eyed Cecil and his imperious wife. The coachman was in complete agreement with her on that score; and he was equally in agreement with her in her suspicious reaction to this unexpected present that had just appeared upon the scene without warning.

Chapter 19

In fact, William was the only one in all of Harcourt who did not question mightily the appearance of the big bay stallion and its groom. And he was the only one who did not immediately condemn the animal as being a nasty, vicious brute, fit only to be a cart horse that would be worked hard enough to keep it too exhausted to exhibit any temperament at all. Indeed, it was a miracle that the horse did not subject the boy to the wicked kicks and nips that it gave to everyone else who tried to approach it. When William appeared, the flaring nostrils relaxed and the rolling eyes focused on him with something akin to trust.

"I think he likes apples," William confided to his sister the morning after the horse's arrival. "Cook gave me a bit of apple tart yesterday afternoon when I was feeling a bit peckish and he licked my fingers. I shall ask Mrs. Hodges if I may take some from the storeroom to give him." Just as William predicted, apples were a huge success and the household grew accustomed to seeing him with his pockets bulging awkwardly as he headed toward the stables.

Caesar, as the horse had been named, seemed to be ready to act like a reasonable creature for a few bits of apple and words of gentle encouragement from his young master. "I shall just let him become my friend first and then we shall see." William was firm in his resistance to Tom Piggott's urgings to put the stallion through its paces. No amount of recounting the stallion's prowess in speed and jumping could dissuade William from following his program of leading the horse around the pastures of Harcourt, acquainting it slowly with its new home and master.

"And in truth the lad seems to know what he is about for the creature is a good deal calmer now, and even lets Jem and Tim near him without getting into a pucker. He won't do the same for Tom Piggott, though. 'Tis clear as the nose on my face that he does not trust the man, nor do I, my lady," the coachman remarked to Charlotte one morning as he drove her into the village.

"I am afraid you are in the right of it, Speen. I too have my doubts about Tom Piggott, but I can hardly send him back to Cecil without some sort of explanation, especially if he was meant to be part of Cecil's gift to William. And I can hardly say that I suspect Cecil of trying to do William a mischief. In the first place, if he *is* trying to harm William, I must prove it and that is best done if I do not put Cecil on his guard by sending his servant back. In the second place, it is not polite to accuse a relative of being havey-cavey, even if . . . even if . . ."

"Even if he is," the coachman replied with all the familiarity of a servant who had helped Charlotte on her first pony and reassured her after all her subsequent falls. Speen considered himself, along with Mr. Tidworth of course, as a father figure for both the Winterbournes, and he was not about to let such a minor thing as a difference in station stand in the way of plain speaking. "For it is my opinion, my lady, that Sir Cecil is up to no good."

"Oh, undoubtedly; though I would not have thought that even Cousin Cecil would have wished any disaster to befall William. However, it does appear that he presented him with an unmanageable horse in the hopes that that is precisely what would happen. Fortunately for William, Cousin Cecil reckoned without my brother's knowledge of horses. We shall just have to make Piggott report back with an account of how changed an animal Caesar is. Why, the beast is practically docile now. That will make Cousin Cecil think twice about making William look the helpless fool."

Privately, Speen thought that Sir Cecil had something rather more dastardly in mind than proving the young earl to be hopelessly incompetent, but he kept his thoughts to himself. Time would tell, and in the meanwhile, he would keep a close eye on William while Jem and Tim did the same for Tom Piggott.

Though she had put a brave front on it for Speen, Charlotte was made uneasy enough by the entire episode that she wrote a long, detailed report to Lord Lydon, a report that held no illusions as to her cousin's nefarious behavior, and then she waited anxiously for a reply, trying all the while to keep a watch on her brother without letting on to the rest of the household her very real fears for his safety.

As far as William was concerned, he could not have been happier. His patience and dogged persistence paid off and soon he was riding Caesar around the pasture and then on nearby lanes, returning every time full of praise for the horse's action and stamina. "You don't often find a horse that walks as well as he gallops, but Caesar is good at all of it," he exclaimed over and over to his sister until she was thoroughly tired of hearing it. In fact, William's only reservation was that he was neglecting poor Duke for his new mount until he had the happy thought that Tom Piggott could exercise Duke for him. "I don't think he likes Caesar much, but he'll like Duke. He is always telling me to ride Caesar because horses need exercise, so I must make sure that Duke gets exercise too."

"That is an excellent idea, dear, and I am sure that Duke understands that at the moment Caesar needs your attention." Charlotte refrained from commenting that Tom Piggott's theories had less to do with promoting the welfare of horses than they did with making sure that William was constantly in the company of a powerful, unpredictable, and potentially dangerous animal. However, she knew that her brother's sixth sense where horses were concerned would keep him from taking unnecessary risks. If, on mounting Caesar, he were to feel the least bit of nervousness on the horse's part, he would stop immediately, not so much to protect himself as to protect the animal's peace of mind, and it was this concern for his mount that would keep him safe.

Speen seemed to agree with Charlotte in her assessment of the situation so that if anxiety for William caused her faith in him to waver, the coachman could be counted upon to reassure her. "Aye, my lady, the lad may not be so bright as some, to be sure," he agreed with her one morning as they watched William and Caesar head off toward the home woods, "but he knows his horses better than any man I have ever seen. Do not fret yourself; he'll not do anything rash, nor will that horse. That animal trusts William and he won't let any harm come to the lad any more than the lad would let it come to him—almost like a dog, that horse is, and he don't like it above half if Tom Piggott gets to close to the boy."

Charlotte smiled gratefully at the grizzled coachman for the sympathy and understanding she saw in the bright blue eyes. "Thank you, Speen. All the same, I wish I would hear from Lord Lydon. I wrote him some time ago advising him of my concerns." She paused to watch horse and rider disappear into the woods. "Undoubtedly he will put me down as a hysterical female, but . . ."

"The marquess is a man who is awake on all suits and he knows you are not one to fly into the boughs over nothing."

Indeed, the coachman was entirely correct in this. Lord Lydon took the letter with all the seriousness that it was written. He did not dismiss his ward's fears as the products of an overactive imagination; however, he had far less respect for the strength of Cecil's character than Charlotte did. In Maximilian's experience, men like Sir Cecil Wadleigh might wish harm to come to others, but they were far too timid to do anything about it, even men with wives as resolute as Almeria.

Though the marquess had no doubt that Cecil considered William unfit to be Earl of Harcourt and looked upon himself as the true heir to the earldom, he did not believe the man capable of plotting anything more serious than creating a situation—a situation that would make it clear to William's sister that her brother needed the supervision that Cecil had recommended all along, and that would make her listen to Cecil's plan for finding a suitably quiet and safe place for William far away from Harcourt. At the very least she might become anxious enough to look to her cousin for guidance and support. Cecil was a grasping, slippery sort of fellow, but he was not, in Max's opinion, an out-and-out villain.

The reply that Charlotte eventually received, while it acknowledged her misgivings, advanced the same opinion as Speen's. Lord Lydon agreed with the coachman that William, while not possessing the intelligence of an adult in most things, was as competent as any adult—more so—in managing even the most difficult of horses. Therefore, Charlotte should feel no more alarm over the gift of Caesar than she would if the horse had been presented to a perfectly normal fifteen-year-old lad. And while Charlotte was gratified by the marquess's confidence in her brother's abilities, she was not particularly reassured by the letter. It was not, and never had been, William's abilities that had troubled her so much as it had been Cecil's motives for sending the horse.

Charlotte agreed with her guardian that Cecil was a spineless toady of a man, but she did not agree that he posed no threat to her brother. Cecil might have no backbone, but his wife did, and the acquisitive instinct was strong enough in both of them to bear them up when resolution failed. Harcourt was too rich a prize for them to give up, and both of them had made it abundantly clear that they considered Charlotte far too strong-minded. They knew that she would never accept their sending William away with a keeper. They had already tried that line of reasoning first, but it had failed lamentably, and the appearance of Caesar and the groom confirmed her fear that they had not given up. A gift as expensive as a high-blooded thoroughbred horse from the tight-fisted Cecil was proof that the man was desperate, and desperate men were known to adopt desperate measures. No, Charlotte did not agree with the marquess at all that Cecil lacked enough pluck to pose any real danger to her brother.

Lord Lydon knew Charlotte better than to risk her indignation by dismissing her fears entirely, and though he sought to minimize them, he urged her to write him again should anything develop further to cause her concern. He did instruct her to direct any correspondence to his estate in Kent, where he was going to inspect improvements made to the stables and check out the progress of the foal recently dropped by his prize mare.

Though her guardian's letter did not accord with the depth of suspicions that Charlotte harbored against Cecil, at least it did not mock them. Kent was not a great deal further away than London, and the marquess had assured her of his immediate presence should she need him. She was forced to be content with that and the fact that she and Speen were on the alert.

Charlotte's misgivings were justified not two days after she had received the marquess's reply when William came in looking as though he had been engaged in a battle with a gorse bush and emerged the loser. His blond hair was tousled and sported a twig here and there while his face had more than a few scratches, but his eyes were alight with excitement and the grin spreading across his face could only be described as exultant.

"Gracious, William, you look as though you have been wrestling with the shrubbery." Charlotte struggled to keep the rising note of alarm from her voice, for he really did look a sight.

"I have, but I didn't fall. Caesar almost bolted, but I stopped him and he minded me!"

"Oh," his sister responded doubtfully. Certainly his appearance belied this interpretation of events. "What happened?"

"We were right by the hanger wood, just trotting along, when there was a big bang and then a whiz and some branches snapped off over our heads. Caesar reared up, but I hung on and then he tried to bolt. He did run a little, but I kept his head up and I talked to him and he got better. He is very strong, but I was able to hold him, Charlie. You should have seen me. Jem thinks it was poachers."

Charlotte was silent for a moment, lost in thought as she tried to recall whether there had ever been poachers at Harcourt. The Winterbournes had always been generous to their tenants and had always taken such responsibility for the welfare of the village that no one had ever needed to poach. At any rate, there had never been anything worth hunting at Harcourt and those who wished permission had only had to ask. The Earls of Harcourt, traditionally more interested in agriculture or politics than in blood sports, had never stocked game of any sort. The most that was to be found was the occasional rabbit, which did not interest anyone.

William, full of praise for Caesar's speed and the smoothness of his gait, was oblivious to his sister's preoccupation and babbled happily on about his horse's strength, agility, and general superiority.

"So you must come riding with me, Charlie, and see how well Caesar does. He is ever so much better. Charlie, Charlie, are you listening to me?"

"Hush, William. I must think." Charlotte's brother subsiding into hurt silence, looked at her curiously. It was unlike his sister to be so short with him. Ordinarily she was always interested in anything he had to say and delighted in his every accomplishment, but now she sat staring into space, her dark brows drawn together in a worried frown.

At last she rose, summoned a half-hearted smile, and patted her brother absently on the arm. "I am proud of you, dear. Now you had better change out of those clothes and get ready for your lessons. I need to speak to Speen."

William sighed. "Do I *have* to? Aren't I old enough to stop lessons? Tim doesn't . . ."

"But *you* need to do lessons. How else will you learn to do all that has to be done to look after Harcourt? That is your job you know."

"Couldn't you just look after Harcourt?"

"But you are the earl now. Remember I told you that now Papa is dead you are the earl?"

"Could you not be earl and let me work with Jem and Tim? I would like that much better."

Charlotte smiled. "I know you would, dear, but you were born to take care of Harcourt. I will help you, though. We shall do it together. Now run along."

Somewhat reassured by his sister's pledge of assistance, William hurried off, leaving her to her own disturbing reflections.

She stood for some minutes, twisting and untwisting one dark curl around her finger. Then with a stifled exclamation of annoyance at her own inactivity, she shook herself and hurried off to the stables in search of Speen.

Chapter 20

The coachman was in the stalls checking on the quality of Tim's cleaning. For Charlotte, just the sight of Speen's rugged face breaking into a welcoming smile and the scent of warm air filled with the tangy, reassuring smells of horses and oats was comforting and went a long way toward thawing the cold lump of fear that had weighed on her heart since she had heard her brother's harrowing tale. Briefly she recounted William's story to Speen. "But are there poachers around Harcourt, Speen? Have there ever been?"

"Not so's I'd recall, my lady. There is nothing worth hunting here and everyone knows that they only have to ask to get permission." The coachman's bushy eyebrows drew together in a worried frown.

"I do not like it, Speen."

"No more do I, my lady. It's too smoky by half. Perhaps I should make sure that one of the lads always accompanies Master William when he goes out riding?"

Charlotte sighed. "But what about Tom Piggott? If one of the lads always rides with William, then it shows that you mistrust Piggott."

"Which I do. That man is no more a groom than Mrs. Hodges is."

"I know. It is most upsetting. However, I am glad you agree with me that something is amiss and it is not all my imagination. Someone does not want William to be the Earl of Harcourt, and I have my suspicions as to who that someone is."

"Aye, there you have it." With a dark look the coachman nodded his head in agreement.

"I think that perhaps the best thing is to leave Harcourt for a while. Lord Lydon has gone to his estate in Kent. Surely William would be safe there and his lordship could advise us. I have his direction from his last letter. Aylesford is not so distant that it would be any difficulty for us to journey there in day." Charlotte paused for a moment, thinking of all the preparations that would need to be made. "I shall write a letter to Lord Lydon advising him of our visit, of course, but I think it is best that we make as much haste as possible and keep our destination to ourselves; we shall just have to arrive unannounced though . . ." Her voice trailed off as she considered possible complications, but only for a moment. "Yes." She nodded her head decisively. "That is what we must do. Will you see to it that the carriage is ready tomorrow? We should leave directly after breakfast. I shall make sure that William and I are ready and I shall spread the tale that we are going to London on business to do with Papa's things. We start off in that direction anyway, so no one will be the wiser as to our true destination. I dare say that whoever it was that pretended to be a poacher would not have the temerity to follow—at least I hope not. Can Jem and Tim be trusted to keep an eye out for anyone who is acting suspiciously?"

"Of course, my lady. The lads are sometimes given to laziness, but both of them are as loyal as you could hope to find, and powerful fond of Master William. You can rely on them completely, but that there Tom Piggott is another matter altogether."

"Yes, well he is one person I want 'specially for Jem and Tim to observe. Undoubtedly he will think that he should be included in this excursion, but you can think of some reason to keep him here, can you not, Speen?"

"My telling him so should be all the reason he needs," the coachman growled, "not that he won't take exception to it. He is a man as holds a very high opinion of himself." One glance at his mistress was all Speen needed to read a confirmation of all his own suspicions in her clear-eyed gaze.

He should have known she would share his views on the new groom. Lady Charlotte Winterbourne was as kind and sympathetic a mistress as one could wish—going out of her way to take care of those who served her—but she was no namby-pamby miss. Her gentleness was tempered with a sharp, observant mind. In spite of having spent all her life in the limited confines of Harcourt, she had been forced by her father's neglect and her brother's weak-mindedness to deal with the world by herself at a very tender age and though Speen, Mr. Tidworth, and Mrs. Hodges had done their best to help and protect her, she harbored few illusions about life or about people, poor thing. She had never had anyone to turn to, what with her father ignoring her completely and that scoundrelly Sir Cecil and his nosy wife working to install themselves at Harcourt.

Speen had high hopes for this marquess fellow, a sharp-eyed gentleman if he'd ever seen one. It had seemed for a while as though he had taken a liking to the mistress and even to the young master, but then one of his lordships' fancy ladybirds from London had appeared on the scene and he had abandoned the Winterbournes too. The coachman winked reassuringly at Charlotte. "Don't you worry, my lady, I shall see to it that Mr. Tom Piggott is looked after. We'll get to the bottom of it all, never fear."

"Thank you, Speen. Now I'd best go supervise the packing." Charlotte smiled gratefully and turned toward the kitchens, her mind full of instructions for filling a hamper for their journey. She did not like the idea of descending on her guardian without so much as a by-your-leave, but if Speen, who had seen both her and her brother through all the disasters of childhood without so much as a blink as he patched up cuts, bruises, and cracked heads, did not scoff at her worries for William, then there was a very real danger facing him. A quiver of panic rose up within her, but she fought to control it by concentrating on all that needed to be done for their departure. Giving way to worry over William was not going to do her or her brother any good.

Speen went back to work in a thoughtful mood. He was in complete agreement with Charlotte's suspicions that her brother's life was in danger and that Tom Piggott, acting as an agent for Sir Cecil Wadleigh, was behind it all. What he was not so sure of was what would happen next or if the trip to Kent would protect William and expose the plots. But at least they would be enlisting the aid of the marquess.

The only one completely unfazed by recent developments was William himself, who recounted his near brush with disaster to anyone and everyone who would listen. By noon, all of Harcourt was aware that the young master, by an act of superb horsemanship, had saved himself from a nasty situation. William's euphoria over his own skill in this dangerous situation was only heightened by the prospect of a trip to visit his guardian.

"We are going to visit Lord Lydon, Charlie? Famous! Will we be in the carriage for hours and hours? Will I get to see London? Can I ride on the box with Speen?" William, sitting on a corner of

Charlotte's bed watching Charlotte and Lucy pack, bounced up and down in his excitement.

"Whoa, William. Catch your breath, dear, so I can answer your questions one at a time." Charlotte could not help chuckling. His enthusiasm was so infectious that even she began to look forward to the change in routine and scenery. The prospect of new sights and different people was enough to make her forget for a while the reasons behind their journey. She folded a paisley shawl and handed it to Lucy, who was packing the valises. "Yes, we shall be in the carriage for some time. No, we shall not be going to London, but to Lord Lydon's estate in Kent, and you will have to ask Speen if you can ride on the box with him." She leaned over to ruffle his hair. "But we shall ask Cook to pack a hamper and, if the weather is fine tomorrow, which I expect it should be, we shall have a picnic."

"A picnic! Hooray! I'll go tell Cook." William jumped up and was out the door before his sister could say another word.

The rest of the day, Charlotte was too preoccupied with instructions to the staff and last-minute packing to wonder how their guardian would take their sudden eruption into his life, but the next morning when, after a hurried breakfast, she at last sank back against the squabs of the carriage, exhausted from having been awakened before dawn by a brother in a fever of expectation, she was assailed by misgivings. Already she could picture the marquess, one dark brow raised in ironic disbelief as she explained their sudden appearance on his doorstep. The reasons behind their flight from Harcourt *did* sound rather fantastical, Charlotte admitted to herself as they rolled down the gravel drive, but fantastical or not, she was not willing to risk William's safety to find out.

She glanced over at her brother's face, which was alive with interest. To him, the entire episode, from his successful restraint of a runaway horse to a sudden journey into Kent, was huge adventure. Charlotte prayed that that was all it ever would be. The thought of life without him, his sunny, smiling face, all his little enthusiasms, the blue eyes so full of love and affection, were all she had. His was the only love she had ever known except for the dimly remembered feeling of her mother, so faint and faraway that she sometimes wondered if it had been real at all.

"Look, look, Charlie, there is Mr. Mapplethorne." William leaned out of the window to get a better look at the gig they overtook as they turned from Harcourt's drive onto the main road. He waved vigorously.

The shopkeeper smiled and nodded as they passed.

"I wish I had told him we were going away. I did not get to tell anyone we were taking a trip, not even Mr. Dashett. Mr. Dashett will wonder where I am. Sometimes he even lets me hold the horses when he is putting shoes on them."

"Well, you will be able to tell him all about your journey when you return, and won't he be surprised?" Charlotte was just as glad that the blacksmith, a greater source of gossip even than the barmaid at the Green Dragon, had not been given the slightest hint of their departure. The less gossip there was, the less likely Cecil was to hear where they had gone from Tom Piggott, or anyone else he might have bribed to keep an eye on the young earl.

"Yes he will be surprised," William replied with great satisfaction, "because I have never been on a journey before, have I Charlie? You went to London, but *I* did not go to London."

"No, you did not go to London, but I was hardly gone at all. If I had been, I would have missed you dreadfully."

"If I am good on this journey, will you take me to London some time? Jem says there are lots of fine horses to be seen there, but it is very crowded."

"I shall take you there some day and you can see for yourself," his sister promised. Then with a sigh of relief at having safely escaped Harcourt and its environs without mishap, Charlotte leaned back and gave herself up to the motion of the carriage, trying to empty her mind of the questions jostling with each other for a place in her consciousness. She had dealt as best she could with the threat to William; nothing would be served by worrying further over it. When she had had time to relax and think calmly, she would consider how to proceed, but for the moment she was simply too exhausted to do anything more than stare blankly at the passing countryside.

They ate lunch atop Crockham Hill, though William, who raced around taking in the magnificent view from every angle, was too excited to do more than swallow a mouthful of the pigeon pie and cold pheasant that Cook had packed. He even ignored his favorite, apple tart, in his eagerness to be on the road again.

Just as the sun was beginning to sink and a light mist was rising over the low places, they entered Aylesford and, after crossing the medieval bridge, stopped to ask directions of a prosperous-looking farmer, who directed them to Lydon Court a few miles beyond the village. "You cannot see the house from the road, but there's no mistaking the gates or the gatehouse," he added, eyeing them curiously. It was rare for the marquess to be at home receiving visitors, and rarer still for those visitors to be a young lady of obvious gentility and a lad whose mouth and nose bore enough resemblance to hers to be either a brother or a cousin.

The farmer's directions were easily enough followed and they were soon drawing up in front of Lydon Court, whose long, low brick facade glowed pink in the soft evening light, the gilded ball atop the central cupola gleaming like a beacon in the last rays of the setting sun. Lydon was not so large or impressive as Harcourt, but it was a good deal older, its exterior having been left virtually unchanged since its construction during the reign of Charles I.

Though lights glowed in most of the windows, there was a strangely deserted air in the courtyard. When a footman finally did appear, followed closely by the butler, both servants wore the slightly startled air of men who had been called upon unexpectedly. Both of them tugged at their coats as they hurried down the steps, as though they had been attending to something else when interrupted by the arrival of the Winterbournes' carriage. However, the greeting was gracious enough and the butler sent the footman with the message to the housekeeper, Mrs. Purdy, to have the bedchambers prepared for the travelers as naturally as though Charlotte and William were frequent guests at Lydon.

"I shall tell his lordship of your arrival, my lady, and have some refreshments brought in," he reassured Charlotte as he led them into the low entrance hall ringed with marble columns below and a portrait gallery above. Charlotte glanced without much success at the portraits above her, for they were too high to make anything out. Her attention was quickly distracted by a burst of raucous laughter from a brilliantly lighted room halfway down the hall along which the butler was conducting them. As they passed the room, she peeked surreptitiously over her shoulder to catch a glimpse of a table littered with wine glasses and the remains of a sumptuous meal.

The guests seated around the table were laughing uproariously, their attention focused on a dark-haired woman in a gown cut so low as to leave nothing to the imagination. She had one arm around the neck of a man who was obviously her companion and one around someone who closely resembled the marquess, though it was too far away for Charlotte to be absolutely certain. The others were leaning back in their chairs and up against one another in a most intimate, provocative manner, one saucy red-haired young woman even going so far as to sit on the lap of a most appreciative gentleman.

Charlotte's eyes widened. So that was what people meant when they whispered disapprovingly about the antics of rakes and libertines. Actually, it did not look shocking so much as it did fun. She would have liked to observe it all more closely, but afraid of attracting the notice of William or the butler with her curiosity, she hastily directed her gaze in the opposite direction at some ancient suits of armor along the wall just as the butler opened the door into the library.

The room into which they were ushered was larger and less intimate than the richly paneled room at Harcourt, but the dying fire was quickly poked into a roaring blaze. Charlotte was grateful for its welcoming warmth, for the chill of the evening had begun to make her wish she had brought a heavier cloak instead of the yellow sarcenet pelisse she was wearing.

"Thank you." Charlotte made herself comfortable on a sofa directly in front of the fire while her brother ran to the windows that surveyed the vast park and the pastures beyond. "Do you think Lord Lydon's horses are still in the pasture, or have they come in for the night? He said he was raising them, you know."

"Yes, he did," Charlotte answered wearily. Ordinarily, she was delighted to join in her brother's conversation, but hours of responding to speculations on the oddly shaped ost houses they passed, or the numbers of sheep, the height of a towering church steeple, and numerous other points of interest along the way had quite worn her out and emptied her of all conversation. For the moment all she could do was stare fixedly into the dancing flames and hope that their guardian would not be too angered by their sudden descent upon his bachelor household.

Chapter 21

Lydon's face as his butler whispered in his ear the news of his unexpected guests' arrival registered all the annoyance that Charlotte had feared. The first spurt of anger he felt at being interrupted was quickly followed by a more rational response as he disengaged himself from the soft arms of the very obliging actress seated next to him. Charlotte was not the clinging, helpless sort of female who needed masculine support or attention. He knew her far better than that. She would not leave the pleasant, comfortable, and familiar atmosphere of Harcourt to go haring about the countryside with her brother unless something was seriously amiss. But that she should appear at this particular moment, when he was entertaining guests, some of doubtful respectability, was unfortunate, to say the least.

Max had run into Tubby Westrup, Jack Standish, and Colly Forsyth at Tattersall's a fortnight ago and had been hailed with delight by some of the choicest spirits ever to pass through the portals of Government House in Calcutta. There had been little difficulty in recognizing them, for the colorful trio was easily distinguished from the rest of the crowd by the outrageous parti-colored waistcoats and bright hues that only an Indian tailor could have been talked into making up as a jacket.

"Lydon, you old dog! You can't have been in London long, for we haven't heard news of any daring curricle races, duels, or legions of lovelorn ladies." Tubby greeted him in his great booming voice and gave him a huge buffet on the shoulder. Tubby, an enormous man of prodigious appetites, had caused his father, the Earl of Claverdon, almost as much annoyance as Max had caused his, and the two of them, after discovering one another at the racecourse in Calcutta, had soon become fast friends.

"Tubby, what brings you here to the metropolis? Surely life in England, even in London, is too flat for your tastes."

"That it is, my boy, that it is. But the pater is doing poorly and wanted to lecture me one last time before sticking his spoon in the wall, and Colly and Jack were making Calcutta rather too hot for themselves, so here we are—and dashed boring it is too. London didn't used to be this flat, but now everyone is so respectable it makes you want to turn up your toes. Why even Mad Dog St. Clair has become a father and is as dull as a parson. Who would have thought it?" Tubby paused in his litany of woe to direct a suspicious glance at Max. "You have not gone and done something stupid like getting leg-shackled, have you?"

Max chuckled. "Have no fear, Tubby. You know me better than that. I prize my freedom too highly to sacrifice it to some woman who would spend the rest of her days trying to turn me into a lap dog."

The four friends had spent a pleasant morning sauntering among horse fanciers of all types, from grooms to dukes, admiring magnificent shoulders here, a noble head there, and recalling some of their more outrageous exploits. The marquess had ended by inviting them all to join him in the country. "For surely you will have set London on its ear by then and will be looking for some cover to run to."

Not wishing to trespass on Lydon's hospitality without giving something in return, Tubby had convinced some obliging lady-birds to take time off from their minimal duties on stage to liven up the house party and they had all journeyed down from London several days before. There was no doubt that the *ladies* had added to the hilarity of the mealtimes, entertaining them all with ribald jokes and tales of life backstage. They had contributed less to the outdoor activities, not being the least interested in riding, fishing, or even touring the countryside in their companions' dashing curricles, preferring instead to lie abed until noon and spend the better part of the afternoon chattering among themselves and dressing for dinner.

In actuality, the gentlemen preferred this state of affairs, as it allowed them freedom to indulge in all the pursuits that sporting-mad gentlemen enjoyed in the country. It had been a relaxing, convivial time, one so reminiscent of the old days in India that Lydon had been able to put all his duties and obligations out of his mind completely. And now, here was one of his duties come to confront him in his refuge. Regardless of the reasons—and, knowing Charlotte, the marquess felt that they were probably entirely justified—he was more than a little irritated at having his sojourn so rudely interrupted.

Scowling ferociously, the marquess pushed back his chair and stalked from the dining room, leaving his dinner partner to transfer her plump, white arms to the neck of Jack Standish instead. His scowl deepened as he strode down the hall to the library and flung the door open. "What in the blazes—"

"Lord Lydon, Lord Lydon, we came all the way from Harcourt to see you and we had a picnic and Speen let me ride most of the way on the box with him." William ran from his place at the window, his eyes shining with eagerness and excitement. "We're here. Isn't it famous? Can I see some of your horses that you are raising? Charlie says I mustn't plague you, but I saw one in the pasture and he is splendid. Will you let me see him?"

Max was no proof against such obvious delight. The hard, angry line of his compressed lips relaxed into a reluctant smile. "Why yes, William I shall show you my stock, but for the moment why don't you go find Griggs? He is in the stables and I expect he will be just as surprised to see you as I am."

The ironic tone was lost on the boy, but not on his sister, who blushed and gripped her hands even more tightly together in her lap. The marquess was not pleased. She had known it would be that way. He was someone who treasured his privacy and independence and who loathed interference from any quarter. She sympathized heartily with this, but William's welfare was of paramount importance; what else could she have done?

"I do not blame you for being annoyed, my lord," she began in a low voice as soon as her brother had raced from the room and clattered down the hall, "and ordinarily I would never intrude, but I . . . we . . . there have been developments."

Max's anger receded as quickly as it had come as he looked more closely at her and laid a firm, but comforting hand on her shoulder. The dark smudges of fatigue under the deep-set eyes, the grayish pallor of her usually glowing skin, and the dispirited droop of her shoulders told him more than he needed to know about her reasons for seeking him out. She was desperate and worried, with no one to turn to. The last remnants of annoyance vanished to be replaced by the strangest sensation of pride that she had looked to him as the person most likely to be able to help her.

His heart turned over at the exhaustion and worry he sensed in her, and his throat was strangely tight. It was a moment before he could say anything. "My poor girl, you have had a nasty time of it, it appears. Tell me what has occurred."

Grateful tears stung Charlotte's eyes. He was going to help after all. It had not been a dreadful mistake to come. Observing first the raucous party in the dining room and then the fierce expression of irritation as he had entered the room, she had begun to doubt the wisdom of her actions and to wish fervently that she had not come. But then the rigid, angry lines of his face had softened and the iciness in those penetrating eyes had warmed. He was still her friend, the friend she remembered from his visit to Harcourt, the friend who had given her strength and support, enough strength and support that she had come running to him when she was at a loss as to what to do next.

"I . . . I do apologize for descending on you without the least bit of warning, but I had no choice."

"I am sure you did not. Now, what is amiss?" Still grasping her shoulder with a warm hand, he sat down next to her and looked deep into her eyes.

The weight of his body next to hers on the sofa, the breadth of his shoulders, the alert expression as he prepared to listen to her story, had an amazingly calming effect. Charlotte drew a steadying breath and began. "I know that this may seem like the most absurd fantasy concocted by an overactive imagination, but William was narrowly missed by a poacher's bullet yesterday." Was it only yesterday? It seemed a week ago. The strain of it all had made every hour before they had reached the safety of Lydon Court seem like a day. And now, recounting it to the marquess, it sounded like such an ordinary event that Charlotte wondered if she had been foolishly precipitate in overreacting to one of the normal hazards of country life. "Now I know that my suspicions were correct, somebody *is* trying to hurt William. We do not have poachers at Harcourt, because there is never anything worth hunting and we have always allowed those who wished it full run of the woods and fields away from the house itself. Somebody is trying to hurt William and I didn't know what to do to protect him, so I had to come here."

Max was silent for a moment mulling it over. "Did you discuss this with anyone?"

"Only with Speen, and he agrees with me that it is too out of the ordinary not to be significant. He too mistrusts the groom that Cecil sent with Caesar. Furthermore, it appears that no one can account for the groom's whereabouts at the precise moment that the entire episode was taking place."

"Hmmm." The marquess already respected Charlotte as a reliable, practical young woman who was not given to exaggeration, but, during his stay in Sussex, he had closely observed Speen and taken the man's measure. It had not taken very long before he had reached the conclusion that the grizzled old servant was more than a coachman to the Winterbournes, but operated as something more along the lines of advisor and protector, particularly for William, who spent as much of his time as possible in the part of the estate under Speen's jurisdiction. In Speen, Max saw another Felbridge and, indeed, his own loyal servant had confirmed this by his reports of what went on in the stables at Harcourt. "If that is the case, then it seems you made a wise decision in quitting Harcourt as quickly as you did. The question remains, however, as to how we should proceed. For the moment, I think it perhaps best that you remain here. I, ah, have been *entertaining* some guests, er, old friends from India, but they intend to leave tomorrow." Max devoutly hoped that he would be able to convince his friends that the brevity of their visit was in their own best interest, that any more rustication on their part would result in a paralyzing boredom.

Stealing a quick glance at her guardian from under her lashes, Charlotte was surprised to see the faintest hint of red stain his cheeks under his deep tan and a slightly self-conscious look creep into his eyes, and she quickly surmised that his guests had intended no such thing. She hastily bit her lip to hide her amusement. It was a rare thing to see the arrogant Marquess of Lydon even the slightest bit discomfited, but discomfited he undoubtedly was. The urge to tease him was irresistible. "Please do not ask them to leave on our account. I should be delighted to meet them. I have so little opportunity to make the acquaintance of anyone except our nearest neighbors, and I have known them all for years. Your friends seemed to be most amusing; certainly you were all enjoying yourselves when we arrived. It would be a dreadful shame to spoil it."

"You saw, then?" Max tugged irritably at his cravat, which he seemed to have tied too tightly. What exactly had she seen and, more importantly, what exactly had she understood?

"I caught a brief glimpse of the ladies, but they seemed to be quite pretty, gay, and amusing, certainly more amusing than Lady Winslow and her daughters or anyone else I meet around Harcourt. They looked as though they would be rather fun to know."

Max choked and pulled harder at his cravat. "Believe me, you would not find them the least bit entertaining."

"But you did. You seemed to find the dark-haired one next to you most diverting, so surely I should do the same."

"But it is *not* the same, believe me." For once in his life, Maximilian was at a loss for words. All his life he had condemned his parents and much of the society in which they had moved for being hypocritical, for maintaining rigidly proper exteriors while they committed every sort of indiscretion, for choosing people as friends based on their social standing rather than on their characters. Now he was about to do much the same sort of thing. But it was different. Charlotte did not understand the implications of it all; or did she? Looking down into those magnificent eyes, he detected what looked to be a mischievous twinkle.

"I suppose that is what Lady Winslow and the others mean when they talk about the scandalous doings of rakes and libertines, but it does not look so very dreadful to me. What is wrong with enjoying oneself? Those ladies seemed to be enjoying themselves, and they were not hurting anyone or causing anyone any harm. I know that you think that a gently brought up young lady should not know women like that, but I am not a gently brought up young lady. In fact, I was not brought up at all, except by myself."

"What is wrong, indeed?" The marquess's lips twitched in spite of the heroic self-control he was exercising. There was no doubt about it, Lady Charlotte was an original. No wonder Almeria and Cecil were desperate to marry her off quickly and force her independent spirit and questioning intellect into a more socially acceptable and conformable personality. As it was, even Max, iconoclast that he had always been, was being made distinctly uncomfortable by her unanswerable logic.

"Your dinner party seemed to be far more entertaining than the few I have ever witnessed."

The wistful note in Charlotte's voice brought him up short. "Believe me, these, er, *ladies* may be enjoying themselves for the moment, but there is not a one of them who would not trade places with you in an instant." Even before the words were out of his mouth, Max knew that they would mean nothing to her because her wealth and social position meant nothing to her. Charlotte was, purely and simply, lonely, and she always had been. Position and wealth had given her nothing that she particularly wanted, and at the moment, they were a source of complication for her, inspiring the envy and jealousy of Cecil and Almeria.

He went on. "And believe me, you would soon find that Tubby, Jack, and Colly, even though they tend to laugh a good deal more than most people, are rather limited in their conversations, which center around two topics, and two topics only—horses and the fancy. Believe me, I know."

"Oh." Charlotte wrinkled her forehead as she concentrated on recalling the scene in the dining room. At first glance it had appeared that everyone was laughing, joking, drinking, and flirting, but the more she pictured it, the more she realized that Lord Lydon, in spite of being physically entwined with his dinner partner, had worn the slightly remote expression of a spectator rather than a participant.

In fact, Max was realizing the very same thing. He had thought he was enjoying himself, but in truth, it was only the memories of India that he was enjoying. In India, he had chosen Tubby, Jack, and Colly as friends more because they tended to avoid the fashionable squeezes and matchmaking mamas as diligently as he did than because of any personal attractions they possessed or common interests they shared.

"At any rate, there is truly no need for them to leave on our account. William and I have no wish to intrude, only to be safe. We shall be quite happy to keep to ourselves and you may carry on as though we were still miles away in Sussex."

"But I do not wish to do so." And, smiling down into the big green eyes, the marquess realized with something of a shock, that this was quite true. He was rather looking forward to showing them around his estate and sharing quiet evenings in front of the fire again with Charlotte. He had missed those evenings, and he had missed her. He had not realized quite how much he had missed her until he had seen the slender figure seated wearily in front of the fire, too weary even to smooth the dark tendrils of hair that had freed themselves from the knot at the back of her head and now curled around the pale, strained face.

Max had to fight the urge to wrap her in his arms and comfort her. It was then he knew that ever since his leaving Harcourt there had always been at the back of his mind a nagging worry over her and an unconscious concern for her welfare. "Speaking of all the miles between here and Sussex, I realize that I am being an abominable host, however unexpected the visit. And you must be quite done up. I shall have Mrs. Purdy show you and William to your rooms and see that you are fed while I attend to my other guests."

He rose as if to leave, but stopped and, gently taking her hand again, raised it to his lips. "Sleep well, Charlotte."

He had spoken so softly that Charlotte did not take in the precise words he had uttered until after he had shut the door behind him, but she sensed their meaning and the concern for her that lay behind them. Hot tears pricked her eyelids as she dropped her chin into her hands and stared into the fire.

Chapter 22

The dining room seemed almost garishly bright to Max in comparison to the flickering flames of the library fire and the fading light of the sunset that had suffused the library with a soft pink glow. And his companions' hilarity was such that they hardly noticed his return. In fact, Tubby, bent double over his partner's ample bosom by a hearty guffaw, did not notice his host at all until he grabbed for his glass of port, missed, and would have slid from his chair had not Max caught him. "What, back already? She must not have been worth it," he exclaimed wiping his streaming eyes.

"What makes you think it was a she?" There was no mistaking the iciness in Lydon's voice.

Tubby goggled at his host's grim expression. "Of course it must be a she; nothing less could make you interrupt such a jolly party as this. No offense intended, old man." Tubby eyed Max uneasily. Lydon did look rather fierce, and Tubby had no intention of aggravating a temper that was legendary on the Indian subcontinent.

The expression of alarm in his friend's eyes brought Max up short. He quickly swallowed his anger to answer lightly, "No such thing, Tubby, it was merely duty calling."

"Duty?" Tubby looked as blank as if Max were suddenly addressing him in a foreign tongue. "Duty? You?"

"Yes. Even I have some obligations, and this one unfortunately compels me to cut short our little party. I am afraid that I shall have to ask you all to leave tomorrow."

"Leave tomorrow! Ha, it *must* be a lady. You would not act so havey-cavey about it otherwise." Colly Forsyth, catching the end of the conversation, hiccuped and waved an empty bottle at the footman, who had stolen in to replace a guttering candle. "And she must be a rare little ladybird if you are so anxious to keep her all to yourself." He winked broadly at Max before turning back to his own companion. "You go ahead and be a dog-in-the-manger, I don't mind, for I've got lovely Bess here." He planted a smacking kiss on the lady's improbably red cheek.

Jack Standish, only a little less jug-bitten than his friends, was sober enough and close enough to Max to observe the muscles tighten in his jaw. "Here now, lads, Max invited us here and he has a perfect right to uninvite us. No need to turn it into a dust-up. I say we move the party to Newmarket to recoup our fortunes, and leave the man in peace. If he has got a duty, he has got a duty, and there's an end to it."

"Newmarket, now there's a thought." Tubby perked up. "It will be a rare treat to see horses run a course in broad daylight after all those early dawn meets in Calcutta. Granted it was better for the horses to run in the cool of the day, but dashed difficult to see anything. I say, didn't Wheatley tell us he had a horse racing there this week?"

"Yes, and a sweet goer according to him," Colly joined in.

The mere mention of Newmarket was enough to turn full attention to the turf, and in less than an hour the party was so enamored of the idea that Max was hard-put to keep his guests from heading out that very evening so as not to waste the daylight hours in travel.

In the end, they decided to leave at the first sign of day, and after having set their servants to packing, sat down at the gaming table to while away the rest of the night.

It was a rather groggy but cheerful crew that piled into their curricles just as dawn was breaking. The ladies, yawning prodigiously, stumbled into the traveling coach to follow at a more leisurely pace, and, lured by the promises of a share in the prospective winnings, settled happily enough into the carriage.

Max retired to the breakfast room to enjoy a hearty rasher of ham and eggs washed down with liberal cups of coffee, and a bit of peace alone with *The Times*. He had barely focused on the "Parliamentary Intelligence" when the sound of running footsteps warned him that his solitary moment was not destined to be.

Seconds later, William came bursting into the room. "I *knew* I should find you here, sir. Charlie told me that you would not yet be up, but I knew she was wrong for I saw all those people leaving. I wish I could have talked to the man driving the black curricle with the red wheels. Did you ever see such a fine rig and such bang-up horses? I wish they had stayed so I might have asked one of them for a ride. They must go like the wind."

"Oh they do. Tubby would never be caught dead with anything but prime cattle. He was known all over India for his horses."

"Was he in India with you?" William's eyes grew round with interest. "I should like to hear his—" He broke off at the sound of approaching footsteps. "It's Charlie," he whispered. "Now I *will* be in the basket, for she told me not to bother you, but I am not bothering you, am I sir?"

Max was forced into a reluctant grin as he rose to hold a chair for William's sister. "No, you are not bothering me."

"I apologize for William. He has been up since before dawn and it was all I could do to keep him from interrupting you until now." Charlotte directed a playfully ferocious look at her brother as she accepted a steaming cup of hot chocolate from the footman who had suddenly appeared to replenish the breakfast table.

William smiled beguilingly. "I know you did, Charlie, but Lord Lydon doesn't mind, do you, sir?"

Max chuckled as he caught Charlotte's eye and hastened to reassure her. "I feel certain you did your best. I am flattered that he sought me out, for anyone who knows me would tell you that I am not fit company before noon."

"But you had already been awake for hours seeing your friends off, hadn't you, sir? I wish they had stayed, for they looked like prime fellows." William could not help regretting the dashing equipage and splendid horses he had glimpsed earlier.

Charlotte echoed her brother. "You see, there truly was no need for them to leave."

"Nevertheless, it was time for them to go." And having effectively ended the conversation, the marquess turned his concentration to the eggs and ham before him.

Charlotte peeked curiously at him. There was a note of finality in his voice that sounded almost angry. She could not fathom it, for it did not seem to be directed at her and William as much as it was at the departed guests. She could not know the conflicting emotions her guardian was struggling with.

First and foremost among those emotions was annoyance at himself for having allowed anything to ruffle his customary mastery of any and every situation—a mastery that gave him an ironic detachment that was the envy of the *ton*. Where was that detachment now? Where had it been when Colly Forsyth had winked knowingly at him and the mere thought of Colly leering at Charlotte had so infuriated Max that he wanted to wrap his hands around Colly's pudgy throat and squeeze and squeeze.

Secondly, he was irritated by both the Winterbournes' blithe assumption that they would have enjoyed the company of anyone who had been his guest. He could just picture the sly grins that would have been exchanged among the trio from Calcutta as they took in Charlotte and her brother, how they would vie with each other to make Charlotte blush or to make William look foolish, though his interest in horses might just have won their acceptance.

Finally, there was anger at his friends for . . . for what? For always being ripe for any mischief, for living every moment to its fullest, for constantly pursuing gaiety at every possible moment, or for reminding him by their presence of what he himself was, or had been, until very recently.

". . . must ask to see the stables . . ." William's voice broke into Max's reverie. With an effort, he forced himself to concentrate on the matters at hand. "I beg your pardon, William, I was not attending."

"Oh, I was just telling Charlie that she ought to see your stables. Griggs showed them to me. They are slap up to the echo, aren't they, sir? I would like some just like that at Harcourt. Charlie says that I am the earl now and I don't want to be the earl if it means I have to do lots of hard things like sums and reading, but I shouldn't mind it if I could have new stables. Could you help us make some?" It was a long speech for William, and he looked somewhat surprised at himself as he paused to gasp for breath.

Oddly enough, the smile that Max had willed himself to assume suddenly felt completely natural. "Why, I expect I could. Perhaps we could take a look at the stables after breakfast. Would you like that?"

"Oh yes, very much." William beamed happily as he applied himself to a generously loaded plate. Now that he had the prospect of a tour of the stables led by the marquess himself, he was rather sorry that he had piled his plate quite so high because it meant there was much more to dispose of before they could begin their tour. Sensing his sister's watchful eye upon him, he did his best to eat slowly in the gentlemanly manner she had assured him that all the Earls of Harcourt before him had done, but it taxed his patience severely.

For her part, well aware of her brother's eagerness to show her the splendors of Lydon's stables, Charlotte confined herself to eat-ing a piece of toast and drank her chocolate so that when William laid down his fork and looked expectantly at her she was able to take her cue. "I am quite ready for our visit to the stables, my lord."

"Of course." Maximilian had been a silent, but appreciative observer of the entire scene. Having spent most of his life alone in the nursery and the schoolroom, only briefly paying his respects to whichever parent happened to be at home, he had never witnessed the interaction of family members who understood one another's needs. He found the give and take between Charlotte and her brother fascinating. It was clear from the occasional glance William cast in his sister's direction that he wished to win her approval by living up to her standards for table manners, but it was equally clear that she was just as eager to please him by the way she hurried through her own breakfast. The two of them were vastly different as far as their capabilities went, but their concern for each other was the same. Maximilian could not remember when he had seen such a demonstration of evident solicitude even between lovers, much less between family members. Watching Charlotte's eyes light up at her brother's enthusiasm, Max could not stifle the tiniest prick of envy at the Winterbournes' closeness or subdue the tiniest pang of loneliness at being outside such a special relationship.

As if sensing his feelings, Charlotte turned toward him with a smile. "Lead on, my lord. Let us see these wonders whose example is no doubt going to shatter the peace and quiet at Harcourt. For I know William will not rest until he is assured that the equine population of Harcourt is as comfortably housed as that at Lydon Court."

"Come along." William tugged at his sister's hand. "You must see the stalls. They are all made of brick instead of wood. Griggs says it is a special sort of brick and that it is easy to clean. And there are almost as many boxes as there are stalls. Griggs says that they are the best stables in the whole of the county. But the main thing is to have them clean, with plenty of light and air. Griggs knows ever so much about horses. I think Caesar will like it here."

By now they had reached the stableyard and William, unable to curb his enthusiasm any longer, hurried ahead to find Griggs.

"I do hope that Speen will not be totally eclipsed by William's new idol." Charlotte shook her head, laughing gently. "And I do hope Griggs is prepared to be looked upon as the source of all wisdom and knowledge. It can be rather wearing. I shall try to keep William in check, but once he takes a liking to someone it is rather difficult to keep him from following that person around like an eager puppy. The best way to keep oneself from going mad is to give him something to do, such as rubbing down horses or currying them. A simple task that he can master but one that requires all of his concentration is the most effective way to protect oneself from being completely worn down by questions."

"What a very good sister you are. William is indeed fortunate in having you to look after him . . . anyone would be fortunate in having you to look after him."

The marquess had paused during his speech and then had added the last under his breath, almost as though he were speaking to himself. He spoke so softly that Charlotte, not entirely sure that she had heard correctly, glanced up at him and was surprised to find the gray eyes fixed on her with an unreadable, but oddly intent expression in them. At a loss as to what he was thinking and suddenly shy and unsure of herself, she blushed and laughed a little shakily. "It might seem that way to you now, but I assure you, you would think otherwise if you were to see me after William to do his lessons, which he says I am forever nagging him about." Charlotte was grateful that by now they had reached the stables where William and Griggs were waiting for them and the tour began. She could remain in the background while the marquess explained to her brother that his growing number of studs and broodmares could enjoy a healthful atmosphere, reaping the benefits of modern agricultural management as well as ancient wisdom.

"It is the most bang-up place I ever saw," William could not help exclaiming again and again.

"Let us hope that the horses agree with you." Lydon chuckled.

"Oh, I am sure they do. Look at how happy they are."

"Happy? I devoutly hope so, but what makes you think they are happy?"

William scrunched up his face so tightly for a moment that the freckles on his nose ran together. "I don't know, but they just are."

"He's a rare lad that way," Speen remarked as he joined the little group surveying the stables. "Always knows what the horses like."

William, Charlotte, and Griggs moved off to look at Caesar's new quarters, but the marquess fell a bit behind, taking advantage of a private moment with the Winterbournes' coachman.

Glad of the opportunity to advance his opinion, Speen did not hesitate to offer it when Lord Lydon questioned him closely as to the recent series of events at Harcourt. "I'll put it to you straight, my lord. That cousin of my lady and the young master is a nasty piece of work if ever I saw one, and his wife is a thoroughgoing meddler. They could not stand it when the old earl was alive and living in London, never taking advantage of the estate, and they truly cannot bear the thought of Harcourt's going to *the idiot,* as Sir Cecil calls him. They used to talk of marrying their useless son to Lady Charlotte, but she would have none of that—told them straight off, too. It is my belief that she is in the right of it to suspect foul play. That horse Sir Cecil sent was as vicious an animal as I have ever seen, and strong. But Master William, he was bound and determined to make friends with that blasted beast, and damme if he didn't. As to the poachers, there was no such thing, and my lady knows it. Lady Charlotte is a mighty unusual female—been taking care of herself and that brother of hers since she was a wee mite. She doesn't frighten easily, but she is frightened for his lordship now. She never would have come asking for your help, sir, if she weren't in a devil of a pucker, for she don't like to ask help of anybody—never has. She is a most independent young lady, if you know what I mean, sir."

Lydon nodded ruefully as he recalled his first encounter with his ward. Having been set straight by Lady Charlotte Winterbourne at the very outset of their acquaintance, he knew precisely what the coachman meant. "And do you agree with your mistress about the threat to his lordship?"

Speen snorted. "If that there gentleman that Sir Cecil sent along with the horse is a groom, I'll eat my hat. He barely knows one end of a horse from the other, and he certainly don't know his way around the stables. Oh, he tries mightily to be everyone's friend so as we won't notice that he doesn't do a bit of work. But you want to watch yourself with a man like that, sir. Lady Charlotte says we cannot send him back yet for then we'll have Sir Cecil down on us in some other way and it is better to stick with the devil you know than the one you don't."

"No, you cannot send the man back. She was right to come to me."

"That is what I said, though she hated something terrible to bother you, sir. But I said to her, *His lordship will know just what to do and his lordship is one as has seen a sight more things than you have."*

"Thank you, Speen. How did she take to that?"

"Well, Lady Charlotte isn't one to put much trust in people, sir, what with the old earl never paying the least mind to her and her brother, but there wasn't much else she could do, now could she?"

"No, there was not much else she could do. We shall see what we can do to protect the earl."

"He is everything to her."

"I know, Speen, I know."

The coachman nodded gravely in agreement, but his heart was lighter than it had been since the old earl had died. For some time Speen had been hoping for a miracle, and now it looked as though his prayers had been answered. His lordship was a fine gentleman—top-of-the-trees and awake on all suits—but more importantly, it seemed as though he genuinely cared about Lady Charlotte. There was a warmth in his eyes when he spoke of her and there had been a wistful, almost tender note in his voice when he acknowledged the love she had for her brother. Speen was not a betting man, but at that moment he would have given odds to anyone who might have asked for them that, given a little time and opportunity, the Marquess of Lydon could come to grow very fond of his self-reliant ward.

Chapter 23

Self-reliant she certainly was, and not about to trespass on Maximilian's hospitality any more than she already had. "Do not worry about me, my lord," she assured him as they finished their tour of the stables. "William and I have intruded enough on your life as it is, and we are perfectly capable of amusing ourselves. If we can but beg your permission to fish in your lake and ride on your estate, we shall be merry as grigs. And now that I know William is safe for the moment, I shall be free to think of some way to stop the dastardly Cecil. I feel sure that I will be able to think of something."

Noting the defiant lift of her chin as she uttered these words, Max was inclined to agree with her, but for the first time in his life, he felt oddly moved to meddle in someone else's affairs. For years women had been trying to make him shoulder all their responsibilities and he had always declined, almost to the point of rudeness. Now, one was clearly bent on handling her own problems, and he was determined to relieve her of them. What was happening here? Had this guardian thing gone to his head?

"Do you have a strategy in mind?"

"No," Charlotte admitted rather reluctantly. "But if I put my mind to it . . ."

"I think the best thing is to send one of my men to Harcourt to observe and see what he can discover. I shall send Will Foster. He is a reliable young man with a good head on his shoulders. If Cecil has gone so far as to have someone shoot at William, then he has gone from the stage of merely wishing for a providential accident to the point of causing such an accident. Having crossed that bridge, he will, I feel sure, stop at nothing now, and each and every impediment to his plan will only serve to make him more determined."

The marquess was entirely correct in this surmise, for at that very moment, the hapless Tom Piggott was standing before a purple-faced Cecil. "You what?" Cecil screamed at him.

"I . . . er . . . missed." The unhappy servant shifted from one foot to another.

"You . . . you . . . blasted idiot! Can you not do anything right?"

"Er, no, sir," the counterfeit groom muttered, his eyes fixed to the floor. "Perhaps you might want to send someone else, sir?" he suggested hopefully.

"No. There is no need to drag anyone else into this. You will return to Harcourt, and at Harcourt you will remain until you have done it right."

"But how, sir?" Thoroughly miserable, Tom Piggott looked to his irate employer for some suggestion.

None was forthcoming. "How am I to know, man? You are the criminal." Reassured that his minion was completely cowed, Cecil descended from being infuriated to being merely irritated. "And do not show your face around here until you have accomplished it, for if you do, not only will you get no money, but I shall turn you over to the magistrate as the poacher I caught red-handed two months ago. In fact, now that I think about it, there is really no reason to pay you at all. Not being transported should be reward enough for the likes of you."

"You are not the only one as could turn someone over to the magistrate, sir." Desperation, coupled with greed, made Tom Piggott more bold.

"No?" Cecil sneered. "And what would you do, inform against me? I think not. It would be your word against mine. However . . ." Cecil, observing the knotted fists and the vein standing out on his fellow conspirator's forehead, knew that he had gone too far. After all, what was to stop the man from heading toward Harcourt and continuing on, not even bothering to carry out their scheme. He gave a falsely hearty laugh. "Come, then, let's not fall out over these matters. A few setbacks are to be expected. You shall have your reward upon completion of your, er, *task*."

By the time Will Foster arrived at Harcourt, Tom Piggott had already returned, with a plausible story for his brief absence—a dying mother. He had fallen to work in the stables with such vigor that the grumbling against him had ceased, though Jem and Tim still could not bring themselves to trust the man, nor did they ever invite him to join them for a convivial tankard of ale in the taproom of the Green Dragon where Will Foster was conducting his investigation.

With Will Foster reconnoitering at Harcourt, there was nothing for Charlotte to do but distract William and herself with as much patience as she could muster until he returned with his report. Determined not to interrupt their guardian's routine, she began the distraction the morning of Will Foster's departure.

"Charlie and I are going fishing today," William announced grandly at breakfast the next day. "Griggs told me that there are fish in the lake and Mrs. Purdy said that we could ask Cook to pack us a picnic."

"Ah. It sounds like a grand scheme. You seem to have made several friends here at Lydon already." The marquess addressed William, but his eyes were on Charlotte and the tender smile in her eyes as they rested on William. She certainly looked a good deal better than she had when she had arrived. In the space of a day her color had returned, the circles under her eyes had disappeared, and the weary slump to her shoulders had vanished. Her usual energetic air had reasserted itself. Max could not help hoping that it was the reassurance of his company that had wrought this change, though his more cynical side told him that it was more likely the simple expedient of escape from the immediate dangers at Harcourt that had done it.

"Griggs lets me help him with the horses. I carried their oats to them yesterday," William volunteered. "And Mrs. Purdy let me cut off the sugar lumps to put in the sugar bowls for her yesterday."

"William is always so helpful that people like him wherever he goes." Charlotte smiled fondly at her brother, who glowed with pride.

Again Max felt a pang of—was it envy?—at the bond between the two of them. He had never allowed himself to feel close to anyone except Felbridge because in his experience, such closeness had merely meant more demands made of him with very little given in return. However, the relationship between Charlotte and her brother was something altogether different; it was a mutual thing and provided a refuge and a haven for both of them against the rest of the world. Not for the first time, Max found himself half wishing that he were a part of it.

This wish grew even stronger as later that day he caught sight of them at their fishing. He was riding back across the fields after inspecting some land that was being cleared for a pasture and happened to pass by Lydon's ornamental lake. They had each removed their shoes and stockings and were sitting companionably next to each other on a log, their poles in hand and their feet dangling in the water. It was such a peaceful, friendly scene that the marquess could not help wanting to be part of it, and he turned Ajax toward them.

William was the first the hear horse and rider approach and he jumped up, waving his pole at Max. "We are fishing, my lord," he announced unnecessarily. "I even found my own worm and put it on the hook all by myself. We haven't caught anything, though."

"Nor will you if you keep jumping up and disturbing all the fish, silly boy. Hello, my lord. Did you have a satisfactory morning?" Charlotte greeted him in the friendliest of tones, apparently not the least bit disconcerted at being discovered with her shoes and stockings off and her bare feet and ankles in the water for all the world to see.

In fact, for the moment, Max could concentrate on nothing else but those elegant, narrow feet with the graceful high instep and the delicate toes sparkling in the water and the slim ankles which, no doubt, led to long, slender legs. He could not decide whether he was charmed or disconcerted by her utter lack of self-consciousness. Most women of his acquaintance, if they had done something so improper in the first place, which was highly unlikely, would have scrambled up the minute they were discovered, would have blushed furiously and made a great show of offended modesty while trying to cover themselves. Charlotte, on the other hand, was clearly enjoying the caress of the cool water against her feet as she waved them gently back and forth, but she was not about to call attention to herself or to deny her obvious enjoyment of it.

The sheer naturalness of her pleasure was completely enchanting and it made the marquess want to do nothing so much as pull off his own boots and stockings, sit down next to her, and plunge his own feet, which were hot from a morning of walking and riding, into the clear water next to hers. He had never been so casual with a woman before and he found the very casualness of it appealing. During his entire life Maximilian could not remember being simply companionable with a woman in a comfortable sort of way. Women had always seemed to want something from him. The unmarried ones acted coquettish and tried to fix his interest and make him pay court to them while the married ones seemed to

want to capture his attention and win him as a lover for the grati-
fication of being thought of as Lord Lydon's latest interest by their
jealous peers.

On the other hand, Max was uncomfortably aware that Charlotte
regarded him as such an avuncular figure that the questionable
propriety of being discovered this way by one of society's most eligible bachelors simply did not occur to her. It was a rare thing,
and Max could not recall a time when he had had no effect whatsoever upon an attractive woman. Perhaps he was getting old—a
lowering thought—or, more upsetting still, perhaps he had turned
into such an insufferable coxcomb so blinded by his own vanity
that he had lost all sense of reality. Had he? Had he lost his attrac-
tiveness to women and simply been too conceited to be aware of
it? No. It had been genuine desire he had seen in the eyes of the
actresses Tubby had brought from London; he was sure of it. Certainly Madame Dufour enjoyed his attentions. And even Isabella,
who had undoubtedly desired him more for the opportunity to become Marchioness of Lydon than for his person, had been unable
to hide the hunger in her eyes. Even at her most provoking, when
she had been holding him at arm's length in order to prevail upon
him to buy her some trinket or escort her to some insufferably dull,
but highly fashionable squeeze, he had sensed her desire. But what
was he doing even thinking of Charlotte in these terms? She was
his ward and nothing more.

"Do sit down and join us." Charlotte patted the space next to her
on the log in a friendly fashion, and Max could not help thinking
again what a lovely smile she had, how deep those green eyes
were—so deep a man could lose himself in them.

"Please do, sir," William chimed in. "You may use my pole if
you like."

"Why thank you, William." Max was genuinely touched by
their eagerness to have him join them. When had anyone wanted
him simply for the pleasure of his company? And how annoyed he
was at himself for giving a second thought to the pristine condition
of his buff breeches as he examined the soft green moss on the seat
they were offering him. Was he becoming as stiff a prig as his father had been?

"We still have some bread and cheese and a bit of tongue left."
William pointed to the basket set carefully away from the water's
edge.

"Thank you. That is most kind of you, but I finished off one of

Cook's excellent pork pies not long ago." However, he did take the proffered pole and, mentally consigning his breeches to the tender care of the laundry maids, sat down on the log as smoothly as he could without getting his feet wet.

The sun was warm on their backs as they sat gazing into the clear water, all of them mesmerized by the light twinkling on the ripples. Max felt himself slowly relaxing until he almost felt as though he were daydreaming. It was difficult to recall when he had experienced such a sense of simple contentment, certainly not for a very long time.

This serenity was soon interrupted by William, who jumped up from his perch on the other side of his sister. "Oh look, sir, you have caught a fish!"

"Why so I have." The tug on the marquess's line was not so strong that he thought he had anything worth keeping, but he pulled in his catch, which turned out to be a rather small carp.

"Charlotte says we must throw the small ones back, but it was very clever of you to catch one, wasn't it, sir?"

"Oh very." Max winked at Charlotte as he carefully unhooked the fish and tossed it into the water before handing the pole back to William. "Now it is your turn. I thank you for the use of your pole, but I really should be going." He was curiously loath to move, however, and he sat there quietly for some time listening to the wind in the willows and the buzz of the occasional bee. It was all so peaceful, and far more entertaining than the mountain of correspondence that awaited him on his desk.

Chapter 24

As the days went by, Lord Lydon found himself pushing work aside more and more often to join Charlotte and William, who seemed to find amusement and pleasure in anything and everything, even something as simple as a walk along the stream that fed the lake or throwing sticks off the decoratively arched bridge over the stream and betting on which stick would appear first on the other side.

The evenings were most often spent in the library discussing the latest news in *The Times* or, if he could be persuaded to tell them, listening to stories of the marquess's life in India. William never tired of hearing about the tiger hunts, though in truth he was more curious about the elephants Lydon had ridden during these outings than in the stalking of the tiger.

William spent as much time as he could in the stables pumping Griggs for any information that he could be persuaded to share on the care and training of horses, though he also spent a fair amount of time exploring the countryside on Caesar.

In the absence of Dr. Moreland, Charlotte did her best to carry on with her brother's lessons, but though she tried valiantly, she did not have the materials at her command nor the vicar's years of experience. Much to William's delight, lessons took a decreasing portion of the day each day.

For William, life was happier than it had ever been and there was only one thing it lacked to make it entirely perfect. One morning at breakfast, before Charlotte had joined them, he screwed up his courage enough to put forth a request. "Charlie says that I am not to bother you, and I promised her I would not, but there is something that I would like to do. I think you would like it too, and I *know* Charlie would . . ." He paused and fixed his guardian with a hopeful look.

It was a glorious day and Max, having decided to forego all the onerous tasks he had planned for himself in favor of riding out with Charlotte and William, was in a generous mood. "Well young man, out with it. What would you ask of me?"

Reassured by the marquess's smile and the teasing note in his voice, William drew a deep breath. "Well, it's like this, sir. Griggs was inspecting the harness for your curricle the other day and I remembered what a nice ride we had in it before and I thought maybe Charlie would enjoy a ride, and maybe you could let her drive it a little the way you let me, and I could come along and sit where Griggs usually sits." It was an unusually long speech and William, aghast at his own temerity, was forced to take a deep, steadying breath at the end.

Max took a bite of toast and chewed thoughtfully. "That sounds like an excellent idea, William. What do you say to doing it today?"

"Hooray! I shall tell Charlie right now!" He chortled as he pushed back his chair to rush off and tell his sister the good news, but remembering his manners, he paused in mid-flight. "That is, if I may be excused, sir."

"Yes, go ahead, scamp. You are likely to burst if you don't." Even though he had become more accustomed to his wards' presence, Max had still not grown accustomed to his own enjoyment of William's transparent delight in such simple things as a curricle ride or his gratitude for every bit of interest that anyone showed in him.

The day was a fine one, with only the gentlest of breezes. The scent of roses was in the air and the sky was a brilliant blue, a perfect day for a drive. William climbed happily into the tiger's seat as Max assisted Charlotte up onto the seat next to him. "Wait until you see how much you like it, Charlie. Maybe you can take the ribbons, but you have to be quite strong."

"Of course she will take the ribbons, but we shall wait until we have reached a good stretch of road." Max flicked his whip over the horses' heads and they were off.

After they had been rolling smoothly along for some time, he turned to her. "Ready? I have gotten them started, now all you need to do is let me help you with the reins."

Charlotte did have a moment of misgiving, for the grays did indeed look powerful, but since both her brother and the marquess appeared to have no doubt of her ability, she said nothing.

Max carefully lifted one hand over her head. "Now, place your hands behind mine and take hold of the reins." Barely loosening his grip he slid his hands back over hers, covering them with his own.

Charlotte did as directed, but in truth, her attention was more taken up with her guardian than with the team she was driving. She underwent the oddest sensation as he put his hands over hers. Their warmth, even through his gloves and hers, was comforting and there was the oddest fluttering in her stomach as she felt the strength of his arms pressing on either side of her waist. The hardness of his chest behind her shoulders was so solid and reassuring. Charlotte had never been so close, so intimate, with a man before, even her father, who had rarely seen her and never hugged her or held her close.

It was all she could do not to lean back and relax in his arms and revel in the sensation of being taken care of, enjoying the knowledge that for once there was someone else who was there for her, to hold her and protect her should anything happen. The tip of his chin just touched her bonnet. "Do you feel comfortable now?" His voice, so near to her ear, was warm and deep, like a caress, and she wanted to give herself up to the feeling of closeness and security, if only for the moment.

With an effort, Charlotte forced her thoughts back to the business at hand and gripped the reins, clenching her hands tightly until her fingers dug into her palms and fighting the languorous feeling that threatened to overwhelm her. She knew that in real life there was no such security, no guarantee that anyone would look after her. Her family, such as it was, never had looked after her, and if they had not, who else would? Charlotte knew that such safety and such belonging did not truly exist, but that did not keep her from wishing for it or for nearly succumbing to the illusion of it. She dug her fingers harder into her palms, so hard that her hands ached with the effort and the tension it created in her arms brought back her concentration.

"Relax, Charlotte, relax. You only need direct. The grays' mouths are so sensitive that they will respond to your every thought. You only need to be ready to hold them should they become frightened. Relax." The marquess's hands, gentle but firm, rubbed some of the tension from hers. They moved up her wrists, soothing, caressing, massaging away the ache and spreading a tingle so delicious through her that she longed for him to continue on up her arms to her shoulders and she was forced to bite her lip in order to keep her mind on the powerful horses she was holding.

At last Charlotte's thoughts cleared, and with a deep sigh, she let herself feel the horses' heads and mouths. That was better. She kept her eyes fixed on the pair's ears, making herself read every little twitch and ignoring as best she could the disturbing awareness of the marquess's body so close to hers.

"There; that is better. Give them their heads. It is not like you to be timid." Max slowly drew his hands away.

"I know it is not, but we do not have such expensive cattle at Harcourt and I am unaccustomed to handling such 'sweet goers', as William would call them." Charlotte laughed shakily. Good, let him think it was nerves that had overcome her instead of the foolishness that had truly afflicted her. She had herself reasonably well in hand now and was beginning to enjoy the sensation of guiding the powerful but sensitive animals and the smoothness of the ride as they glided past hedgerows bursting with green. Though she had no intention of springing someone else's horses, Charlotte could feel the speed they were capable of and found just the thought of such speed exhilarating.

She drove for several miles in silence, her eyes riveted to the unfamiliar road and her arms sensitive to every motion of the horses, and soon—blessedly soon—she was able to forget everything in the rhythm of the horses' hooves, the freshness of the sweet-scented air, the sun warm on her back, and give herself up to the pleasure of driving.

Charlotte was a natural horsewoman, the marquess reflected as he watched her ease into driving. After her initial and uncharacteristic nervousness, she had relaxed and become one with the team as he had known she would. There was an intuitive sensuality about her that, aside from her obvious intelligence, made her aware of things that most people never noticed. What other people had to learn, she seemed to sense instinctively, and in no time at all she had the team moving along as easily as if there had been no change in driver. He glanced at her as she sat there, her back straight, her arms at the precisely correct angle. She was a slender little thing, but there was a strength in her and a vitality that he had never felt before in a woman and he was drawn to it, almost mesmerized by it.

Strength was not a quality Max had ever looked for in a woman. He had always wanted them sophisticated, willing, voluptuous, and blatantly sexual—until now, that was. There was something damnably attractive about a woman who held a powerful team so easily but whose slim form radiated an energy and a bond with the natural world that was completely sensual. Her arms formed a fluid connection through the reins with the horses and her entire being was devoted to sensing their every thought and movement, yet he could see her delicate nostrils flare as she took in the heady scent of the surrounding countryside and see the sweep of her thick, dark lashes against the smooth cheek as she glanced from the road ahead of her to the woods and fields on either side to the tips of the horses' ears. He watched her bosom rise and fall under the white fichu of her severely tailored carriage dress as she savored the breaths of fresh air.

Observing her patent enjoyment of the out-of-doors, Max was again reminded of her bare feet dangling in the water and his own breathing became slightly irregular.

"How do you like it, Charlie? Aren't they the most bang-up pair you have ever seen?"

Both Charlotte and the marquess were so immersed in their own thoughts that they had been forgetting William's presence entirely. Charlotte glanced up rather guiltily at her guardian before replying. "That they are. I am so glad you had the notion of asking Lord Lydon if we could go for a drive." She spoke in a normal enough tone, but a self-conscious blush stained her cheeks. It was not like her to ignore her brother so completely and the expression she had seen on the marquess's face as she had looked up at him told her that he too had been lost in some sort of reverie. It had been rather unsettling to look up from the reins to find him regarding her strangely, almost as though he had never seen her before. The expression in his eyes was oddly intent, as though he were talking to her or at least reading her thoughts.

The recollection of some of those thoughts made her blush even more, bringing a glimmer of amusement to the marquess's eyes. So she had been aware of his scrutiny, had she? Did she suspect the nature of his thoughts? Perhaps Charlotte was more of a woman than she liked to think. And just how aware of women and men and their relationships was she?

She had always spoken of marriage in such disparaging tones and had made it so abundantly clear that she had no very high regard for men—understandable in the light of the men who were her relatives—that Max had thought her completely ignorant of such things. Now he wondered. A complete innocent would not have colored under his gaze the way she had.

One wheel of the curricle hit a largish stone, jarring Max out of this dangerous train of thought. What was he doing even entertaining such ideas? Charlotte Winterbourne was an inexperienced young girl, and his ward at that. Anxious to direct his thoughts somewhere else, Max turned to William. "If you would like to try your hand at it, we could stop at the next crossroads where there is a place wide enough to turn around and you may drive us home. Would you like that?"

"Would I? Oh yes, sir!"

"That is," Max turned to Charlotte, "if you do not mind. I shall change places with William."

"You be the tiger?" William's astonishment was comical to behold.

"I expect Griggs would allow me to do so just this once. He is secure enough in his position not to feel threatened so long as I do not make a regular practice of it."

"You'll see, Charlie, how I can hold the horses just like Lord Lydon. He taught me just the way he taught you, by first putting his hands over mine on the reins and then letting go."

Stealing a sidelong glance at his ward, Max surprised another conscious flush. Good. She had felt something as he had clasped those delicate hands in his and held his arms on either side of her. It had been disturbing enough as it was to find himself so very aware of her as a woman; it would have been more disturbing still if she had felt absolutely nothing in return.

They reached the crossroads. Max descended and took the horses' heads as William climbed down. It was a relief to leave Charlotte's side. The closeness of the shared seat had been altogether too distracting. But as he took his place in the tiger's seat Max realized that this relief had been short-lived for now, though he could not see her face, he was offered an excellent view of the trim waist and slim hips, which proved to be equally as distracting as proximity had been.

With an effort he forced his mind back to the activity of the moment—driving the curricle and William's ability to guide the team. It had been rather a rash decision on the marquess's part to move back such a distance that he could not easily grab the reins should anything go wrong, but then, he had been rather desperate to divert his thoughts from the woman next to him. Changing places, as drastic a measure as it was, had seemed to be the only solution.

Fully aware of the awesome trust his guardian had placed in him, William concentrated so hard on maintaining perfect control of the horses that sweat was trickling down his cheeks by the time they reached the gate to Lydon Court, but he managed it perfectly, coming to a smooth and easy stop on the gravel drive. He let out a sigh of relief. "I did it, and you were not even next to me, were you, my lord?" He exclaimed proudly as he handed the reins to Griggs and climbed down. "I drove us all the way back, Griggs, and Lord Lydon was not even next to me."

"Very good, sir. I knew you could do it, sir."

"We had ever so much fun. Charlie drove too. And you liked it, didn't you, Charlie?"

"That I did."

"Do you think we could have a curricle, Charlie?"

This was too big a decision, and Charlotte was not thinking as clearly as she would have liked, but she could not resist the eager expression in her brother's eyes. "Let me think about it, dear. It is a rather big decision," she temporized.

Any answer that was not an outright negative was enough to satisfy William, and he went off happily to the stables with Griggs and the horses.

"You are a very good sister." The marquess gave Charlotte his arm as they made their way up the steps.

"He has so little that he can excel at that I feel I must encourage those things where he can. However, I have no idea of the expense of it."

"Let me think about it for you and see what I can do."

"Why thank you." How easily he offered his assistance and how easily she had accepted it, Charlotte marveled to herself. Things had changed a good deal since their first prickly encounter, or, for that matter, since his initially stormy reaction to their appearance at Lydon Court. Perhaps her father had been right after all in choosing the marquess as guardian.

Chapter 25

In fact, having Lord Lydon as a guardian could even be rather pleasant, Charlotte thought as she and the marquess sat down to a game of chess in the library that evening. She had never really had anyone to turn to for advice before. Speen, Mrs. Hodges, Mr. Tidworth, and Mr. Sotherton had always been there to answer questions about the practical aspects of running the estate and Dr. Moreland was a fund of knowledge where Greek, Latin, history, mathematics, or even botany were concerned, but none of these people, devoted as they were, could offer much in the way of worldly wisdom, and that was the area where Charlotte most needed help. Her father should have been the one to make up that deficiency, she thought as her hand hovered over her queen, but he could not even be bothered to acknowledge her existence, much less answer the letters she had faithfully sent to him over the years.

"A scowl that ferocious bodes ill for my hapless rook," Max remarked as he studied her face in the firelight. Concentration was not an expression he was accustomed to observing on female faces. He found the intensity with which Charlotte devoted herself to anything intriguing and her total lack of self-consciousness delightful.

"What?" Charlotte looked blank for a moment. "Oh . . . no, I was thinking of something else."

"Something else? You could think of something else at this critical moment?" Max raised his eyebrows in mock dismay.

"I, well . . . yes," Charlotte admitted a trifle sheepishly.

"What a lowering thought. I am quite undone." The marquess shook his head sadly.

"I suppose it is rather appalling to you that I was not attending, accustomed as you are to females' undivided attention."

"Vixen." Max grinned appreciatively. "But I deserve it. I admit it; I have grown shockingly puffed up. However, I assure you that any female attention I may command is not due so much to my person as it is to my position. If I were a haberdasher, for example, I should attract no notice whatsoever, but were I twice as old as I am now with a club foot and a squint, I should probably attract no less interest."

Charlotte could not help chuckling. The idea of the dashing Lord Lydon as a haberdasher was incongruous in the extreme, but there was no hiding the bitter edge in his voice and it gave her pause. It had never occurred to her that he would do anything but revel in his reputation of being irresistible to women.

Tilting her head to one side, she examined him more closely. The sardonic grin, dark brows, mocking expression, and high cheekbones certainly gave him the look of a rake, but the eyes betrayed him. Instead of the cynical gleam she had half expected to see there, she saw bleakness, and a loneliness as deep as her own.

It was only the impression of a moment, and then he laughed, raising one dark brow. "I assure you I still enjoy myself. Whatever the motivation behind it, the results are the same."

He was his usual ironic self again, but Charlotte had seen the vulnerability underneath. That moment of understanding, brief though it had been, gave her the courage to ask something she had been unable to ask before. "What was my father like?"

Her voice was so low that at first Max was not even sure that she had spoken at all, but looking at her he could read the question in her eyes, in the tension of her body, and the whiteness of the knuckles that now clutched her knight, and he sensed how difficult a thing it was for her to ask. He was silent for quite some time, searching for just the right words, words that would reassure her without lying to her. "He was a very private man, a brilliant politician and card player, a stimulating conversationalist when he felt comfortable enough with someone to take the trouble to talk to him. But essentially he was a solitary person, someone who worked very hard for the things he believed in, but who did not waste much time on purely social affairs."

"But did you like him?" Now that she had asked the question, she was pathetically eager for information, and Max's heart went out to her.

"Yes I liked him. I trusted him, and that is saying a great deal, for the worlds I have lived in are such that one can easily be destroyed if one places trust in the wrong person. He was not an easy man to know, but he saw and appreciated many things about me that the rest of the world did not."

"He respected you."

"Yes, I think . . . yes he did." Looking across at the serious little face, Max could see that she understood all that he was trying so awkwardly to convey about what it was like to discover someone who saw the real man beneath the rank and the reputation, someone else who was deeply interested in trade and finance instead of being bored or appalled by it, someone who knew exactly what it took to do what Lydon had done, to succeed as he had succeeded.

"I wish . . . I wish he had respected me."

"I do too." Max longed to reach out to her, to pull her into his arms and hold her close, to smooth away some of the hurt he heard in her voice and saw in her eyes. Any father would have been proud to have a son who had accomplished what Charlotte had—running Harcourt, looking after the land and people who trusted in the care of the earls of Harcourt. Hell, his own father would have given anything to have a son like that. That a young woman had done it all was all the more extraordinary. "But he did choose someone to look after you who does."

There was a smile in his eyes and a warmth in his voice that spoke to her more than words. Ordinarily, Charlotte would have bridled at the thought of someone looking after her and in the beginning she had, but something had changed. It was different now. The marquess was not speaking of looking after her physical well-being as much as he was about looking after her soul and making sure that he protected, not so much what she was, but who she was, from Cecil and Almeria, and anyone else who wanted to turn her and William into something they were not. Perhaps, in some small way, her father *had* cared about them. After all, he had appointed the marquess as their guardian when he very easily could have ignored them completely and left them to the tender mercies of the Wadleighs.

"Thank you." Unaccustomed to such a feeling of closeness with anyone except William, Charlotte felt suddenly shy and at a loss as to how to reply, but she did not need to. Her expressive face told him everything and Max felt oddly happy sitting there watching the glow of the fire on her skin and the shadows cast by her lashes on the curve of her cheek.

The thought of Cecil, however, brought Charlotte quickly back to reality. In the security of Lydon Court and the freedom from her daily responsibilities, she had almost forgotten the threat hanging over William. "Have you heard anything back yet from the servant you sent to Harcourt?" Charlotte broke the silence, glad of the excuse to divert the conversation away from herself. She felt just the tiniest bit uneasy with the intimacy she suddenly felt between them.

"What?" With an effort, Max broke out of his reverie. "Oh. No. But I did not expect to hear immediately. I asked him to be discreet, but to make a thorough investigation—not just into the question of poachers, but into anything that seemed out of the ordinary. I do not expect him back until the end of the week."

"You do not think I am imagining things, do you? Cecil may seem to be just a prosy old windbag, but I think he truly believes that he deserves to inherit Harcourt and that William stands in his way."

"Whether or not you are correct in your suspicions is less important than protecting William, so it is best to act as though Cecil were capable of anything. If you are wrong, there is no harm done, and if you are right, you have protected your brother. However, while you are here at Lydon, my task is to see to it that you enjoy yourself to such a degree that the thought of Cousin Cecil does not cross your mind from one day to the next."

"That is too kind in you, my lord, to act the host to two uninvited guests who caused the end of a party which must have been far more amusing to you than anything William and I have to offer."

"Yes, I am a paragon of gracious hospitality, in fact. But you need not remark on it with such surprise. Just because I do not haunt the gathering places of the *ton* does not mean that I am totally devoid of social graces, you know."

"Well if you are going to protect yourself against being caught in the parson's mousetrap by letting the world think of you as a sad rake, then you must be prepared to suffer the consequences of being thought of as antisocial," Charlotte responded unsympathetically. But both of them were thinking back to the evening Charlotte and William had arrived. She was wondering how much she regretted the departure of his friends, and he was marveling at how quickly he had forgotten that they had even been there. It seemed so long ago and part of another life.

Actually, everything but the present with Charlotte and her

brother seemed part of another life. Max kept telling himself that since they would be leaving soon and since they had so little opportunity for enjoyment he ought to devote himself to making their time at Lydon Court a pleasant one. But in truth, he was more than happy to lay aside the rest of his affairs to spend time with them, and more than happy to ignore the fact that he was working to make it a memorable visit for himself as well as for them.

And as the days passed, Lord Lydon was to be seen less and less in his study and more and more in the company of his wards. Their enjoyment of their first driving lesson had been such that he continued to teach them, gratified by their natural ability and the quickness with which they both picked it up.

He also set up an archery range on the lawn in front of the library. William did not take to archery as easily as he had to driving, and occasionally became frustrated. "I shall never get it," he complained one warm afternoon as his arrow missed the target entirely.

"Of course you will. It is just that you are not so accustomed to this as you are to other things. Just do not try so hard. You would not force a horse at a fence, now would you? It is the same with archery or anything else; you must concentrate until it feels right and you can picture it all without looking at it. Now try again, slowly . . . wait until you can feel it . . . There, you see? You hit the target."

"I did, didn't I?" William looked pleased. He turned to his sister, who had been quietly watching the lesson. "Now you try, Charlie."

Both William and his sister let out a crow of delight as her arrow flew straight to the target and buried itself in the bull's-eye.

"A well-brought-up young lady would never run the risk of upsetting a gentleman by besting him at anything, especially an athletic pursuit." The marquess shook his head in mock dismay. He picked up his bow, sighted along the shaft, and let fly. Much to his disgust, it landed a considerable distance from the bull's-eye. "Blast!"

"You won, Charlie, you won!" William was even more excited than his sister who, though not as vocal as her brother, was visibly pleased with herself.

"And only a perfect hoyden would take pleasure in beating a gentleman, not to mention letting him see it." Max shook his head sadly, his eyes dancing.

"Perhaps, but if I were a proper young lady you would not be able to enjoy the archery because you would be wondering if I were hoping to charm you into making me an offer."

"Touché. There is a great deal to be said for honesty. Brutal honesty, however, is another matter."

Not certain of whether or not he was truly offended, Charlotte colored and opened her mouth to apologize, but Max took pity on her. "Relax, I am only teasing you. Actually, I have never had a woman compete with me before and I find it extremely refreshing. Though I cannot say how I would take defeat on a regular basis, I find it only adds to your charm that you are extremely skillful at something."

"My charm?" Charlotte looked so dumbfounded that Max could only laugh and ruffle the dark hair that, freed from the confines of the cottage bonnet she had tossed carelessly on the ground, curled around her face.

"Yes, your charm." He strolled over to the target and pulled out the arrows. "And for tomorrow afternoon, may I suggest an activity in which I am certain to excel because it requires nothing more than brute strength, which I feel quite sure I possess in greater abundance than you do? I suggest that we row on the lake."

There was a challenging gleam in his eye, but Charlotte was still too taken aback at being told she had charm to respond to it.

Chapter 26

The following day was even warmer than the previous one and the idea of spending the afternoon on the water was infinitely appealing. Charlotte was glad to shed the heavy bombazine carriage dress she had worn for the driving lesson that morning in favor of a white India muslin walking dress trimmed with straw-colored satin. The bodice was cut rather lower than most of her dresses, which made it even cooler, but she did take the precaution of bringing a muslin shawl for protection against the sun and in case the breeze over the water turned out to be fresher than she anticipated.

After their driving lesson, William had hurried off to his bedchamber with a great deal of purpose. Charlotte wondered at this, for ordinarily he liked to seek out Griggs and regale him with every last detail of his lesson. But his mysterious behavior was soon explained when he appeared after luncheon holding a folded paper boat. "Speen taught me how to make boats back at Harcourt, so I made one to try here when we go out on the lake."

"A capital idea. I remember that Felbridge taught me a similar design when I was your age. May I see it?" Absorbed in examining William's toy, Max was oblivious to the effect that this simple speech had on William's sister.

A lump rose in Charlotte's throat and her eyes misted over so that William and the marquess merged into one blurry mass in front of her. Outrageous and irreverent though the marquess's behavior might be in the eyes of the fashionable world, to her brother, he was kindness itself. Charlotte very much doubted that at the age of fifteen Lord Lydon would have done anything but sneer at paper boats; however, at the age of seven or eight he might very well have been as intrigued by them as his ward now was. As always, he made William feel appreciated and comfortable with who he was. Not for the first time Charlotte noticed the warmth in the marquess's voice when he spoke of Felbridge. Though her guardian had no obvious family ties, it was clear from the way he spoke of the man that Felbridge meant more to him than anyone else did.

They soon reached the charming little boathouse at the edge of the water. William and the marquess launched the boat and the marquess assisted Charlotte in taking her seat in the bow. He took the oars, and at his direction William climbed into the stern and pushed off. With a few swift strokes the marquess had set them gliding smoothly toward the middle of the lake.

"Please may we go to the island?" William begged.

"We can go around, if you like, but at the moment the ducks are nesting there so I do not like to disturb them. Perhaps if you look closely you may see some ducklings."

Mollified, William kept his eyes glued to the shore as they circled the little clump of rocks and trees in the middle of the lake, but he could see nothing.

The warmth of the sun and the rhythmic plunk of the oars in the water made Charlotte feel pleasantly drowsy. She trailed one hand in the water and stared dreamily into its depths, letting her mind wander as freely as the white fluffy clouds drifted in the brilliant blue sky overhead. She was practically dozing off when she heard her brother exclaim, "Oh, my boat!" There was a violent lurch to starboard, and the next thing she knew she was tossed into the water in which she had so leisurely been dipping her fingers.

Gasping with the sudden shock of it, she untangled her arms from her shawl and struggled to right herself. Since she and William had been taught to swim by Speen, she was not at all worried. The water, being shallow, was not too cold and, given the warmth of the day, it was pleasantly refreshing once she had gotten over the surprise of it all.

Checking to see if William and the marquess were all right, she grabbed onto the boat, which had turned completely over, and, using that for support, stretched her feet down. They touched the bottom with ease and she stood up, chest deep in the water, and wiped the dripping curls away from her face.

William and the marquess were also struggling to their feet. "I didn't mean it, I didn't mean it, Charlie," William apologized when he had caught his breath. "I dropped my boat into the water and I didn't want to lose it. I'm sorry, Charlie, I really and truly am."

"I know you did not mean it, dear," Charlotte reassured her brother with a watery smile. "But you must remember what I told you back at Harcourt about staying in the center of the boat and not making any sudden movements." Seeing that he was still distressed, Charlotte splashed over to her brother and put one arm around him. "There, there, dear. There is no harm done. It was just a bit of a shock, that is all, but I am afraid that your boat has gone for a voyage of its own." She pointed to the little craft which, pushed by gentle waves, was rapidly making its way to the island. "I wonder what the ducks will make of that?"

Reassured, William laughed and shook the water out of his hair. "Yes, I wonder what they will think of that." Then he tucked his arm under hers. "We are having an adventure, aren't we, Charlie? Did you hear that, sir? We are having an adventure," William sang out gaily.

Wiping the water from his own eyes, Lydon shook his head in a bemused fashion. "I expect we are." Stunned by the entire episode, Maximilian was undergoing a series of startling revelations that seemed to be rendering him entirely incapable of thought or action. Accustomed to being in command of every situation, and being the one people looked to for a solution to every crisis, he was oddly put out that no one seemed to be asking him to do anything in this one. Charlotte appeared not to be the least ruffled by her unexpected dunking, and William had turned immediately to his sister for guidance. Instead of being counted upon, the marquess was merely superfluous.

Glancing over at Charlotte to see if she needed assistance, he had been confronted with a dilemma of another sort—he could not take his eyes off her. With the water glistening in her hair and transforming the fine muslin of her walking dress into a second skin, she looked like Venus rising from the sea, and it quite took his breath away. He gasped for air as though someone had tipped him a leveler in the stomach. What had come over him? He had seen scores of women in all states of undress; what was it about this one that affected him so? Steady, man, he told himself, she is your ward.

But then Charlotte turned to him, laughter sparkling in her eyes. "I had not thought to go swimming, but it really is rather refreshing on such a warm. day." Max's heart began to pound in a way it had not since his salad days. She was so blithe and calm about the entire episode, accepting it and dealing with it in a way he could not imagine another person doing, except himself. She was entirely without embarrassment, obviously enjoying the cool water without the least thought for what it was doing to her clothing or her coiffure. For a wild moment he wondered if she even cared that her dress was practically transparent.

"Perhaps we had better make our way to shore, for I do not think that even the three of us together can right this boat, do you my lord?"

"Ah, er, no."

Charlotte slowly began to wade toward the nearest shore, but in water that high it was rather slow going so she gave up and swam as best she could, with William splashing along behind her. Finally, reaching shallower water, she stood up, the folds of her skirt clinging to her like the drapery of a Greek statue.

Max followed more slowly, trying valiantly to keep his eyes on William, on the shore, on anything but the long, delicious curves of her slender figure as she rose from the water. Her naturalness was enchanting, and her obvious enjoyment of the water only made his throat tighten as the picture of her totally unencumbered by clothes, free to frolic in the lake, flashed unbidden before him. Drops of water on her skin gave it a pearly glow that made him long to reach out and caress it, to run his hands down the smooth, slim column of her neck and . . . what was he thinking? She was his ward. He was supposed to be her guardian, not her ravisher. But slow, delicious ravishment was all he could think of at the moment.

It took a supreme effort of will even to breathe normally. Conversation was certainly impossible. Fortunately for Max, a gentle breeze ruffled the water and Charlotte pulled the sodden shawl she had been dragging from the water and wrapped it around her shoulders. That snapped him out of his trance. He made his way over to her, stripped off his own coat of Bath superfine, and placed it over the shawl, pulling it close around her. However, it took all his self-control not to pull her into his arms and plant kisses all over her soft red lips and down her white throat.

Charlotte turned to glance up at him. "Why thank you. But there really is no need. I am warm enough and you have only your shirt, which is thinner than my dress." This was quite true, for she could see the outline of the muscles of his arms and the dark hair on his chest through the wet linen of his shirt. Charlotte had never realized what a physically powerful man the marquess was. Until this moment, if she had thought about it at all, she had attributed his assurance and air of authority to his vast worldly experience and clever mind, but now she realized that these were only part of it. The broad shoulders, muscular chest, long, lean legs, and strong, capable hands played no small part in his imposing presence. All of a sudden her knees felt weak and she had the wildest urge to lean against that chest, gathering warmth and strength from his solidity. It was most unlike her, but she supposed it must be a reaction to the shock of being dumped without warning into the water.

"Here, Charlie, here is a bit of log you can step on to get out." William, who had moved on ahead of them and searched the shore to find the best place to emerge, now pointed it out proudly to them.

"Thank you, William. That was very clever of you," Charlotte responded, grateful for the distraction that broke the almost palpable tension between her and the marquess. It was as though she had been aware of him with every fiber of her body, and the intensity of it had been almost overwhelming. Certainly it had been extremely unnerving and Charlotte, never having experienced anything like it before in her life, was a little afraid of it. Just after her mother had died she remembered wanting to have her father hug and hold her as her mother had done, but he never had. He had never so much as held her hand or kissed her good night and she had never again allowed herself to long for anything so much as she had for that.

The feelings rushing over her now had filled her with that same desperate yearning, and it frightened her to think that after all these years of raising herself to be an independent and rational creature, able to look after both herself and William, in the blink of an eye, or in this case, a tumble into the water, she could find herself right back where she had started from fifteen long, lonely years ago.

"What will we do about the boat, sir?" William's question to the marquess was equally as restorative to his guardian as his finding a place to climb out had been to his sister. With a sigh, half of regret, half of relief, Max gave the coat on Charlotte's shoulders a final pat, as though his hands had been resting there only to make sure the coat was well and firmly placed and not because he ached to touch her.

"I shall ask some of the lads from the stable to bring one or two of the plow horses from the home farm and hitch them to the boat and drag it in. The bottom of the lake is solid enough so they should be able to keep their footing, and it is not so deep as to make them nervous if the lads can just float it close enough to shore to right it."

"I should like to see that."

"And so you shall, but I think your sister would agree with me that we should go and exchange these wet things for some dry ones; do you not think so, Charlotte?"

"Charlotte." Hearing her name on his lips startled her and she looked up at Max in some surprise. It was a mistake, for his eyes were smiling down into hers in such a way that she felt as though he could see right through her, right through his jacket and the thin muslin dress to her heart, which was absolutely pounding. Surely he must be able to see her knees threatening to buckle again. For the life of her, she could not tear her eyes away, but remained staring up at him as her throat grew dry and her cheeks grew warm. "Yes," she croaked. "I mean, certainly we must do that. It is very warm outside at the moment, but a cloud could come along or a puff of wind and we should feel rather cold." What in heaven's name was wrong with her? First she was tongue-tied as a school-girl and now she was babbling like an idiot. Surely it was not the shock. She had gotten into scrapes, suffered cuts, bruises, falls, accidents of all kinds without being the least affected by it, but now she was all at sea. At last, drawing a deep breath, she was able to tear her eyes away from Max's and, planting one foot firmly and deliberately in front of the other, made her way toward the house.

Chapter 27

Maximilian let her go, but a secret smile of satisfaction spread slowly across his face. So she had felt it too. She was not indifferent to him. Good! It was bad enough to ache for her as he ached for her now, to be possessed with the overwhelming urge to bury his hands in the shining dark hair and press his lips to hers, but it would have been unbearable to feel that way if she herself felt nothing. But he had seen the telltale signs, the green eyes turning deep emerald with desire, the delicate flush on her cheeks, the fluttering pulse at the base of her throat. Charlotte might not recognize such signs herself, much less admit to them, but they were there.

Maximilian followed Charlotte and William at a more leisurely pace, but as he climbed the steps to the terrace outside the library he paused, his hand on the latch of the French doors. If he entered, he was sure to encounter someone—Mrs. Purdy, one of the footmen—and he would be forced to speak to them. His mood would be broken, and he did not wish it to be. Just for the moment he wanted to savor it, to enjoy it to its fullest.

He turned to gaze back over the lake and his eyes lighted on the overturned boat. The sight of it brought him back to reality with a jolt. What was he thinking? Charlotte was the daughter of his friend, his ward, entrusted to his care, depending on him for his support and guidance. And all he could think of was ravishing her.

Heretofore, Max had confined his amatory exploits to women of the world, women experienced in the art of dalliance. He had never desired, never allowed himself to think about the young, the innocent, the inexperienced. That only led to expectations and responsibilities that he was not about to take on. Besides, the idea of making love to someone who had no skill or experience, someone who was likely to resist or, at the very least, regret it, had never held any attraction for him; it had seemed more like work than pleasure. Why now, suddenly, did innocence and inexperience seem so appealing?

To think that he would be the first to kiss those full soft lips, the first to make her body experience the delights of passion, now made it all the more desirable. Charlotte's blushes, her lowered lashes, the look of surprise in her eyes made the attraction all the more powerful because the lack of dissembling made it all the more real. Skill on the part of one's lover meant the ability to deceive—such was not the case with Charlotte. The desire she felt was mirrored in her face, and its presence in her only made him want her all the more.

However, it could not go on. As her guardian, unsought as the responsibility had been, he owed it to her to protect her from men like him. He was there to insure her peace of mind, not to threaten it. How he longed to threaten it, just as she threatened his. How he longed to fill her thoughts as completely as she was filling his.

"Ahem . . . my lord?" Max barely heard the footman addressing him, though the man was standing practically at his elbow.

"Yes?"

"Begging your pardon sir, but Will Foster is here and he said you asked to see him the moment he returned."

"Yes, yes I did. Have him wait for me here in the library. I must get out of these wet things. Oh, and Lumley?"

"Yes, sir?"

"Tell some of the lads from the stables to hitch up some of the plow horses and pull the boat from the lake, would you?"

"Yes sir, very good sir."

Will Foster. Max opened the door to the library and headed for his bedchamber and dry clothes. Here was news that would distract him from the dangerous territory into which his thoughts insisted on straying.

He changed hurriedly and was soon back in the library. "Well, Will, what news have you to report?" The vigorous toweling he had given himself before putting on dry clothes had cleared the cobwebs from his brain and allowed him to push aside his disturbing reflections to become his customary energetic self.

Will's broad, ruddy face looked drawn and tired. "Well sir, I put up at the Green Dragon, like you said, and I got to be on pretty good terms with folks in the taproom, told them I worked for a wealthy banker who wanted to build an estate in the area. People were friendly enough, and I even had the opportunity to speak with some of the lads in the stables at Harcourt, but there was nothing to find out except that they do not care overmuch for the new man, Tom Piggott. He keeps pretty much to himself, does not seem very knowledgeable about horses, and the general opinion is that he has been sent by Sir Cecil to spy on Lady Charlotte and her brother in order to prove that his young lordship needs the guidance of an adult."

"They *have* the guidance of an adult. *I* am their guardian."

"Of course you are, sir, but this here Sir Cecil wants to prove that you are always absent and are not fulfilling your duties in the proper manner, or leastways, that is what most people think."

"No, I have the audaciously improper notion that two people who have been managing by themselves for years, quite nicely thank you, are not suddenly in need of the help of some outsider who is totally unfamiliar with Harcourt and its people."

"As you say, sir, most everyone seems to feel that Lady Charlotte is entirely capable of taking care of it all herself."

"Yes, and then some. Was there any mention of poachers?"

Will shook his head, a perplexed frown wrinkling his face. "No one had heard of such a thing. The Winterbournes always have allowed people to hunt on their land, so perhaps it was just someone from the village out hunting who fired the shot and was afraid to own up to nearly missing the earl, but there was nothing out of the ordinary that I could find."

"Thank you, Will. I have no doubt you have conducted a most thorough investigation. Now go and get some rest."

"Thank you, sir." Will took leave of his master and headed toward the kitchen, eager to have a bite of apple tart that had smelled so enticing when he had come in from the stables.

Max remained for some time staring unseeingly out the library windows. The men had arrived to pull the boat out, but he did not even notice them as he mulled over the information that Will had brought him. It did not appear as though there was any immediate threat. If there had been any truly suspicious characters or suspicious activity, someone at Harcourt would have noticed. Surely if he sent someone back with Charlotte and her brother to watch over both of them, they would be safe enough. After all, how safe was Charlotte here? She had begun to dominate his thoughts in such a way that he knew it was better for him to send her away, and where else could she go but to Harcourt? Did he dare send her there? Max rang for a footman and continued to stare out at the expanse of green lawn stretching before him.

"Yes, sir?"

"Could you please take word to Lady Charlotte that I am in the library and wish to speak with her at her convenience."

"Certainly, sir."

Never one to spend a great deal of time on her dress, Charlotte was already changed, all traces of the accident completely eliminated, by the time the footman knocked on her door, but after receiving the marquess's summons she lingered in front of the looking glass, patting in a stray curl here and there, and fiddling with the lace of her collar. She still needed time to recover her composure before she could meet her guardian with the customary easy friendliness she had shown him before their sudden dunking.

She still could not get out of her mind the expression in his eyes as he had looked at her, nor could she wipe out the image of the muscles rippling under his shirt as he had gently placed his coat around her shoulders, and she could not stop the curious quivery feeling that came rushing over her at the thought of him. She leaned closer toward the looking glass examining herself more carefully and not with a great deal of satisfaction.

She wished her mouth were smaller. The eyes looked well enough, but the lashes were too thick and dark and her hair was too curly. She pulled the collar again and sighed at her reflection. Now that she thought of it, she really was too thin. It would have been nice to have some curves under the fall of lace on her chest, curves like those of Lady Hillyard—not that she wished to look quite so obviously enticing as that lady—but it would be nice to appear as something more than just a slip of a girl. Would she never grow up? Odd how she had never noticed such things about herself before, nor had she ever felt so dissatisfied with her appearance.

In a corner of the bedchamber, picking up her mistress's sodden things, Lucy glanced surreptitiously at Charlotte. It was most unlike her ladyship even to consult a looking glass, much less examine herself in one. Ordinarily, Charlotte never gave a second thought to the way she looked or, if she did, it was only to appease her maid and only out of concern for Lucy's reputation. What had occurred to effect such a change? A sly smile crept over Lucy's face, and she bent down quickly to hide it as she retrieved a wet stocking. It could only be his lordship who had wrought such a transformation. Come to think of it, ever since they had been at

Lydon Court there had been a sparkle in Lady Charlotte's eyes and a lightness in her step that she had never seen before. The maid wished fervently that she had Cook or Mrs. Hodges to discuss this delicious state of affairs with her. Lucy was sure she was correct in her reading of the signs, but still it would be nice to have someone with whom she could share it.

Giving a final tug to her collar, Charlotte let out a dissatisfied sigh and descended to the library, taking several deep breaths along the way. By the time her hand was on the door she had herself well in hand and was her usual calm, collected self, until the marquess, rising to greet her, smiled at her with a special intimate smile. Then she suddenly felt hot all over even though she was still somewhat chilled from her dip in the lake.

"I have some good news for you." Max gestured toward a chair on one side of the fire and seated himself on the other.

Charlotte sank into it gratefully, for her knees were feeling peculiarly unsteady. She was thankful that the glow from the fire hid the flush that surely must be obvious. What on earth was wrong with her?

His lordship, however, did not seem to see anything amiss. "Will Foster reports that he has scoured the countryside around Harcourt and has not been able to discover any reports of poachers or other undesirable persons in the vicinity. He has also made discreet inquiries about Tom Piggott, and has come to the conclusion that though the man is certainly spying on you for your Cousin Cecil, there is no evidence that he is trying to do anything more than discredit you and prove that William needs more care than you can offer. Perhaps that is the case. Perhaps he is merely trying to scare you rather than harm William. I know, I know"—Max held up an admonitory hand as he saw the spark of anger kindling in Charlotte's eyes—"Cecil is all sorts of a scoundrel, but we have no proof, and we can do nothing without proof. Let me send Will back with you. Surely you could use another servant somewhere, and he can keep an eye on things."

Charlotte digested this slowly. She did not know what to do. On one hand, she was uneasy about William's safety and she felt protected at Lydon Court. On the other, she knew they could not run away forever and though she felt physically safe with her guardian, her peace of mind was most definitely at risk. She could not live with a man who, simply by looking at her, could make her feel as she was feeling now. Surely a pulse as rapid as hers and breathing so irregular were not at all healthy for a person.

Max saw her indecision and it tore at his heart. He reached over and tilted her chin to look deep into her eyes. "Charlotte, I promise you I will let nothing happen to you or to William. Do you believe me?"

Charlotte sat as if mesmerized, unable to look away, but afraid to look into his eyes, which had the strangest expression in them. It was as though they were speaking to her, asking her something, something she was not sure of, and it made her feel all fluttery inside. Slowly she nodded.

"Good girl. We shall get to the bottom of this if I have to hire an army to protect you. Now I must speak to Will and make some arrangements of my own." He dropped a gentle kiss on her forehead and was gone, leaving her to stare blankly into the fire feeling strangely bereft.

It was some time before Charlotte could pull her scattered wits together, but at last she rose. There was packing to be done and orders to be given to Speen and Lucy, but somehow she was finding it difficult to concentrate on anything but the warmth of the marquess's lips on her forehead and the look in his eyes as he had promised to protect them. She was in the grip of an odd sort of lethargy that made her long to remain right where she was, savoring the feelings of being cared for and watched over, feelings she had never had before in her life.

At the same time, a tiny voice in the back of her mind was telling her to get up and go away before she grew to like such feeling too much. At the moment it was too new, but oh she could grow accustomed to having someone to turn to with problems that seemed too difficult, someone to hold her when she was exhausted. It was a dependency to be avoided at all costs, for no one knew better than she did that life was not that way, that the only person she could count on to take care of her was Charlotte Winterbourne. Painful experience had taught her that thinking or hoping anything else was merely setting herself up for further hurt and disappointment.

With a wistful sigh, she rose from her comfortable seat by the fire and headed toward the stables where she was sure to find her brother as well as Speen.

Chapter 28

The next morning after breakfast, a subdued little group gathered on the drive. The previous day, when informed of their plans, William had wailed unhappily. "But I don't want to go back to Harcourt. I like it here. Can't we stay with Lord Lydon, Charlie?"

Charlotte, who longed to express very similar sentiments herself, smiled sadly at her brother. "I am glad you enjoyed yourself, dear, but we must get back to Harcourt. Jem and Tim will have been missing you, and certainly Duke has been wondering where you are."

"Oh." William had stirred the hay in Caesar's stall with his foot and hung his head dejectedly for some minutes. Then he had brightened. "Could we not ask Lord Lydon to come back to Harcourt with us?"

"That would be nice, but this is Lord Lydon's home and he has a great deal to do here and in London."

Speen, who had been examining one of the carriage horses in the next stall, thought that his mistress's voice sounded hardly any less sad than her brother's at the thought of leaving Lydon Court, and he nodded his head knowingly. Her enjoyment of their stay at Lydon had not been lost on the coachman. Like Lucy, he had observed the disappearance of the preoccupied frown she had been wearing lately and the ease with which she smiled and laughed. He did not have to look far for the cause. He could tell from the way she relaxed immediately when the marquess was around that at last she had found a friend, someone she could count on, someone who could advise her and help her, someone who made her feel as cared for as she did for her brother, and, in Speen's opinion, it was about time she had such a person in her life.

In bidding farewell to Felbridge, Speen had discovered that the Winterbournes were not alone in their lack of enthusiasm for their return to Harcourt. "We shall certainly be much quieter here at

Lydon Court, Mr. Speen," Felbridge had replied to Speen's thanks for the hospitality. "I have not seen his lordship so diverted for quite some time."

"Nor her ladyship so carefree."

Felbridge nodded meaningfully at the coachman. "I believe we understand each other, Mr. Speen." The faintest of smiles warmed the coachman's craggy features. "I believe we do, Mr. Felbridge; and may I say we look forward to seeing you at Harcourt in the not-so-distant future."

It was Felbridge's turn to smile ever so slightly. "I believe you may, Mr. Speen."

Not only was William distressed at having to part with the marquess, he was suddenly struck by another unhappy thought as their carriage drew up in front of the marble steps. "Griggs! I must say good-bye to Griggs." And he turned to rush down the stairs toward the stables. A firm hand gripped his shoulder, stopping him in mid-flight.

A curious smile played about the marquess's lips as he held his ward captive. "If you wait a minute, lad, I believe Griggs will be here directly."

The smile was not lost on Charlotte, but she could not fathom the significance of it; however, she did not have long to wonder at it for there was a crunch of wheels on gravel and they turned to see Griggs pulling up in the curricle.

"Are you going with us then?" William asked his guardian eagerly.

"No, lad. As you can see, this is not my team."

"Whose is it?"

"Well, er, the horses are mine. I use them for my traveling carriage and when I need an extra team, but the curricle, I believe, is yours."

"*Mine!*" Too astonished to do or say anything more, William stood rooted to the spot, his face pale with suppressed excitement.

"Er, well yes, it is yours, but I thought you might want to share it with your sister since she too has done well at her driving lessons. Griggs will follow you to Harcourt in the curricle and then he will return here with the horses."

These last words were entirely lost on William, who had hurried down the last few steps to examine the miracle that had appeared before him. But in a minute he was back to grab his sister's hand. "Come look, Charlie. Look, it is painted yellow just like Lord

Lydon's and everything is just like his. Griggs says it is made by Barker, the very same coachmaker that made yours, sir."

"But of course."

William was off down the steps again to look and exclaim and admire the finer points of the coachbuilder's art, but Charlotte remained with her guardian, too overwhelmed to say anything. "No one has ever given us anything before," she whispered at last. "I . . . I don't know what to say except . . . thank you." Her eyes shining with unshed tears, she reached up and kissed his cheek.

"There is no need to thank me. There is so very little that I am able to do for you." Max looked down at the face turned up to his, alight with gratitude, the soft lips parted in surprise, and it seemed the most natural thing in the world to kiss them. "Good-bye, Charlotte. Take care of yourself," he whispered back before pressing his mouth to hers. He had meant it to be a simple farewell kiss, but the moment her lips parted under his, he could not help himself and he pulled her into his arms. All the worry he endured on her behalf and all the longing overcame him and he pressed her to him as if he could give her some of his strength, as if holding her close could soothe all the confused and conflicting emotions he had suffered since she had come to Lydon Court.

Charlotte, on the other hand, was aware of nothing except the solid reassurance of his embrace as she clung to him, the warm firmness of his lips as they gently caressed hers, and the strength in the arms that held her. She wanted to stay like that forever, cared for and protected. Then she heard her brother's shout to Griggs. "Is it not the most bang-up rig you ever saw?" Her mind came dizzily back to the present.

What was she doing? There was no such thing as security and safety like that. It was all an illusion; no one could give her peace and protection except herself. If she were not careful, she would lose that self in the illusion and then, when it was shattered and she saw it for the illusion it was, she would suffer the same terrible sense of loss, the same hopeless longing she had suffered years ago for her absent father. Once was enough. She never wanted to endure a pain like that again. "It is wonderful, William," she responded brightly and, pulling herself quickly away from the marquess's embrace, she hurried down the steps to get a closer look and share in her brother's excitement.

William's simple joys had always been her pleasures. Losing herself in his happiness had always been her solace. Keeping him safe and happy was what had made her happy, and it would continue to do so, she told herself as she listened to his catalog of the finer points of the vehicle.

"Perhaps you would like to drive it part of the way home," Charlotte suggested as she admired the powerful spring, the gleaming yellow paint, and inhaled the delicious smell of new leather upholstery.

"Do you think I could?" Her brother looked eagerly from Griggs to the marquess, who had followed Charlotte's precipitate flight at a more leisurely pace.

"Do whatever you like, you're the master. And you'll never find a better tiger than I am to be with you on your first long journey." Griggs winked broadly at him.

"Oh, sir, may I?"

"As Griggs so rightly puts it, *you're the master.* You may do whatever you like, but I do think it would be nice of you to offer your sister a chance with the ribbons. It is a present to her as well."

Again his eyes were fixed on her with that secret sort of smile in them. It made Charlotte uneasy and breathlessly happy at the same time. "Oh, no, I prefer to ride in the carriage at a leisurely pace and enjoy the countryside. William may wear himself to a fare-thee-well tooling along at a slapping pace, but I shall relax and let Speen do the work." Charlotte could have kicked herself for allowing the marquess to affect her in such a way. Her voice came out all squeaky and she sounded as odiously missish as the Winslow girls. It was high time to leave before she turned into a perfect ninny. Summoning as much dignity as she could, she held out her hand to her guardian. "Thank you so very much for everything. It has been a delightful stay."

"I am glad you enjoyed it." Max's voice was formal, as formal as hers was, as he bowed over the hand she extended to him, but his eyes glinted with amusement. So she had been unnerved by his kiss. Good. So had he, but he was not going to let her forget it easily. Pressing his lips against the cool smooth skin of her hand, he whispered, "I shall miss you, you know."

Her green eyes widened and she blushed adorably as she turned and climbed into the carriage. He closed the door behind her and gave the signal to Speen, who whipped up the horses and headed down the drive before Charlotte had a moment to react or to collect her thoughts.

As they rolled on down the drive she was doubly grateful for the curricle which was occupying her brother's attention and allowing her to be alone with her confused jumble of thoughts and feelings.

Whatever had possessed her to kiss the marquess like that? Though it was true that he was her guardian and she had made the gesture in the same manner as she would have to a favorite uncle, it had certainly not ended that way. His kiss in return had not been the least avuncular, nor had her reaction to it been that of a niece. It was a great blessing she was leaving, for who knew what could have happened next?

Charlotte leaned back against the squabs of the carriage and tried to concentrate on all the things that would need looking after at Harcourt. Her efforts to focus on her responsibilities did not meet with a great deal of success, however, for her mind kept wandering back to their good-bye. All she could think about was the warmth of his lips on her hand and the look in his eyes as he had said *I shall miss you, you know.* Would he miss her? She would miss him, she admitted unhappily to herself. But would he miss her? She very much doubted it; why, in no time at all he would probably invite his friends and their ladies back to Lydon Court to pick up where they had left off when Charlotte and William had burst in upon them. With beautiful, amorous women around, the marquess was not likely to spare a thought for his dowdy, unsophisticated ward, and would he miss her? Charlotte thought it highly unlikely.

Chapter 29

She was entirely wrong, however. The marquess was in a rather gloomy state of mind as he climbed slowly back up the stairs after bidding them farewell. Riotous parties and beautiful women were the farthest things from his mind as he made his way back to the library. He had a vague notion of tackling some of his correspondence and looking over reports from London that lay on his desk, but in truth, he was retreating to the library because that was where he pictured Charlotte the most often. They had spent their evenings there playing chess or talking, and as he took his place in his chair by the fire, he could picture her sitting in the one opposite as she had so many times, leaning forward with her feet tucked under her, eyes bright with interest, her face eager as she debated this topic or that political question with him, enjoying the challenge of pitting her mind against his.

Max ran his hand through his hair distractedly. Why was he so affected by the Winterbournes' departure? He was acting like some moonstruck youth instead of a man who had been on his own, making a name for himself since he was eighteen.

There was a muffled knock on the door. "I've brought your mail, sir." It was Felbridge. At Lydon Court the butler ordinarily brought the marquess his mail and had been on his way to do so when he had been waylaid by Felbridge. "I shall be happy to take that to his lordship, Mr. Hickling, as I am on my way to consult with him on several items."

"That is most kind of you, Felbridge." Though he was technically head of the household at Lydon, the butler accepted Felbridge's superior claims as the marquess's chosen companion unquestioningly.

In truth, Felbridge had nothing in particular to discuss with his master, but he was consumed with curiosity. The marquess had been dressed for riding when he bade farewell to the Winterbournes, and usually he spent the morning riding around the estate checking horses, fences, and fields and indulging in the physical exertion that would clear his mind for more intellectual pursuits in the afternoon such as reading the paper, keeping up with correspondence, and in general tending to his affairs. Felbridge had placed himself strategically in the window of his master's dressing room so he could keep an eye on the Winterbournes' departure. As he checked over the marquess's freshly laundered cravats he had been surprised to note that the marquess, instead of proceeding to the stables after waving them off, had turned back toward the house.

This was not at all like Lord Lydon, who had also been uncharacteristically taciturn last evening as Felbridge had helped him undress and also this morning when he had shaved him. His lordship's silence had not been the silence of a man at peace with himself and the world, but more reflective, as though he were grappling with some complex problem. Felbridge knew that his master had been ignoring his correspondence from the City lately and had therefore ruled out any problem connected with business. None of the servants had mentioned any difficulties related to Lydon Court or its tenants, which left Felbridge with only one conclusion: His master's somber mood was the result of something personal. Felbridge did not have to look far for the answer.

He had observed his master quite closely during the Winterbournes' visit and had seen the marquess's spirits rise as he began to slack off from his usual routine and indulge in some of the diversions with which Charlotte and William had chosen to amuse themselves. It had been a different sort of pleasure that Felbridge had witnessed this time. It was not the uproariously high spirits Lord Lydon enjoyed when carousing with his friends, nor was it the half amused, half ironic air he wore after an evening with one of his highborn mistresses, a beautiful opera dancer, or any of his other interesting ladybirds. No, this was a quieter sort of enjoyment, something verging on happiness—a state quite foreign to Felbridge's cynical master and one the servant had despaired of the marquess ever attaining. But these last few days, as Lord Lydon had participated in the Winterbournes' simple pleasures, there had been an air of contentment that surprised Felbridge, acquainted as he was with his master's restless spirit. Now the visit was over and with it, apparently, Lord Lydon's peace of mind. But Felbridge had not yet seen enough to convince him one way or the other—hence the offer to deliver the letters and avail himself of another opportunity to evaluate his master's state of mind.

Max's fit of abstraction was such that he had not heard the knock on the door and he gave quite a start when Felbridge addressed him.

"Oh . . . the mail, er, thank you. You may leave it here." He shoved aside some papers on the table at his elbow, but remained staring blankly into the fire.

"They are off, sir, are they then?" Felbridge spoke in the conversational tones of a long-trusted friend and servant.

"What? Oh, yes, they have gone. The curricle was a great success."

"I am glad of that, sir. Were Master William and Lady Charlotte surprised?"

"That they were." The marquess smiled at the memory of William's excitement.

"It was most kind of you. I hope they enjoy it."

"I am sure they will." There was a wistful note in Lord Lydon's voice that sounded perilously close to loneliness, something that Felbridge had never heard before from his master, a man whose lack of family and romantic ties had heretofore been something to celebrate rather than regret. But regretful was decidedly the mood that the marquess seemed to be in at the moment. Though the servant sympathized with his master's somber frame of mind, he also rejoiced at it, for it had seemed to him, after much critical observation and one or two carefully casual conversations with Mr. Speen, that Lady Charlotte and her brother were precisely what his lordship needed to make his life complete.

"I believe the staff will miss them. The place will seem quiet now that they are gone; with them here it seemed like a home." Felbridge's eyes were riveted on the marquess's face, alert for even the tiniest change in expression that would reveal the true nature of his feelings.

"Something it has certainly never felt like before, I assure you." The sardonic note was more pronounced than ever, as though Lydon was realizing just how much he had missed in his isolated childhood now that he had finally seen what a real family could be, even though it was just brother and sister.

Max stared intently into the fire for some time and Felbridge, sensing that there was still something left that the marquess wished to say, remained waiting quietly, patiently, for whatever it was. The marquess had never been one to confide in or ask for help from others, but to the man who had known him since he was a child, even the most oblique remark could contain a wealth of information. "I have asked Griggs to accompany them and take a look around Harcourt before he returns," he said at last.

So that was it. In spite of Will Foster's report, the marquess still worried that something threatened the young earl and his sister. "Griggs is a very clever man. He will get to the bottom of things if anyone can. He is awake on all suits, is Griggs. Lady Charlotte and her brother could not be in better hands."

"I hope so, Felbridge, I hope so." The marquess turned to the desk behind him, pulled out a blank sheet of crested stationery, and scrawled a few lines on the heavy cream paper. The conversation was at an end. Felbridge bowed and shut the door quietly behind him.

So his lordship was worried, was he. Good. That meant he might journey first to Harcourt to check up on things before returning to London. The marquess was an excellent manager of the estate and he invested a good deal of time and effort in it, but in the end, he always tired of country life and returned to the metropolis for amusement. However, the last few times they had been in London it had seemed to Felbridge, at least, that Lord Lydon had not been enjoying himself as much as he had been seeking distraction, making the rounds from the theater to the gaming room at Brooks's to the boudoirs of enticing women in a frenetic attempt to capture the adventure and sense of purpose he had found so easily in India where every word and every decision was fraught with difficulty and challenge.

For his part, Felbridge almost hoped that Griggs would find something that required the marquess's presence at Harcourt and would catapult him out of this uncharacteristically somber and reflective mood.

Max finished his letter, sealed it, and left it on the corner of his desk for Mr. Hickling to collect. That done, he surveyed his desk with a jaundiced eye. He really did not feel particularly like doing anything. The letter had merely been an excuse to get rid of Felbridge and his acute powers of observation. The man saw entirely too much and Max, who did not particularly wish to examine his own state of mind at the moment, certainly did not wish to have anyone, even his oldest friend, doing so for him.

He really ought to invite Tubby, Colly, and Jack back and pick up where they had left off when interrupted by Charlotte's unannounced visit. But somehow the thought of obviously lascivious women and the hearty cheerfulness of his friends left him cold. Perhaps returning to London would be the thing. Certainly the divinely alluring Madame Dufour could be counted on to amuse him. That also seemed rather stale and bloodless. Max could picture it all now: the delighted surprise, the intimate dinner, the come-hither look in the dark eyes, the seductive way she would shrug her shoulders or gesture so as to make her revealing décolletage even more revealing.

Until now, Madame Dufour's skilled dalliance had attracted him, but now it seemed so practiced, so artful that it lost all enticement for him. There was no challenge or charm in inspiring such feelings in someone who had indulged in them for years with scores of men. He wanted to bring the light of passion into the eyes of someone who had never experienced desire before, heightened pulses to someone who had never known what it was to want a man.

Max was for Madame Dufour what any attractive man would be for her; it was the game that meant something to her, not the person. For the first time he could ever remember, Max wanted to mean something to someone. He would not let himself think who or what that person would be, but he could not banish the vision of green eyes sparkling with grateful tears or a softly whispered *thank you.*

Where were they now? Had they reached Crockham Hill or Edenbridge yet? Had he been mad to send them home to possible danger, or would he have been mad to let them stay when he was growing daily more attracted to the young woman he was supposed to be protecting, not entertaining tantalizing thoughts of her soaking wet in a thin muslin gown or swinging her bare feet in the water.

Max groaned and rose to his feet. It was time to go out riding, to engage himself in as much physical exercise as possible so he would be too exhausted to think or to speculate. At least he had sent Griggs along. But could he trust Griggs to be as quick to sense danger and to react as he would be? Should he have gone himself? Max paced the carpet in front of the fire. No, he told himself, it was better that he had not gone, for his presence would have warned anyone bent on wrongdoing that the Winterbournes' guardian suspected something. It was better to lull the perpetrator of the accidents, if there was one, into a false sense of security so that they could catch him and put an end to it all.

Chapter 30

The marquess need not have worried; the Winterbournes could not have been in better hands than Griggs's. The tiger's sharp eyes missed nothing as they bowled along toward Harcourt. They were constantly scanning the countryside and the road ahead of them for danger of any kind, from any direction. Occasionally he would offer a comment such as *Drop yer hands, sir* or *Give them their heads a bit . . . that's it,* but he never seemed to take his eyes off the road or the fields on either side. Griggs had been duly impressed by the seriousness in his employer's voice and the anxiety in his eyes when he had been given his instructions to keep an eye on the Winterbournes at all times. In all the marquess's wild escapades, the curricle races, the sparring matches, even a duel, Griggs had never seen his lordship anything but laconically at his ease, his voice never rising above a bored drawl. This worried guardian, his face tense with concern, was a stranger and Griggs had promised with unusual solemnity not to let the young earl out of his sight during all his waking moments and to report immediately if he observed even the slightest thing out of the ordinary.

"Stay as long as you need to," the marquess had instructed his tiger, "and let it be thought that you have come to Harcourt to continue with the lad's driving lessons and consult with him about improving the stables. Say whatever you have to, but I want his sister to know that he is being looked after. He is everything to her and she has suffered enough as it is."

"Yes sir. Of course sir," Griggs had replied with awed seriousness, but behind the keen eyes and sharp, foxy features his mind was working busily. So that was the way the wind blew, was it? Concerned as Lord Lydon was for the safety of the boy, it was really her ladyship's happiness that dominated the marquess's thoughts. Any fool with eyes in his head could see that. Griggs had turned away to hide a sly smile. According to his guess they would all be reunited fairly soon, because the Marquess of Lydon was a man of action and he would not be able to sit idly by and let others do his work for him, especially where someone as important to him as Lady Charlotte was concerned. He would soon become impatient at having to rely on secondhand reports and would journey down to Harcourt to satisfy himself that everything that could be done was being done. In the meantime, Griggs intended to do his best and keep a weather eye out for trouble.

Thus it was that several days later as he and William were entering the stables, Griggs, ever watchful, glanced up just in time to see two slates, jarred loose by William's opening the door, slide from the roof toward the lad's head. Without a second thought, the tiger, only a step behind William, hurled himself at the boy, pitching both of them onto the floor of the stable.

"What happened?" Round-eyed with astonishment at this strange behavior, William picked himself up off the floor.

"Begging your pardon, sir, but those two slates was heading right for your head; they would have given you a nasty crack if they had hit you."

"Oh my." Dazed by the sudden turn of events, William stood glued to the spot digesting this bit of information while Griggs crept silently back out the door and, hugging the building, peered around to the back. No one was in immediate sight, but he established that there was a window opening from the loft above through which someone could very easily have gained access to the roof.

He turned and made his way back stealthily into the stable and climbed the ladder to the loft. The hay on the floor made it difficult to tell whether or not anyone had been there recently, but it did appear that the hay on the floor in front of the window had been pushed off to either side and the wood on the sill was slightly scuffed as though someone had stood upon it to gain footing for the roof. He looked down and surveyed the stableyard, being careful to stand back far enough from the window so as not to be seen from below. He still saw no one, but there was a cart next to the wall behind the stables that offered easy access to the wall and there was a spinney on the other side in which a man could easily hide. It would have been useless to follow. Anyone who had climbed the wall would be long gone by now.

It must have been someone from Harcourt, Griggs reasoned, as he climbed back down the ladder; because only someone very familiar with the routine of the household would know that the sta-bleyard was likely to be empty at this time of day while Jem and Tim were cleaning out the stalls, Speen was in the village with a wheel that needed a new rim, and the maids, who had been hang-ing out the laundry in the yard the day before, were busy with iron-ing.

"Are you all right, lad?" Griggs's pointed features were made even sharper with concern; he was truly fond of William. To be sure, the lad was a trifle slow, but he was as gentle and kind a soul as one could hope to meet and his love of horses alone would have endeared him to the tiger even if he had been completely witless.

"Yes . . ." William was still stunned by the shock of it all. He looked up uneasily at the ceiling. "Do you think any more will fall? We must tell Charlotte. She will have it fixed."

"That she will." Griggs was torn. He wanted to stay and calm the boy, but at the same time he felt that something should be done immediately and he certainly did not want to leave the lad alone. "Let us go find Jem and Tim. They can help you harness the horses and I shall just go and have a word with someone about the roof." William agreed and was left under the watchful care of the stable-boys while Griggs sought out Lady Charlotte.

He found her in the library, and the instant he appeared she knew something was amiss. Her face paper-white, she rose quickly from her desk, knocking off a pile of papers in her haste. "My brother?"

"Is perfectly fine, my lady," he assured her hastily. "But it was rather a near thing." Griggs hated to be the cause of such an anx-ious expression in those eyes. "I mean, it was just an accident— two slates from the roof that fell—but it should be fixed."

"But *you* do not think it was an accident." Though she was nearly dizzy with the relief that had followed the first cold shock of fear, Charlotte pulled herself quickly together to deal with the problem at hand.

"No, my lady." The tiger could not help admiring the brave and efficient way she mastered her emotions and took control of the situation—a very special young woman was Lady Charlotte Win-terbourne.

"Do you have any idea what caused it?" Charlotte could not bring herself to ask *who*.

"I could not see anyone, my lady, though from talk I have heard around the stables, I have my suspicions."

Charlotte nodded. They both had their suspicions.

"My master asked me to keep an eye out for anything unusual and I should return to Lydon Court at once. His lordship will want to deal with this himself immediately."

"Ah." Charlotte hesitated, hating to ask for the marquess's help yet longing for the reassurance of his company.

Griggs was pleased to see her worried frown lighten at the mention of the marquess. "Then with your permission, I shall be on my way. I left Master William with Jem and Tim at the moment. Mr. Speen told me that they can be trusted."

"Thank you. I shall keep him close to me or he will be with Speen until I hear from Lord Lydon. And Griggs . . . ."

"Yes, my lady?" The tiger paused as he was about to shut the door behind him.

"Thank *you*. My brother owes you his life, and I owe you an incalculable debt of gratitude."

"I was just following orders, my lady," he replied gruffly. "Besides, I am fond of his lordship; we all are."

She smiled mistily at him. Griggs had no trouble seeing why his master was so concerned for her; she was a taking little thing, with worries too big even for a grown man, much less a young woman. And yet, with all that she had on her mind, she had taken the trouble to thank him for reacting as anyone might have done when things started hurtling off the roof at them.

Griggs would have preferred to have saddled up directly and headed off for Lydon Court, but a moment's reflection made him change his mind. Whoever was behind this was far more likely to tip his hand if he thought his villainy was going undetected. A sudden departure immediately following such a near miss might reveal Griggs's suspicions. Better to prepare the household by alluding publicly to his departure and leaving the following day as though it had always been agreed that he would return then to Lydon Court with the horses lent by the marquess for the curricle.

Whistling as he crossed the stableyard, Griggs exuded a blithe lack of concern as he went to retrieve William from Jem and Tim. It was a crying shame, it was, that someone wished to harm such a nice lad, open, honest, and appreciative of everyone—qualities that, to Griggs's way of thinking, were in all too short supply in the world.

Though Griggs's careful assumption of insouciance might have fooled anyone who happened to see him, its effect was lost on one observer. Skulking in the shadows of the carriage house, Tom Piggott cursed his bad luck as he surveyed the shattered slates. Griggs's suspicions, or lack thereof, had no effect on him as the panicked refrain *Whatever shall I do now? Whatever shall I do now?* played over and over in his mind. The time for circumspection was past. He was doomed. Either Sir Cecil would expose him and he would be transported, a fate as horrible as death to the timid Piggott, who had found life away from his own square mile of existence in Somerset trying enough, or he would be caught for trying to injure the young earl and an even worse fate would befall him. He had suffered such an agony of apprehension from the moment he had left Wadleigh Manor that at this point he did not much care what happened; he just longed for the suspense to be over.

First he had had to deal with that brute of a horse, then there had come residence in an unfamiliar household where he was distrusted by everyone, who could see in an instant that he had no more affinity for animals than a windmill. Jem and Tim, the two people with whom he had had the most contact at Harcourt, had made no secret of their scorn for him. All the others had followed suit and Tom Piggott had disliked them just as heartily in return.

He slipped through the door into the carriage house and eyed the shiny new curricle. Surely an inexperienced driver could be made to have an accident in such a sporting vehicle? He only need to procure a saw and arrange some time alone in the carriage house. Perhaps he was not in such dire straits as he had thought.

Chapter 31

Griggs left the next day, waved on his way by a woebegone William, who ran alongside the horses as they trotted out of the stableyard. "But now I have no one to teach me how to drive."

"Don't worry lad, you know what to do. All it takes now is a bit of practice, and no one but you can do that."

"But I shall miss you."

The tiger could not help but be touched by this. He was unable to recall a time when anyone had expressed the least interest in his whereabouts. "Take your sister driving with you," he tossed over his shoulder as he urged the horses to greater speed down the drive toward the main road.

Cheered by the thought that his sister might replace Griggs as a driving companion, William was about to go in search of her when Speen strolled over with the suggestion that he and William take Duke and Caesar out for some exercise. "Duke has been rather neglected since Caesar arrived, and even Caesar has not been out so much what with your driving lessons and all. What do you say, lad?"

"Ride? With you, Speen? That is a bang-up idea. Let's go now." Thrilled by the prospect of being honored with Speen's company, William did not stop to wonder why Speen, instead of Jem and Tim, was offering to ride with him, or why the usually busy coachman was able to find the time for such a ride, but excited by this special treat, he bounced along happily beside the coachman as they made for the stables.

For his part, Speen was glad it had been so easy to turn William's thoughts away from the curricle and the loss of Griggs, but Charlotte had been most emphatic that William was to be in either his company or hers at all times, and at the moment, she was tied up with Mr. Sotherton, the agent having ridden over to discuss draining some more fields and a few repairs being made to tenants' cottages.

With Speen and William off riding and Jem and Tim off at the tanner's looking for leather to mend a broken harness, Tom Piggott was at liberty to enter the carriage house. The saw he had purloined from the gardener's toolshed was hidden under his jacket and it took only a matter of minutes to saw partway through several spokes in one wheel of the curricle. "There," he muttered to himself as he wiped telltale sawdust from the spokes and the saw, "let us see this *accident* fail." He returned the saw to the shed and then, retrieving the small bundle of belongings that he had hidden carefully under some boxes in the harness room, he crept out of the stables and, checking in either direction to see that he was unobserved, climbed the wagon by the wall, hoisted himself over, dropped down, and made for the spinney that had sheltered him once before.

He made his way to the edge of the spinney and then, out of view from the house and the stables, he was free to lope through the park until he reached the main road where, catching a ride from a passing tinker's wagon, he began his journey back to Somerset and Wadleigh Manor. The next evening he was so convincing in his portrayal of the inevitability of William's demise that Cecil paid him begrudgingly and sent for his wife.

"It is time, Almeria," he gloated to her as he warmed himself in front of the fire. "Tom Piggott assures me that *this* time there is no possibility of things going awry. We must journey to Harcourt so that we are there at the most critical moment to offer sympathy and support."

"Do not be a fool, Cecil. Any man who blunders so much that he is caught poaching by *you* is not likely to be successful at accomplishing a task of such a delicate nature. We will journey to Harcourt, but we will take Tom Piggott with us. If anything is amiss, he will bear the blame, not we."

Cecil reddened. As usual, Almeria was right, but there was no need to speak to him as though he were a complete fool. After all, it was he, Cecil, who had thought of Tom Piggott. It was he, Cecil, who had made all the arrangements. It was all very well for her to criticize him after the fact. "Very well," he muttered, "we shall take him with us to Harcourt."

The Wadleighs were not the only ones making their way to Harcourt. From the opposite direction, the Marquess of Lydon was bearing down on Harcourt with the wrath of an avenging god.

Upon reaching Lydon Court, Griggs had tossed the reins to one of the stableboys and told him to look after the horses while he went immediately in search of the marquess.

Max had only to hear of the slates crashing from the roof before he sprang into action. "I *knew* it. Lady Charlotte is absolutely right! She has been all along. The man is an out-and-out villain, which is precisely why I sent you along with them back to Harcourt. The only thing I did not do, which I should have done, is go there directly myself, but I shall do that now. Will you see to it that my curricle is made ready? Then you may rest from your journey for I shall take Felbridge. We shall travel light and send for anything we need."

An hour later, accompanied by the faithful Felbridge, the marquess was springing his team on the road to Harcourt. Had he been a complete idiot for not accompanying Charlotte and William himself when they had left? What would he find when he got there? He prayed that Charlotte, with her good sense and her suspicions already aroused, would keep William at her side and inside, until Max got there, for danger there undoubtedly was.

In one respect Charlotte was following her guardian's wishes, and after William had returned from his ride with Speen, she had agreed to go driving with him. "Griggs says that I know all he can teach me and that all I need is practice," her brother had announced as they rolled smoothly down the drive. "We always start off slowly and then go faster when we reach the main road." They approached the gate and William was silent, biting his lip in concentration, as he carefully negotiated the turn. Once through the gate and on the road, he heaved a sigh of relief and allowed the team to pick up speed.

"That was very good of you, dear. I . . ." his sister was remarking when there was a thump, followed by a loud crack, and the carriage suddenly dropped precipitately.

Charlotte, completely taken by surprise, grabbed frantically for the edge of the seat, missed, and was tossed clear of the carriage and onto the grassy bank at the side of the road. She had only a moment to realize what was happening as she tried to keep from falling, and then the world went black.

Struggling to hold the horses in check, William was not aware of his sister's plight until he finally pulled the team to a standstill;

then he looked around to the empty seat next to him. "Charlie! Charlie!" he shouted. Fear for his sister made him oblivious of the horses for once and he dropped the reins, jumped down, and ran back along the road frantically shouting her name.

It did not take long for him to spot her inert form lying on the bank. "Charlie, Charlie, are you all right?" He dropped to his knees by her side and, seeing an ugly bruise on her forehead and a few bright red drops of blood on her pale cheek, he burst into tears. "Charlie, Charlie," he sobbed, grabbing her hand and holding it to his face. "Please wake up, please wake up."

William looked frantically about for someone to help him. The sun was sinking and the air was beginning to chill. Fortunately, the horses remained where he had left them, but he had no idea of what to do. Charlie had always been the one who had known what to do and now she was just lying so quietly, not moving a muscle. He burst into fresh tears of despair.

However, it was not long before he heard the clip-clop of horses' hooves and the rumble of wagon wheels and he looked up to see a farmer's cart approaching. Dropping Charlotte's hand, William scrambled up and ran into the middle of the road. "Please help me, please help me."

"Whoa there. Steady boys." The wagon groaned to a stop. "Good heavens, it's his lordship. What's amiss, lad?"

"Oh Mr. Dashett, it's Charlie. I am afraid she is badly hurt." Overjoyed to recognize a friend, William eagerly grabbed the blacksmith's hand as he climbed down from the cart and made his way over to Charlotte. Gingerly, the blacksmith felt her pulse and laid his head upon her chest, where the steady beat of her heart and the regular intake of breath were reassuring sounds.

"She's not . . . she's not . . ."

"Nay, lad. Her heartbeat is sound, just a little bit of a knock about the head. What do you say you and I tie up these horses and then we take your sister back to Harcourt." The blacksmith's presence had a steadying effect on William, who did as he was told, and in no time at all they had secured the horses and laid his sister as comfortably as possible on William's coat in the cart. "No, you sit back there and hold her head. I don't expect Farmer Wadhurst will miss his cart for a while yet. Lucky thing I was returning it to him so I could happen on you, eh, lad?"

William did not reply, for he was concentrating on holding his sister's head so carefully that it could not be jarred.

In no time at all they had reached Harcourt. Charlotte was taken to her bedchamber and the doctor was sent for and Jem and Tim dispatched to retrieve the curricle. William wandered about at a loss as to what to do until Mrs. Hodges, realizing that he had not eaten anything but a very light luncheon, had a fire lighted for him in the library and a tray sent to him.

The doctor, a kindly man who had brought both of the Winterbournes into the world and had treated every illness they had ever had, found him there and sought to reassure him. "She has had a bit of a bump on the head, that is all. Nothing else is hurt. I shall come and see her in the morning." He laid a comforting hand on William's shoulder. "Don't worry, lad, she will be right as a trivet in no time."

But William was not reassured. He had never felt so alone in his entire life. Charlotte had always been there to help him and now she wasn't. He did not know what to do and he sat staring sadly into the fire in the library until the sound of wheels on the gravel drive aroused him. He ran to the front hall and the minute he stepped outside under the portico he recognized the curricle. "Lord Lydon, Lord Lydon, you came!" He ran down the steps and cast himself at his astonished guardian.

Max let the boy cling to him for some minutes, then gently disengaged himself, keeping a steadying hand on his shoulder. "Hold on a minute, William, what is amiss here?"

"It's Charlie." William's eyes filled. "She is hurt. I thought you knew and that is why you came."

"No. How . . . yes, that is why I came. Now why don't you tell Felbridge here what has happened and I shall go see your sister." The marquess watched until William was safely under Felbridge's wing and then turned to the butler, who was directing the footman with the marquess's bag. "Lady Charlotte?"

"This way, my lord."

She seemed so small and fragile lying there in the great Tudor bed that had been her mother's. Lucy, her maid, sat beside her bathing the pale forehead with lavender water. She rose and curtsied when she saw the marquess. "It's that glad we are to see you, sir. She has been stirring and muttering a bit."

"The doctor?"

"Has been to see her. He says we are to keep her quiet and warm and that she'll come around. I do hope it is soon, sir; her brother is fair beside himself. He blames himself, but Jem and Tim say it is not his fault. The carriage was tampered with."

"We shall see what we can do. I will sit with her awhile."

"Very good, sir." Silently Lucy closed the door behind her, leaving the marquess to stare down at the slender form upon the bed. Slowly, quietly, he lowered himself into the chair and took one slim hand in his. The blue veins stood out against the soft white skin and the long fingers were so delicate he could have crushed them in his own. She was always so full of life and energy that he had not realized until now how fragile looking she was. "Charlotte," he whispered as he bent over her, his breath ruffling the dark curls spread out over the pillow. "Charlotte, my love, wake up." *My love,* where had that come from?

But sitting there, watching the rise and fall of her breathing underneath the embroidered coverlet, he knew. He loved her, had loved her almost from the moment she had berated him for not fulfilling his guardianly duties.

He loved her, and he had failed her dreadfully. He had known that whoever had made the first attempts on William's life was bound do to so again. He had thought he could protect her by sending Griggs, but he had known from the wistful look in both her and her brother's eyes that they had wished he would accompany them to Harcourt. Why had he not? What had he hoped to prove by remaining at Lydon? That he did not love her? That he was not going to become involved after all these years of living an independent and virtually carefree existence? That he refused to be under any obligation to a woman? How ridiculous a pretense it had been, when he had done nothing but think about her from the moment her carriage had rolled down the drive. And the memories of her were endless and tantalizing: the defiant tilt to her chin as she had scolded him for avoiding his responsibilities, the tender look in her eyes when she spoke of her brother, the green fire that burned in them when she was challenging him at chess or arguing politics, the slender feet splashing in the water, the feel of her in his arms, the warmth of her lips under his.

He should have followed her, he should have protected her. Max wrung out the cloth of lavender water and gently wiped her brow. "Wake up, Charlotte. Wake up, my love."

Chapter 32

"Wake up, Charlotte. Wake up, my love." Who was calling? She could barely hear. Her head ached dreadfully, her throat was dry and scratchy, and her eyelids felt glued together. "Wake up, Charlotte." She tried to turn her head toward the sound. It was a mistake, for it began to pound even more and she felt horribly dizzy. "Wake up, my love." She struggled to open her eyes and at last, as though she were a long way under water swimming toward the sunlight, she surfaced. The face hovering over her came into focus.

"Lord Lydon?" Where was she? She thought she remembered leaving Lydon Court. She blinked and looked around. No, the hangings on the bed were the familiar blue damask and the furniture warmed by the flickering firelight was the furniture of her own bedchamber. She was home at Harcourt. Then why was she in bed?

"Hush, love." A gentle finger was laid on her lips. "You have had an accident, but you are fine now." The gray eyes looking down at her were alight with tenderness and the hand that smoothed her brow was gentle and comforting.

She heard the door opening and Lucy appeared. "Oh, my lady, you gave us a scare, you did. The doctor said if you woke up you were to stay very quiet." There was an air of decision about the little maid that suggested she had prepared herself to meet resistance on that score from her energetic mistress. But Charlotte merely sighed and lay back against the pillows. She was too dizzy and weak to make sense of it all.

There was a rustle of bedclothes and she felt a hot cheek laid next to hers. "William?" There was no answer but a sob as he flung his arms about her neck.

He held her tightly for some minutes and then let go to wail, "I did not mean to hurt you, Charlie, truly I did not."

"It was not your fault, my boy." The marquess's voice was deep and reassuring. "Only an excellent whip could have held the horses the way you did. It was an unfortunate accident."

"I would not hurt Charlie. I love her more than anything in the world."

"We all do, William. Now it is time you get to bed, you have had a trying day."

We all do, William. What had he meant by that? Charlotte was too tired to think and she drifted back into the darkness.

The next time she woke it was broad daylight. Sunlight was flooding the room. Her head still hurt, but only in one spot which, her exploring fingers discovered, was covered by a bandage. The terrible all-encompassing ache was gone and she did not feel so dizzy. Carefully, she raised herself from the pillows. The room swam before her a bit, but soon righted itself.

More surprising than the condition of her head was the sight of the marquess leaning back in a chair next to her bed, his eyes closed and his long legs thrust out in front of him. Judging from the lines of exhaustion etched on his face and the dark shadow of unshaven beard, he had spent the night there. How long had he been there? How long had she been there?

The movement in the bed caught Max's attention. He was instantly alert and bending over her. "How are you, my poor girl?" He slipped a strong, supporting arm behind her shoulders.

It was so heavenly to be held that Charlotte had the wildest urge to allow herself to appear weaker than she actually was simply to enjoy the feeling of being taken care of. It was the whim of a moment, however, and quickly banished. "I . . . I believe I am all right. What happened?"

"You and William were out driving in the curricle when the wheel on your side cracked. By some miracle, and a good deal of pluck and skill, William held the horses, but you were thrown out and knocked unconscious."

She frowned in an effort to recall the hazy set of events before she had been plunged into darkness. "Ah yes, now I remember. We were not going very fast and there was a loud crack. I tried to hold on, but . . . what happened to the wheel? I do not remember the road being bad."

"Nor was it." Max's face was grim. "Speen, Jem, and Tim went to fetch the horses and curricle after the blacksmith arrived back here with you and William. They examined the road and the carriage thoroughly and came to the conclusion that some of the spokes of one wheel had been sawn most of the way through so no matter how smooth the road was, the wheel was bound to have broken the next time the curricle was driven. They showed the wheel to me and I agree with them that that is what must have happened."

"But how? Who?"

"Apparently Tom Piggott is nowhere to be found. He has not been seen since Griggs left, and when Griggs and William last drove the curricle all went well. Speen has felt uneasy about Tom Piggott for some time, and certainly all of the accidents occurred after his appearance at Harcourt. I believe that it is time I have a word with Tom Piggott and his erstwhile employer."

"Cecil," Charlotte murmured as she raised a hand to massage her forehead. "I always suspected Tom Piggott, but what was I to do? I tried, but . . ." Her voice trailed off and, to her horror, a tear rolled silently down her cheek.

Max pulled her close. "Hush, love. You did all you could, and it is thanks to your vigilance that William is al . . . er, *safe* now. I blame myself for not acting sooner, but I shall now." He pulled a handkerchief from his pocket and gently wiped her cheek. Then, cupping her chin in one hand, he looked deep into her eyes. "I promise you, I shall take care of you and William and you shall be safe from now on, even if I have to spend every waking moment at your sides. Now get some more rest, there's a good girl." He laid her gently back against the pillows, touched her forehead with his lips, pulled the curtains, and silently closed the door behind him.

He had barely shut the door to Charlotte's bedchamber when William came scurrying down the hall. "Lord Lydon, Lord Lydon, there is a carriage coming up the drive and it looks like Cousin Cecil's."

"Does it now," his guardian replied with grim satisfaction. "Let us go and welcome him, lad." Max's sardonic smile boded no good for the Wadleighs. Laying a hand on the boy's shoulder he walked briskly down the stairs, through the hall, and out to the portico, where the Wadleighs' traveling carriage was just pulling up.

A wretched-looking Tom Piggott climbed down from the box to open the door for Cecil, who alighted with an imposing air of ponderous self-importance. He turned to help his wife, who cast her eyes around with satisfaction before allowing him to take her arm and lead her up the steps.

Their majestic progress was brought to an abrupt halt by the appearance of William and the marquess. Cecil's eyes bulged, and his jaw dropped as his gaze lighted on William. He opened his mouth to speak, but was forestalled by a sharp jab from his wife's bony elbow.

"My lord," Almeria chirped, "how delightful to see you. We were just on the road to London and thought, as we were passing by, that we would call at Harcourt to see how everything was doing." Completely ignoring William, and with Cecil gasping in her wake, she swept behind Tidworth, who had appeared to usher them into the library, and order refreshments.

Stopping a moment to murmur in a footman's ear and to direct William to go with the man to find Speen, the marquess followed them to the library, where he motioned the Wadleighs to the sofa in front of the fire and then took his place facing them, his hands clasped behind his back his face rigidly impassive.

"I do not wonder at your surprise at seeing William. No"—he raised a hand—"do not bother to deny it, I witnessed your start of shock when you saw that he was still alive, and I saw your wife stop you from uttering some inadvertent and incriminating remark. Do not be harsh on Tom Piggott for failing to carry out your orders. He did what he was told, but it was Charlotte, not William, who is lying upstairs." Their horrified expressions told him all he needed to know and he smiled grimly. "No, she is not dead, no thanks to you, but it is only by a miracle that no one was killed, which means that I need not feel compelled to turn you in to the magistrate as murderers."

Cecil opened his mouth to protest, but was stopped by the sound of footsteps in the hall. Speen threw open the library door and a cringing Tom Piggott, flanked by Jem and Tim, was hauled in.

"You miserable cur, how could you?" Cecil snarled.

"Hush, Cecil," his wife interrupted. She turned to the marquess. "Quite obviously our former servant has been misbehaving again. Cecil caught him poaching and threatened him with transportation, but the man was so miserable and Cecil so softhearted that he gave him a second chance. He thought that by sending him away he was providing him with the opportunity to make a new start. Equally obviously, he was mistaken as he so often is."

"Yes. Almeria is quite right. I—"

"Silence!" Lydon snapped. "Now, Tom, you are under my protection from this moment on. Nothing that the Wadleighs threaten you with, or have threatened you with in the past, can harm you. I

can help you start afresh. If, however, you lie to me, I have far
more power than *this*"—he waved a contemptuous hand in Cecil's
direction—"miserable cur, to ruin you. I know you have been unhappy with what you have been called upon to do and I am prepared to forget everything and perhaps find you a place on one of
my estates or one of my ships if you will but tell me the truth."

Poor Tom was only too eager to do so. "I was to make sure that
an accident happened to the lad," he blurted out. "But I didn't want
to do it. He was a nice enough lad and I had nothing against him,
but he"—he pointed a shaking finger at Cecil—"said he would
have me hung, or transported at the very least and I . . ." Here the
miserable man broke out into sobs of woe.

"Very well." Max turned to Jem and Tim. "Take him to the stables and lock him up. I will get a signed confession later and then
he is free either to go or to seek employment under me. In the
meantime . . ." The marquess turned back toward the Wadleighs,
who were looking less and less self-confident by the moment. "In
the meantime, I shall deal with these two.

"As guardian of Charlotte and William, I have no wish to see
their relatives, even ones as despicable as you are, dragged through
the courts. But that is the *only* reason I have not sent for the magistrate already. If you wish to retain your freedom and your reputation in the future, you will refrain from having any contact
whatsoever with my wards. And should anything happen to either
of them, if one of their horses even so much as casts a shoe, you
will both be turned over to the authorities, believe me. You need
not wonder whether or not I am powerful enough to do it. I am.
And how will I know what is happening where the welfare of my
wards is concerned? It is very simple. I am making Charlotte Marchioness of Lydon, and William will make his home with us. So
you see, I shall be instantly aware if one of them so much as trips
and falls. Now I feel that I have ruined my day quite enough with
your company. I bid you good day." And without a backward
glance at the pair on the sofa, the marquess strode from the room.

"Well of all the—" Almeria began huffily.

But for once, her husband was not about to be pushed around.
"Hush Almeria. We are fortunate to be allowed to remain in England. Let us return to Wadleigh and be thankful."

"The word of a servant, faugh! You may grovel, Cecil, but I
shall—"

"You *will* be silent. Now come." And Cecil, having assumed authority over his wife for perhaps the first time in his life, was able to hold up his head with a surprising amount of pride, given the circumstances, as he marched her out to the carriage. After all, he was still the heir to Harcourt and the present earl, though alive, was not likely to marry, and even less likely to have a son.

Chapter 33

Though he had spoken confidently to the Wadleighs about making Charlotte his marchioness, Maximilian was not in the least sure that he would be able to convince Charlotte herself as to the absolute necessity of this. While he was man of the world enough to be relatively certain that she was attracted to him, he was by no means confident that this attraction held any significance beyond that. And while it was true that she had recently turned to him for help with her present problem, he had a rather nasty suspicion that in general she preferred to rely on her own intelligence and that she was inclined to consider him in the light of an uncle rather than a lover, not to mention a husband.

Her comments on men in general had been rather pithy and to the point. He recalled from their previous discussions on marriage that she had no use for men, had never known one besides Speen that she could depend on. He knew that she was not about to risk getting hurt again. Not for the first time, Max cursed his erstwhile friend Hugo Winterbourne, who had created a daughter who was enchantingly natural, admirably resourceful, and not about to let any man into her life.

Following the Winterbournes' departure from Lydon Court, Max had spent several restless, lonely days unable to enter into any activity with any sort of enthusiasm except wondering how Charlotte and her brother were faring or casting back in his mind to all the times he had enjoyed her companionship—the evenings in front of the fire, the long rides, the intense discussions. And Max had come at last to the appalling conclusion that he missed her abominably, and now having suffered the agony of sitting by her as she lay unconscious, he knew without a doubt he wanted to marry her.

It had begun as the simple ache of desire and the wish to make her experience all the delights of the passion that he sensed lay within her. That had quickly passed to be replaced by a desperate tenderness, a longing to take care of her, to share everything with her, to look at life through her eyes and to show it to her through his. He wanted to expand her world, to take her all the places she wanted to go. Yes, he even wanted to show William the places he too wanted to see—the Tower of London, St. James's Park. It would give Max himself a great deal of pleasure to see these things with new eyes, to enjoy them more than his jaded soul had allowed him to enjoy them the first time.

He wanted to share all this with her, and he wanted to share it forever. It was a new way of looking at things for him, and the idea of marriage took some time to get used to, but the thought of it made him surprisingly happy. Heretofore, other people in his life had kept him from doing the things he wished to do. Charlotte, on the other hand, made everything he did that much more enjoyable by her presence there. Once the decision was made, Max's feeling of loneliness and ennui passed and he felt lighthearted.

So here he was, having decided to ask her for her hand, now how was he to broach the subject? With William safe and Cecil and Almeria disposed of, it was time to turn his attention to Charlotte. True, there was still Tom Piggott to be dealt with, but the longer he spent as a prisoner the more likely he was to cooperate, and Max needed time to think.

After checking with Charlotte's maid to assure himself that the invalid was sleeping comfortably, Max strolled out to the stables and ordered Ajax to be saddled up. There was nothing like a long and punishing ride to clear the mind.

He did not return until late afternoon and did not see Charlotte until evening when she appeared for dinner. Accustomed to being active and in the center of things, she had quickly grown tired of being an invalid and, overcoming all Lucy's protestations, had insisted on dressing and going downstairs for dinner. "Oh my lady, the doctor said that you were to rest," Lucy had protested tearfully.

"I have rested, Lucy, until I am bored beyond expression. I *must* get up or I shall go mad." Charlotte slid gingerly out of bed. The room did not spin before her eyes, but remained reassuringly stable. "There," she remarked with satisfaction, "I am not even dizzy. Now help me into the bath and then fetch my peach sarcenet, if you would be so kind, and the white lace shawl. I believe I shall take some fresh air on the terrace before dinner."

There was nothing more to be said. Lucy knew her mistress well

enough to recognize when her mind was made up; further remon-
strances would be useless.

It was on the terrace that Lord Lydon found her. Charlotte was
gazing out over the park as the bluish mist floated over the vast
green expanse of lawn. The sky was a delicate pink and the air soft
and heavy with the scent of roses from the garden at one end of the
terrace.

"I am delighted to see you so quickly recovered." The phrase
sounded hopelessly still and formal. Damn! Max could not remember a time when he had failed to charm a woman and now,
here he was, as awkward as though he had never spoken to one before in his life. A hideous silence hovered between them. "Perhaps
you know that the Wadleighs have been here and, er, left."

"Yes, William mentioned something of the sort." At last she
turned to face him, but she could do no more than glance quickly
up at him and then she focused again on the park beyond.

"I promised Tom Piggott my protection if he spoke the truth and
he confessed that he had tried to, ah, *dispose of* William, but that
it was Cecil who had ordered him to do so."

"Ah." Charlotte could think of nothing to say. Her throat was
dry and her heart was pounding. Had she gotten up too soon after
all? No, her head no longer hurt her and she was not dizzy. She had
even removed the bandage and allowed Lucy to bathe the bruise
and cut with lavender water. No, it was not the bump on her head
that was making her feel so strange; it was the intensity in the gray
eyes fixed so steadily on her, and it was the hazy memory of the
gentle way he had held her when she was semiconscious and the
tender words he had whispered. Had he meant it? She wanted to
know, but at the same time she was afraid to know.

"Charlotte?"

At last she looked up at him. He gathered her hands into his and
drew her close. "They are gone. They will never bother you and
William again."

"Thank you," she whispered faintly. She could feel his breath
ruffling her hair, and she longed for him to hold her tight against
the reassuringly broad chest, but instead he disengaged one hand
and cupped her chin and raised it to look deep into her eyes.

"I am so sorry that they bothered you at all. I should have been
here to watch over you, to protect you. It never should have happened." His voice was raw with pain. "But I promise you I shall

never leave you alone like that again. I shall always be with you to protect you."

She shook her head, giving a tiny, inarticulate murmur of protest.

"I know, I know, you have taken care of yourself and William quite successfully all these years without my help and you do not need it now, but I *want* to help. I . . . there is no other way to say it . . . I love you."

Her eyes flew open in surprise.

"Is that such a shocking thing? How could I have spent so many happy days with you, shared as much with you as I have, and not love you?"

"But . . . but Lady Hillyard, the other ladies at Lydon Court . . ." At last Charlotte had found her voice.

"*The other ladies,*" he echoed wryly. "*The other ladies* were a diversion, an antidote to boredom, call it what you will, but it was a purely physical thing. They meant nothing to me, nor I to them. You mean something to me, everything to me—friendship, companionship, and . . . love. I want to mean the same to you."

"Oh." Charlotte did not sound entirely convinced.

"What can I say, but that I love you? I cannot explain it more than that, but that is what love is, inexplicable. I never experienced it before; certainly I did not seek it and I could not have known what it was until I felt it. But I feel it now, and there is no doubt in my mind that I love you. I want to be with you forever." Gently he tilted her chin and softly touched his lips to hers. He *must* make her understand. He felt the warmth of her mouth under his and all the longing and emptiness he had suffered without her washed over him. He pulled her into his arms, sliding one hand up her back to the nape of her neck and burying it in her dark hair while the other tightened on her slim waist. With a groan he kissed her harder until her lips parted under his and her body melted against him.

Charlotte could not help herself. Her body had been craving this ever since she had kissed him good-bye at Lydon. The warmth of his hands through the thin material of her dress made her feel alive again, as though somehow, since she had parted from him, she had been sleeping and now she was fully awake. Without understanding it she knew her body longed for his, for the solidity of it, the strength of it.

Slowly her hands crept up his chest and around his neck. She clung to him and gave herself up to the delicious feeling of being wanted, of wanting and being fulfilled all at the same moment. The vague sense of emptiness that had been plaguing her since her return to Harcourt was gone, washed away by the joy of love and desire. She did love him, she did desire him; she knew that now.

Max raised his head to catch his breath. "Marry me."

"Marry you?" Charlotte was brought up short. She had wanted the moment to last forever, to forget about the world and its problems and revel in the joy of being close to him.

"Yes, my love. It *is* customary, you know."

"But, but . . . I never thought of it."

"I am well aware of that, but I am asking you to think of it now."

Charlotte's thoughts were in a whirl. Leave Harcourt, leave William, give up the well-ordered life she had created for them both? A cold shiver of doubt ran through her. "I don't know. Could we not just . . ."

"No we could not. Charlotte, my love, I do not just desire you; I want you to share my life. I want to share yours, its joys and its sorrows. I want to be together. At last I know what it means not to be alone in the world." He was losing her. A knot of fear gripped his stomach as he read the uncertainty in her eyes. How ironic, after all these years of avoiding women who wished to hold on to him, that he was now desperately, and so unsuccessfully, trying to do just that. "Charlotte, think of William." Max played his trump card. He knew it was unfair, but he was so sure that he was doing the right thing he did not care.

"William?"

"He likes me, he trusts me. I like him. He enjoyed being at Lydon Court and he will need a man in his life as he grows older. With the best will in the world, my love, you cannot help him with some things."

"You would have William with us?"

"But of course I would. You would not think, you could not think . . . Surely you know me better than that, Charlotte. I would never offer you a home and not include William. I would never dedicate my life to you and not to William too."

"Oh, oh . . ." She sniffed audibly and hunted frantically for a handkerchief.

"Fortunately, these days I have them in ready supply." Max pulled a clean white square of linen from his pocket.

"And I have been a regular watering pot."

"Change affects all of us in different ways. Come along. It is time for dinner. I shall not press you any more on this. It is a momentous thing and it is unfair of me to want an immediate answer."

"Thank you. I fear I am not used to this sort of thing. I am not very equipped to deal with it." Charlotte gulped and gave the marquess a watery smile.

"I should hope not." He drew her arm through his and led her into the dining room.

Chapter 34

The marquess was as good as his word. All through dinner he kept up the flow of conversation, telling William more about his plans for breeding his horses, praising him on his handling of the curricle, sharing stories of his own accidents and near accidents, and did not refer once to their conversation on the terrace. Nor did he mention anything about the decision to Charlotte when he bade her good night. He did not need to; she could think of nothing else.

All that night she tossed and turned. She wanted to say yes. She wanted to be part of the companionship and sharing he spoke of. She had missed that after leaving Lydon. Somehow life had seemed rather dull and routine after she had returned to Harcourt. All the things she had formerly enjoyed—riding, reading, taking long walks in the countryside, sitting lazily in the sun and fishing with William—seemed to have lost their appeal. And problems had been just that, problems, with no one to help, instead of challenges to be explored and discussed as she had done with the marquess. She had felt restless and dissatisfied. Even her body, which until now she had taken for granted, had seemed out of sorts. The simple pleasures in which she had indulged—bathing in the lake, riding hell-for-leather through the fields, walking briskly on a fresh summer morning, or strolling in the dusk and watching the sun warm the stones of Harcourt with its last slanting rays, had all been less pleasurable, less fulfilling since she had returned from Lydon Court, and what had been a full life had seemed oddly empty.

The marquess's reappearance had changed all that. Indisposed as she had been when he arrived, Charlotte still felt more alive than she had in all the time since she had left Lydon Court. When she had opened her eyes to see him smiling down at her, had felt his arm around her shoulders and his hand on her forehead smoothing away her hair, all the ache and weariness from the accident, all the listlessness she had felt since leaving Lydon Court had simply evaporated and the emptiness had vanished.

She admitted it to herself now. The symptoms that had been plaguing her since her return to Harcourt could all be attributed to missing the marquess, pure and simple. He had said he was in love with her; was she in love with him too. Deep down inside she had sensed that, but she had not allowed herself to recognize it until he had held her and kissed her, and then there was no longer any ignoring it.

But that was for now, for this particular moment. What about the future? Could she bear it when she lost it again? If she allowed herself to give in and build someone else into her life to the point that she relied upon him for love and companionship, for sharing problems with her and helping her cope with things, then, the agony of it all when he was no longer there would be worse than it would have been if she had not allowed herself to enjoy it at all. The pain of losing it would be far worse than the pain of never having had it. She knew that sort of pain—had lived with it for years—and she knew she could continue to live with it. But that had only been the unfulfilled longing for a mother and father. This would be far worse; it might destroy her altogether, and she could not afford that—for William's sake.

The worst of it was that during this agony of indecision, all this tossing and turning, Charlotte had the most overwhelming urge to run to the marquess for comfort and advice. He would understand what she was going through. He had been through it all himself. He knew what it was to be alone, with no one but himself to count on. He knew what it felt like to be self-reliant, dealing with things in one's own way without the interference of others. And he knew the enormity of what he was asking her to do, to trust someone else, to allow someone else into a carefully ordered world; for he himself had faced that same enormous decision. However, he seemed to have made that decision; she could not.

Charlotte got out of bed and padded over to the window. The moon lit up the park and the fields below, outlining the dark shadows of the enormous, spreading oaks, gleaming on the pond. All her life she had longed to see the world beyond Harcourt; now someone was offering that to her and she was afraid to leave. She had always scorned people, like the Winslow girls, who governed their behavior by *what is done* and *what is not done*, for accepting the status quo, but was she now not guilty of the same thing, clinging to the safety of what she knew, of what had been, and turning her back on what might be? Sighing, she returned to the bed and lay there staring at the canopy overhead, hoping against hope that inspiration would come to her, for she could not seem to think her way out of this muddle as she had thought her way out of muddles before.

Charlotte was not the only one who was wide awake. Max, too, was unable to sleep, but unlike Charlotte, he had not even made the pretense of going to bed. Instead, he sat fully clothed in front of the fire in his bedchamber, a glass of brandy in his hand. *Think, Lydon, think,* he urged himself over and over. *You have never let anything or anyone get the best of you before this; you will not do so now over the most important thing in your life. There must be a way!*

He glanced at the portrait over the fireplace. It was a young boy with a gun and his dog. The clothes were from a previous generation, but the face was vaguely familiar. Recognition dawned. Of course, it was Hugo! It was Hugo who had plunged him into this mess, asking him to look after his son and his daughter, a daughter whom he had made independent and self-reliant to a fault, a daughter who was afraid to . . . That was it! It was Hugo who had plunged him into this mess, and it was Hugo who would get him out of it.

Max leapt out of the chair, nearly spilling the brandy in the process. He knew what he had to do now. Setting the glass down, he pawed feverishly through his valise until he found the packet of letters he had meant to show Charlotte. They would speak for him. With a sigh of relief, he retrieved his brandy glass, gulped down the remainder of its contents, and threw himself fully clothed onto the bed.

The next morning the marquess was up betimes, certain that Charlotte would seek to clear her mind with an early morning ride. He waylaid her in the hall as she was heading toward the stables, hat and crop in her hand.

"Come with me." Grasping her hand, Max led her downstairs and out into the rose garden where, without ceremony, he pulled her down next to him on a stone bench. "Read these. I think they may help you to think about what I have asked you to think about."

"Letters?"

"From your mother and father to one another."

She looked at him curiously for a moment, then did as he asked, frowning at first, and then with increasing eagerness, until she had read through every one. He sat silent, gnawing his lip in impatience. At last she finished. Still clasping the letters, her hands dropped into her lap and she gazed unseeingly at the garden in front of her for what seemed like a very long time. "He did love us . . . after all," she whispered at last.

"Yes, he did." Max ached to touch her, to hold her and reassure her, but he held back. She had to work this out by herself.

"So it was not that he did not love."

"No, I do not think he did not love." Max produced the miniature he had found with the letters.

Charlotte gasped. "But it looks like me!"

"Very much so."

"Then why?"

"Would you like to know what I think?"

She nodded mutely, begging him with her eyes to help her.

"I think that he could not bear losing her, and that you were too painful a reminder of what he had lost. Now, loving you as I do, I understand how it could have happened. If I were to lose you, I would feel that my life was not worth living, but unlike your father, I would cling to anything, everything, that reminded me of you. I do that now. Every time I see a field I think of riding with you; every time I see a pond I think of fishing with you; every time I see a book I think of talking with you. Everything now has meaning for me because now somehow everything reminds me of you. For your father, it was just the opposite; he could not bear to remember. If I had been your father, I would have cherished you, as I *do* cherish you. I love you, Charlotte, and I think, I hope, you love me."

"I . . . I do love you, only I am afraid of losing . . ."

"I know. I am afraid of that too. In many ways it is much easier to be alone. When one is alone and does not have anyone, there is nothing to fear; when one loves as much as I love, there is everything to fear. However, when one is alone, there is also less to enjoy. But love gives us very little choice in the matter. We already love, we cannot help that. You never question your love for William, do you? It is just there and you take happiness in that. Could you not do the same for us?"

"But William?"

"William is part of you, part of us, and I think that if I were to ask him, he would have no trouble in answering the question of whether or not I could be part of his life forever."

Charlotte's brain was in a whirl. So much had happened and what was she to make of it all? What was she to think? She looked up at Max to ask him for more time to sort out her jumbled thoughts, but was stopped by the look of understanding in his eyes. He knew all the doubts and fears that were plaguing her. They were plaguing him too, but he was ready to face them, to take up the challenge.

He was right; she was already in love with him. She could not help it, she had no choice in the matter. A tremulous smile stole across her lips. "Yes . . . Yes, I think I could," she just managed to say before he crushed her in his arms. And the wonderful feelings that washed over her made a mockery of all her hesitation. Why had she tried so hard to think when all she had to do was to let herself go and feel the rightness of it all?

Chapter 35

"Charlie, Charlie." William's voice echoed from the library. Fortunately her brother usually gave fair warning of his approach, which gave Charlotte time to pull herself from the marquess's embrace and smooth back the dark tendrils that had broken free from the knot at the back of her head and were curling wildly around her face. William. How was she going to tell him about her and the marquess when she herself had not quite adjusted to the idea?

She need not have worried about broaching the subject. The moment he was close enough to observe his sister's expression, William came to a dead halt, forgetting everything but the strange look on her face. "Are you all right, Charlie?"

"Why yes, dear. What makes you think that anything is wrong?"

"Well . . ." He paused, screwing up his face in an effort to express himself. "Well, your eyes are all shiny, and . . . and your face is all pink."

"Ah . . . We . . ." Charlotte groped for the words to tell him, but they would not come.

"What your sister is trying to say"—the marquess shot an amused glance at his tongue-tied ward and wife-to-be—" is that she has done me the very great honor of agreeing to become my wife."

"She is your wife? Famous!" William beamed.

"Well, not yet, dear, but I will be. We must have a wedding first."

"Soon." Max amended, smiling at her in a way that made her knees weaken and her heart pound.

"Oh. I should love to see a wedding." William digested this. Then the happy smile dimmed as he considered all the implications of this announcement. "But where will you live, Charlie, and . . ."

At last his sister found her voice and hastened to reassure him.

"Wherever we live, you will always be with us. But I expect that we shall live some of the time at Lydon Court and some of the time at Harcourt." She glanced up shyly at Max.

"Undoubtedly. But I would also like to take the two of you to London and any other place you might like to visit."

"London? Famous!" The smile was back on William's face, broader than ever. "I must tell Speen." He headed toward the stables, but paused in mid-flight to turn back toward his sister. "May I, Charlie?"

"Certainly, dear."

He ran off joyfully toward the stables shouting, "Speen, Speen, Charlie is to marry Lord Lydon and I am to live with them and we are to visit London."

"And now, my love," the marquess said, pulling Charlotte back into his arms, "you are well and truly committed, for once Speen is told, there is no turning back. In fact, I do rather feel as though I have been somewhat remiss in not asking his permission."

"Or Felbridge's."

"Lord yes! Though if I know Felbridge, he has been aware of the state of affairs for some time and I would even hazard a guess that he knew I was madly in love with you even before I did."

"Mmm." Charlotte sighed with satisfaction as his lips came down again on hers.

Indeed, neither Speen nor Felbridge exhibited the least bit of surprise at this happy news. "And so we are to become part of one another's establishments, Mr. Felbridge," Speen remarked when he encountered the marquess's henchman in the stableyard later that day.

"So we are, Mr. Speen." Felbridge allowed himself a conspiratorial grin. "Which, I believe, comes as no surprise to either of us."

"None at all, Mr. Felbridge, though, if I may say it, it will be an honor to serve with you."

"Thank you, Mr. Speen. I assure you, the feeling is mutual."

And secure in the superiority of their foresight, they parted amicably to return to their respective duties.

The rest of the world received the news with varying degrees of surprise and enthusiasm.

The atmosphere at Harcourt was generally ecstatic. Cook sighed gustily over the leg of lamb she was dressing while Mr. Tidworth unbent so much as to confide to Mrs. Hodges that it had long been his fondest wish that a gentleman would appear for his young mistress. "Though even *I* could not have hoped for such a fine gentleman as his lordship, Mrs. Hodges," he admitted humbly.

"I do believe that none of us could have dreamed such a thing, Mr. Tidworth," the housekeeper responded generously.

The joy was by no means universal, however. In a slim house in Brook Street, the occupants were again treated to the sound of smashing Sèvres as Lady Hillyard hurled not one, but two figurines into the fireplace. "Married! Married!" she shrieked. "To that chit? Why she knows nothing of the world, and as for fashion, she has none."

"Calm yourself, Madame." Marie hovered out of her mistress's range, clutching a bowl of lavender water and soothing compresses. "Just look at the beautiful bouquet that Lord Atwater sent you this morning. And yesterday it was magnificent peaches and grapes from the hothouses on his estates. Such a noble estate, and of far greater antiquity and importance than most others in England."

It was not until very late in the afternoon that the maid was able to lull her mistress into a restorative nap, for Isabella was so upset that only the most forcible representation of the damage that could be done to lovely eyes and an exquisite complexion by continued outbursts of rage was effective in quieting her.

"Fool," Marie hissed at Nancy, who had stationed herself just outside the door that the weary maid was finally able to shut behind her.

"But how was I to know she would fly into the boughs over a letter?" the unhappy housemaid wailed.

Marie sniffed haughtily. "A true lady's maid knows that a letter from a relative with whom Madame never corresponds, a relative who lives in the country, quite close to where Madame happened upon milord and his ward, is a letter that at the very best will revive unfortunate memories, and at the worst . . ." She glanced significantly at the door and shrugged.

"But what was I to do? You do not mean I should have destroyed it?"

"*Exactement.*" And turning on her heel, Marie marched down the stairs, leaving Nancy to the miserable reflection that she would never rise to the august position of lady's maid, it requiring a great deal more circumspection and discretion than she could ever imagine herself possessing.

Nor was Lady Hillyard the only person who found herself to be less than delighted by the approaching nuptials. Almeria, upon alighting at Wadleigh after their rout from Harcourt, could not help uttering a disparaging sniff as she cast a scornful eye over that medieval pile, a pile that seemed to demand an increasing share of the tenants' dwindling rents for its repair and upkeep. "With a fortune such as his, he could have no possible use or need for a place such as Harcourt. It is a waste, a shocking waste." And having accused Lord Lydon of the ultimate sin, she shut her mouth with a snap and marched off to her bedchamber to relieve her spirits by bullying her maid, then the housekeeper, and finally, the butler himself.

Nothing could have prevailed upon the Wadleighs to accept an invitation to the wedding of the Marquess of Lydon and Lady Charlotte Winterbourne, which was indeed fortunate as they were not invited.

It was a small and select group invited to the chapel at Harcourt one fine July morning. Chief among these were servants from Harcourt and Lydon Court and a few close neighbors.

The air was redolent of flowers, and the humming of bees and chirping of birds added to the general air of celebration. There were no attendants for either party, only the groom, resplendent in breeches and dark blue coat of Bath superfine and looking more imposing than ever next to his slender bride, who appeared almost ethereal in a gown of white net shot with silver over a white satin slip, the spidery gauze of her veil held in place by a wreath of roses.

There was not a dry eye in the place as they exchanged vows; even the stalwart Speen, not to mention, Jem, Tim, Mr. Dashett, Griggs, and Felbridge, could be seen blinking rapidly and having recourse to pocket handkerchiefs.

"*I* would not be in her shoes for the life of me," Emily Winslow whispered to her sister as the radiant bride swept past their pew on the arm of her husband. "Once a rake, always a rake, they say." She pursed her lips in a righteous simper.

"How do you know?" Selina cast a saucy smile at the marquess. "It might be quite enjoyable to be married to someone who makes himself so agreeable to the female sex."

"Selina, Emily, do try for a little countenance," Lady Winslow quelled them with a frown.

The service, simple and short, was soon over, and the bride and groom emerged into the sunlight surrounded by a group of friends and well-wishers. They paused on the steps outside the church where Max, having rid himself of the most troublesome of his wards, bent down and kissed her heartily in front of the beaming crowd of servants and villagers.

"I may have lost a ward," he whispered gently into Charlotte's ear, "but I have gained a happiness I never thought possible, my wonderful wife."

Charlotte's unladylike chuckle was drowned by the peal of church bells announcing the union of the Marquess and Marchioness of Lydon.